SCALES

A FRESH TELLING OF BEAUTY AND THE BEAST

ALYDIA RACKHAM

Subscribe to Alydia Rackham's website NOW and get
a FREE digital copy of one of Alydia Rackham's epic
novels delivered right to your inbox!

http://captainrackham.wixsite.com/alydiarackham

The Curse-Breaker Series

Scales:
A Fresh Telling of Beauty and the Beast (Book 1)

Glass:
Retelling the Snow Queen (Book 2)

Tide:
Retelling the Little Mermaid (Book 3)

Curse-Maker:
The Tale of Gwiddon Crow (Book 4)

Excalibor:
Retelling the Legend of King Arthur (Book 5)

For Jaicee
Without whom this tale would never have been told.

CHAPTER ONE

"ONCE UPON A TIME"

"S*nakes!*"

The shriek ripped down a wide stone corridor near the kitchens of Tirincashel, followed by the battering of fleeing footsteps. Eleanora threw herself back against the wall as Hattie, a plump kitchen maid, barreled past her, skirts hiked up in her thick hands.

"Run, Princess Ele!" Hattie puffed, her face red, her eyes wide, her bonnet askew. "There are *snakes* in the larder!"

"What?" Eleanora called after her. "What kind of snakes?"

"Blue asps!" Hattie shouted back, her voice pitching to a screech. "Dozens and dozens of them!" Her words dissolved into a trailing howl as she rounded the corner to sound the castle-wide alarm. Eleanora frowned, watching her, then gathered up her long green skirt and trotted down the hall in the exact direction Hattie had come from.

A winsome, slender fourteen, Princess Ele made little sound as she darted across the worn gray stones, through the alternate light and shadow created by the line of tall windows to her left. The scent of lavender washed past her face. Her long black hair flagged out behind her as she hurried faster, listening. She swung around the corner to her right and hopped down a short staircase, then darted onward, past the rustling torches.

Up ahead, light shone from a doorway—and clanging, crashing and shouting rang out to meet her.

"Get back, get back, Ailse! You're in the way!" a rough voice ordered—Ele recognized it as Pather's, one of her father's huntsmen.

"Sorry!" Ailse stammered, and stumbled backward into the hallway, almost tripping on her long skirt. The young, thin woman wore the plain white-and-tan cotton clothes and cap of a kitchen maid, and her eyes had

7

widened with panic.

Ele's feet pounded now, and Ailse jerked around and caught sight of her.

"Princess, you mustn't come any closer!" she cried, throwing out her hands to stop her.

"I want to see!" Ele insisted, grabbing the doorframe of the larder and swinging around it—

Pather, a short, thick, dark-bearded man in softened leather, stood with his back to her, facing the hung baskets of onions, apples and herbs, his attention bent toward the feet of the wine casks that neatly lined the dirt floor. In his left hand he held a short club, and in the other, a gleaming hatchet.

Hsssssss...!

Ele's blood ran cold as the sound shivered through the air. And at last, her attention caught on the writhing tangle near Pather's feet.

Four asps, flowing like ink, wound and wended around each other, their scales twinkling in the lamplight, seeming to change hue even as they moved—from deepest midnight, to the ripple of the ocean at noon, to a shimmering silver.

But their eyes glowed red, like low embers, and their flickering tongues looked like needles of obsidian.

"You women need to get back," Pather warned, adjusting his grip on his hatchet. "I don't want—"

One of the snakes reared up.

It suddenly lifted half its body to waist height, and its neck flared with silver spines. Its eyes blazed like fire, and its jaw spat open, revealing long, black fangs.

Pather swung his hatchet.

He struck the snake down and his blade connected with the ground— the snake's head lopped off.

Ele slapped her hands over her mouth as her heart gave a painful pang—

"Don't kill them!"

The other snakes exploded with snapping, hissing with the fury of bees. Pather ignored her—

And cut them all to pieces.

8

Thud! Thud! Thud!

Their blood splattered across the casks.

The room fell silent. Pather, panting, righted himself, and hefted his weapon. He turned around, and glanced at Ele, then at Ailse. Sweat ran down his pale face.

"Are the two of you all right?"

Ele didn't answer. She stared at the shreds of dead animal lying strewn behind him.

"I'm...I'm all right," Ailse replied faintly. "Thank you, Pather..."

Pather's heavy brow frowned, and his attention sharpened.

"Ailse, you look white."

Ele turned to look at her...

Just as the young woman's skin turned ash-gray, and she collapsed.

"No, no, no!" Pather cried, throwing down his club and hatchet and leaping forward. He clumsily caught her, and the two of them fell to the ground. Ele leaped back and hit the doorframe.

"She's been stung!" Pather cursed as he hastily laid Ailse down and frantically began feeling all over her arms. Finding nothing, he then tossed the hem of her skirt aside...

To reveal a silver spine stuck through the skin of her ankle. A spine that oozed dark purple liquid.

Pather went still, staring at it.

Then, slowly, he covered his face with his hand.

A day later, Ailse died. She never regained consciousness after she collapsed in the hall. And as her family, friends, and the royal household watched, her skin turned from ash to gray, to the tone of stone, and at last her heart stopped. She was given a kindly burial by the king, for she had been a cheerful and helpful maid for five years.

Ele's heart ached. And in the span of that day, she had ceased to feel any sympathy at all for those wicked blue asps, or any other creatures of like kind.

9

Chapter Two

"There Lived a Minstrel"

Seven Years Later

"No, you can't wear that dress," Oralia snapped, tossing her long, golden curls as she snatched the scarlet-and-silver gown out of Ele's hands. She lifted her chin and her sky-blue eyes flashed before she spun around and marched back to her four-poster bed, which was covered in fluffy white pillows and comforters. "You have black eyes and black hair and not a pinch of color in your face," Oralia went on in her swift, bird-like tone. "You would look like death. Even worse than you look right now, in that *sack*."

Ele glanced down at her long-sleeved, loose-fitted beige dress and cream apron.

"Do you expect me to garden in a ball gown?" she asked as she folded her arms, sure to use her low, smooth voice to make her sound even older than her sister—though she only exceeded her by one year.

"You shouldn't be gardening at all," Oralia declared. "You'll be dirty and smelly and brown and your hands will get rough—no one will want to marry you."

"You really oughtn't order me around," Ele answered, a hint of warning in her tone. "It's *my* dress and *my* birthday—I should to be able to wear what I want."

"No," Oralia shot back, ignoring the warning. "I've told you—*I* am planning everything. Including what you're wearing."

Ele considered an answer, then bit her tongue and sank down in a short chair near Oralia's wardrobe, watching the shorter, blonde girl rush and fuss through her lavishly-decorated chambers, tossing dresses, undergarments and jewelry onto her bed.

Oralia was beautiful. She had a charming, glowing face, a lovely figure, and cascading golden hair that was the envy of every woman in the realm. And her eyes constantly sparkled, she had long, black lashes, dark eyebrows, and an elegant, effortless way of moving that almost looked like dancing. She also used a bright, endearing tone of speech with the servants, subjects, and their parents—a tone that Ele *never* heard when the two of them were alone together.

"I think the tapestries are a bit much," Ele remarked, resting her elbow on the armrest and her chin on her hand. "I can't see the walls."

"The tapestries are gorgeous," Oralia answered.

"Yes, but you have all of them, now," Ele said. "Did you leave *any* in Mother's room?"

"Mother doesn't *need* them," Oralia retorted. "She said so herself."

"You have six lamps in here, too," Ele observed. "*And* the gold mantel lions from Papa's old chambers..."

"Listen," Oralia huffed, straightening and facing her. "I like pretty things. I like pretty things all around me. And I especially like pretty things that other people aren't properly appreciating!"

Ele watched her for a moment, a low pain traveling down through her chest.

"Is that what you thought of Roderick?" she asked quietly. "That I wasn't properly appreciating him?"

"Tosh," Oralia waved her off and straightened a bright pink frock. "He and I are not even close to betrothed. You can certainly have him back if you like."

"Perhaps I would," Ele murmured, not taking her eyes from her sister. "If he would even look at me."

"Ha! Well, *perhaps* he will tonight," Oralia said lightly. "I'm going to be paying *my* attentions to the new bard we hired—you remember, the one I heard at the fair and made Papa call to court?"

Ele's brow furrowed.

"No..."

"Amberian, Master of Lute and Song!" Oralia sang the name, scooped up a dress and pressed it to her heart. "Though—everyone calls him Amber. Not sure why. They say he looks like it, but I have no idea

11

what *that* means." She sighed and gave Ele a dreamy look. "Wait until you hear him *sing*, Ele. You've never heard anything like it in your life. And people say he can compose songs right upon the instant, if you give him a line and a subject." She twirled around, and the frilly skirt flared out around her. "I fell quite in love with him at the fair. Tonight, I'm going to have him write a song about me."

"Oh, good," Ele sat back in her chair. "Just what I wanted for my birthday."

Oralia giggled and stopped spinning.

"Your birthday present is your new dress!" she said.

"My new dress?" Ele asked, surprised. "It's finished?"

Oralia gave her a sly look.

"It's just been delivered to your room."

Ele sat up straight, then looked at Oralia sideways. But Oralia just grinned and twirled again. Ele hesitated, then got to her feet and hurried out of the room, hearing her sister laugh behind her.

"Oralia hates me."

"What?! What makes you think that?"

"Look at what she's given me to wear to the feast." Ele held up the dress she had found waiting for her on her own bed: a bright orange gown with large ruffles all down the front of the skirt. It had not been wrapped, hung or folded.

"It...doesn't have sleeves," Ele's mother—a tall, chestnut-haired, beautiful
woman with striking green eyes—raised an eyebrow and put her hands on her hips. "She said she was finished making it..."

"She did not make it," Ele countered, tossing the dress down on her emerald bedclothes. "She got it from the trolls."

"I might believe that," her mother replied, sighing and fingering the skirt of the orange dress. "If trolls wore clothes."

Ele sighed as well and ran her hand absently down through her own long hair, studying her mother's winsome, brown-clad figure. Ele frowned.

"How do you braid your hair like that?"

"Four strands," her mother answered absently, pushing her own long, thick plait out of the way—the end of it brushed the rug.

"Can you do that with mine? For this evening?"

"Mhm," her mother nodded. Then, she glanced up at her daughter. "What are you going to wear?"

"I will not wear this," Ele pointed at the hideous orange dress. Mother paused, and watched her, a weight seeming to settle around her.

"Today is your birthday, Eleanora. Today, you're of age, and have as much authority as I do."

Ele's head came up, her attention caught by her mother's tone. She watched Mother's eyes as she solemnly gazed back at her.

"Your commands to those beneath you cannot be overruled," Mother went on. "And your father and I will uphold all of your decisions. The kingdom now expects you to behave with the mind of a queen." Mother reached out and took Ele by the shoulders, speaking low and warm. "You know the law. Papa and I will now step back from you, so that you may be ruled by your own heart and mind. And we are eager to see what you will do."

"So...what does that mean?" Ele asked. "Regarding the dress?"

Mother winked at her.

"You may wear whatever you like."

Ele smiled back, relieved deep down within her as she watched Mother leave. She listened to her footsteps fade away down the corridor. Then, she sighed, sank down and laid on her back on her wide, canopied bed. Her headboard rested against the stone wall, and just to the left of it stood a wide window, through which the afternoon sun poured. The light washed over Ele as she lay there, gazing at her empty ceiling, breathing in the scent of the cinnamon and cloves that she always enjoyed keeping in a small bowl on her vanity. She diddled her fingers, her gut slowly tightening, until an aching knot formed.

Roderick would be at the feast tonight. As Father's bravest and finest knight, it was out of the question to exclude him from royal festivities. And he would be following Oralia around all evening, even if she *was* chasing the minstrel...

"Hmhmm...Hmmm...Hmhm"

Ele's brow furrowed, her attention sharpening.

A low, melodic tone drifted through the slight crack in her window.
A voice.

Slowly, she sat up.

She climbed off the bed and circled it, then approached her window.
Carefully, she pressed her fingertips against the lowest pane, and the
window swung open. She rested her arms on the cool stone sill, and
glanced down into the bright courtyard just one story below.

Other than the guards at the gate, the broad courtyard was deserted—
except for a single person. He sat on the steps of the well, in the shade of its
little canopy, with a butter-colored lute resting across his lap. He carelessly
plucked the strings—they jingled pleasantly within the stone enclosure.
Ele's gaze fixed on him, and she couldn't look away.

He wore fine, tanned leather, much of which had been dyed playful
colors. He also had on walking shoes, but no hat. She noticed this
peripherally, though, to the rest of his soft and unusual aspect.

His skin was a warm, southern tone—black eyebrows and lashes. He
had a handsome face, tilted to the side as he attended to his lute. His short,
curly hair bore a mix of colors: some strands of deep russet, others charcoal,
others like the embers of a low fire, others like burnished gold. He struck a
chord, then took a deep breath...

And began to sing, all for himself.

And Ele's heart rose to the clouds.

> *"If a gold coin lies down*
> *In the shaft of a well*
> *And deep water hides it*
> *Its worth can you tell?*
> *If the shadows conceal it and moss makes its bed*
> *Is this gold valued less*
> *Than upon a king's head?"*

Even dressed in childish lyrics and a lilting tune, she had never heard a
voice like it. Like the sunshine on a summer's day after a wash of delightful
rain. Like a river laughing downhill through shimmering stones. Like a lit
hearth in the evening after a long day of hiking through the snow. Like
cider and honey, like candles at twilight, like wind off the ocean, like bells
resounding through a valley...

Like nothing in the world. The more she searched her heart for comparisons, the fewer she found that even came close. She held her breath as she listened, chastising even her heartbeat for distracting from the song.

His fingers moved deftly across the strings, and he lifted that voice once more, with an ease that made Ele beam with delight.

"So mark well my words now
Remember this tune
Lest the world tries a falsehood
To lead you untrue
No matter the depths of the black water cold
The coin is still worth all its true weight in gold."

His fingers lifted off the strings. The last notes echoed and settled into the courtyard, as if coming home to roost within the walls. The young man sighed, and moved to stand up.

"Will you be playing that tonight?" Ele's voice startled the echoes—but she smiled even more broadly as the surprised young man hopped to his feet, and his eyes found hers. Eyes of the brightest brown—almost coppery.

She knew who he was. This had to be Amberian of the Lute. But Ele suddenly realized why the name "Amber" was the only one that suited him.

"Hullo!" he answered her, a reflexive smile lighting his features. Then he laughed. "I didn't know anyone was up there."

"I was hiding," Ele confessed. "I didn't want to interrupt you."

"Oh, I was just practicing." He swung his lute strap over his shoulder.

"It was beautiful," Ele told him, a sudden lump in her throat. His smile brightened, and he briefly ducked his head.

"Thank you."

Ele blinked. Modesty? With *that* voice?

"Has...Has someone come to invite you in?" she asked.

He looked up at her again, and shook his head.

"Not yet. I think they've forgotten me."

"No, no, no," Ele chuckled. "I have it on good authority that Princess Oralia is dying to see you." She straightened and held up a finger. "Stay put—I'll go see to it that someone opens the doors for you."

"What should I do then?"

Ele stopped.

"Hm?"

His coppery eyes searched hers—earnest and open.

"Once I come in," he clarified. "I've never sung for a king before. And...I've always found it's a good idea to ask other servants what to expect before I enter a new house."

Ele's face flushed, and she opened her mouth—

Then stopped herself. Smiled slowly.

"That's probably wise," she answered. She lifted her chin. "Well...If I were you, I'd get settled into my quarters first, and be careful to memorize the way, since all the passages twist in that corner of the castle. And, at dinner tonight, I would stay in sight of the king and queen—I know they'll want to hear you. After that, when the dancing begins, get clear of the knights. They don't have any patience for minstrels, especially if they've been enjoying the mead."

Amber's brow furrowed—worry crossed his gaze.

"Or," Ele suddenly added. "If....you need to escape entirely, there is a library just off the dining hall. I've hidden there myself." She gazed at him again, unable to keep the warmth from her tone. "But I'm sure it won't come to that. You'll do very well."

Amber drew himself up, and the tension eased from his shoulders.

"Best of luck," Ele said, straightening to withdraw into her room—though her heart gave an odd pang. "I need to be going."

"Will you be there this evening?" Amber called. Ele stopped.

"Yes," she said. "I will."

"I'll see you soon, then!" he waved at her. Her grin widened, she waved back, pulled in and shut the window. After standing for just a moment, staring across her room, she drew her head up in decision, and made for the door.

CHAPTER THREE

"WHO DANCED WITH A PRINCESS"

Ele walked quietly down the cool, torch-lit corridors, her floor-length, homespun green gown rustling with her steps. It had long, fitted sleeves, simple gold embroidery around the scooped collar, a slender waist and a flared skirt. It was comfortable, and nothing more formal than a day dress. She also wore no jewelry at all, and her mother had braided her hair without ornament.

Ele's cold fingers closed as she heard the sounds of the party—voices, clanging dishes, shuffling feet—roll toward her down the stone hall. Rich scents drifted around her, too: breads, pheasant, boar, venison, ciders, wines, and roasted nuts. Her stomach clenched even harder. She slowed and bit her cheek. Halted. Slid her right foot backward.

"Eleanora!"

She jerked, her hand flying to her heart. It hammered against her ribs as a tall figure blundered out of the shadows to her right and came to a panting halt. She could halfway see him in the torchlight—slender and handsome, with dark hair and vibrant blue eyes. Eyes she had often compared to the spring sky. He wore the leather and dress jerkin of the knighthood of the royal house. And the sight of him sent pain shooting from her chest out to her fingers and all the way down her back.

"Roderick," she gasped, lowering her hand and giving him a look. "Are you trying to frighten me?"

"No," he quickly gave a half smile. "No, I was looking for you."

She watched him.

"Why?"

"Well, your *father* is looking for you, for one," he said, finally catching his breath. "And I also hoped I'd have the honor of sitting next to you this evening, and dancing with you at least twice."

Ele stared at him, but he only gazed back at her, and smiled.

"The seating is arranged," Ele carefully reminded him. "You've been assigned to Oralia's right hand—she did that herself—"

"Never mind her," he waved it off. "You and I are still good friends, are we not? And I've neglected you lately. Besides, Oralia is otherwise occupied. With party business."

Ele frowned—

"A prince of realms did hold a ball,
Forced to marry, against his will
But to the ball, a lady came
All else forgot but this lady fair

And he must dance with her, oh—
And he must dance with her
Throw over all the kingdom's worth,
But he must dance with her."

A voice—as pure as refined gold and as rich as aged wine resounded through the feasting hall ahead of her, silencing the chatter and hushing all the guests to listening. She glanced at Roderick. His smile faltered. Ele drew in a deep breath. It hurt badly.

"You don't want to spend time with me," she realized. "And you wouldn't. Except that Oralia is sitting with the minstrel. Isn't she?"

Roderick blinked.

"No," he shook his head. "I mean—She is? I hadn't noticed. I...How did you...?"

Ele's gut twisted and her fists clenched.

"You want to make her jealous," she said. "Pretending to pay court to me so she'll come to you."

"No, Ele—" Roderick held up his hand.

"I am a princess of this kingdom," Ele snapped, her eyes stinging. "You will address me as 'your royal highness,' 'princess' or 'my lady.'" Suddenly, her whole body broke out in shivers, and she had to fight to form her next words. "But not now," she managed. "I do not wish to see you or anyone for the rest of the evening." And she charged past him, away from the feasting hall and down a dark, narrow corridor where no one but

18

the servants ever walked.

"She was so fair, she was so sweet
He was stricken with true love
But when he asked, she would not tell
The name her mother gave.

He fell in love with her, oh—
He fell in love with her
Throw over all the kingdom's worth
But he fell in love with her."

Amber delicately pressed the thin strings of his lute with his fingertips, watching their progress as he plucked with the other hand. The notes reverberated through the wooden chest of the instrument, shimmering through the large, towering banquet hall. He sat on a low, comfortable stool with the wide granite fireplace to his back. The crackling flames behind him warmed his jerkin, almost humming along with the tune. He smiled to himself, took a deep breath, and kept singing.

"At midnight's strike, she fled from him
And left behind her shoe,
The prince despairs of finding her
But he vows that's what he'll do."

As he sang, he lifted his head, and glanced around the room. Torches lit it, as did tall, white-wax candles atop gold and silver sticks. The three long food-and-wine-laden tables had been arranged in a U, with its open end toward him. The king and queen sat directly across from him in tall, wooden chairs. Queen Lilian was beautiful and stately, with dark hair and emerald eyes that sparkled as she watched him, her fingers lightly entwined. King Herrard sat back, a small, pleasant smile on his bearded face. He reminded Amber every inch of a lionesque monarch—with a blond mane

19

of hair, weather-beaten features and warm brown eyes. Both royals wore splendid comfort—scarlets and golds unrivaled anywhere else, with glimmering jewelry on their hands and throats. At the other tables sat courtiers and knights also dressed in glittering garb—many of the women wore elaborate hats and headdresses. They all listened to Amber, eating quietly if their appetites demanded it, as the flamelight played across their finery, the cutlery, and their attentive gazes. Amber's attention once more caught on the royal table. The chair to the right of the queen stood empty. As did the two chairs to the king's left. He could only account for one of those vacancies.

For on a fur rug right next to his feet sat princess Oralia, dressed in scarlet embroidered with white, and diamonds dancing at her ears and upon her fair throat. Her gold hair, in endless ringlets, spilled down her shoulders all the way to the floor. She watched him fixedly with radiant blue eyes, her perfect, blushing face tilted toward him. Amber kept singing.

> *"And he must find her soon, oh—*
> *Yes, he must find her soon*
> *Throw over all the kingdom's worth*
> *But he must find her soon."*

With a gentle flourish, he finished the song and lifted his right hand off the strings, smiling down at the gleaming face of his lute.

"Ah!" the courtiers exclaimed—a half-sigh of pleasure—and burst into applause. Amber raised his head and met several of their happy glances as cheering rang through the rafters. The king and queen rose to their feet, and the king struck his hands together mightily, grinning from ear to ear. Amber got up, and bowed to them at the waist. When he straightened, he found the king still beaming, and shaking his head.

"Though I spent my boyhood and youth in the north with my father, living amongst the fellowship of Caldic Curse-Breakers," he boomed. "And night after night, around their enchanted fires, I listened to their music— music spun from the weavings of the wind, and the tones of the very morning light itself..." He held out a hand to Amber. "I have *never* heard such a song as that. How proud I am that *I,* of all fortunate men, am blessed to have the finest voice in all the land grace my humble halls."

The court burst into another round of clapping, nodding firmly to

Amber and to each other. Amber inclined his head to him, his heart swelling.

"And how proud I am," the king shouted over the noise. "To have a daughter with such impeccable taste—and cheerful stubbornness—that she insisted I bring him here, to delight us this evening and forevermore!" He gestured broadly to Oralia, fondness glowing in his features. She hopped to her feet, and gave them all cute curtsey, at which the courtiers laughed.

"And now," the king went on. "As we have all eaten our fill, I pray that the other musicians come forth to play for the dancing!"

A wilder cheer went up as the four-piece ensemble shuffled out with their pipes and drums, and began arranging their chairs and stools. The roar of the hall billowed over Amber, as well as the thousand delicious scents from the feast, and warmth bloomed through his chest. Maybe now he could go to the kitchen and get some food—he hadn't eaten all day—and come back out to watch some of the dancing—

Fingers grabbed his wrist. He swung around.

Oralia had hold of him with both her hands, and she tilted her head coyly at him.

"Come, Amber!" she cried, pulling close to his face. Lavender perfume washed over him.

"Come dance," she enticed, smiling beautifully. She slid her hand down and interlaced their fingers. "I've been waiting all evening to dance! Please?"

"With me?" he cried.

"Of course! Why not?" she insisted.

"Ha," Amber laughed. "All right—if you say so."

"I do," she answered resolutely. "Come!"

Amber managed to set his lute down on his chair before she pulled him toward the group of courtiers who had lined up in the center of the room. Amber filed in next to the men and faced the iridescent princess, who gave him a saucy look as she took her place. The musicians tuned, paused—then burst into song.

With a grin, Amber sprang into the dance—Oralia followed immediately. They swung and swirled together, weaving expertly between the other colorful dancers as the music soared to the ceiling. They met in the middle, he wrapped his arm around her waist and they spun wildly—

both let out ringing laughs. Oralia's golden hair flung out behind her like a glorious flag, her skirt flaring like flower petals. The dance blurred around them, and they easily kept pace with the quick rhythm, out-dancing everyone else on the floor.

The music built to a frenzied beat—Amber's heart pounded in his ears—and finally, the players finished with a sweep of gusto. The seated courtiers began to clap first, then the panting dancers. Amber applauded, nodding at the fevered musicians, then sent a happy look to Oralia—

Who promptly stepped to him and pressed her lips to his cheek in a quick kiss. His face went hot.

"I'm off to get a drink," she told him as she skipped back. "I will find you for the next dance!"

Amber could only get out a laugh before she darted off through the crowd. Shaking his head, Amber made his way to a long side table where sat a large bowl of cold, red punch, along with several empty silver goblets. He picked up a goblet, hefting its weight in his hand, and reached for the ladle—

A hand slapped down on his left shoulder. An arm draped across his back. Amber instantly went still. His head came around to the right—

A knight. Back-haired, lean and wolf-like, with piercing blue eyes. Right next to him. With his arm around him.

And he stared straight back at Amber, his gaze like ice.

Amber's heart thudded once.

The knight's mouth twisted into a semblance of a smile, but it didn't look real.

"What are you doing over here, bard?" the knight asked, his voice deep and calm.

"I'm...getting a drink," Amber answered, his brow slowly furrowing as he watched those wintry eyes.

"Oh, you are," the knight's eyebrows raised. "Why?"

"I'm thirsty," Amber replied. The knight's hand tightened on Amber's shoulder.

"And why is that?" the knight pressed.

"I have been dancing."

"Ah. I see. That's interesting," the knight said casually. "Because I thought I was hallucinating earlier, when I saw the princess dancing with a *servant.*"

22

Amber's jaw clenched. The knight's crooked smile grew.

"And I was convinced my vision was continuing to blind me when I saw a *servant* approach a table meant for courtiers and royalty. I'm so glad you've confirmed the truth. I thought I was going quite mad."

Amber said nothing. But his free hand closed into a tight fist. The knight's grip tensed further.

"I'm not exactly certain what corner of the woods you're from, lad— but in civilized places, there are such things as codes of conduct, and expectations for folk of various stations. And in *this* kingdom," He leaned close, and hissed in Amber's face. "Servants do not *touch* princesses. Neither do they pollute the food or drink of their betters. Now, I know you are a newcomer, so I will release you this one time." The knight withdrew just slightly. "Just remember this, Fiddler: keep your station, and you'll get to keep your fingers. Understood?"

A needle-like chill traveled down through Amber's gut. He didn't pull his eyes from the knight. Neither did he nod.

He stepped back. The knight let him go—and any semblance of smile vanished. Amber turned, strode across the room, picked up his lute from off his chair, and hurried around the standing mantel toward a short corridor, praying there would be a door at the end of it that led to something besides a broom cupboard.

Ele sat on the rug in the corner of the library to one side of a desk, knees hugged to her chest, staring absently at the flames in the broad fireplace across the room. All around her, the tall shadows of the tome-packed library stretched to a darkened ceiling. The crackle of the embers filled the silence. She counted her breaths, drawing in the scent of burning cedar and book-dust, absently running her thumb back and forth against her opposite forearm. She sighed. Her whole ribcage ached.

The door latch off to her left clacked. She sat up.

A quick, heavy sigh rushed through the quiet—hard footsteps intruded, the door squeaked and then clanked shut. Low panting followed, and then...

The person stepped in so that Ele could glimpse him around the desk.

He entered the soft light from the hearth...

Tall, dark and warm—hair of twilight and autumn, clothes of a traveler, a lute in his hand. His brow twisted, and his gaze seemed faraway. He heaved another sigh, and raked his hand through his curls.

"So you *did* have to escape," she noted.

He jumped, whirling around, his hand slipping on the lute so it gave a disconcerted *"twang."* Ele felt herself smiling—though it hurt—and climbed tiredly to her feet.

"I'm sorry," she laughed. "It's just me."

His startled eyes found her, and he blew out his breath as his frame relaxed.

"You keep scaring me," he said, recovering a faint grin. "It's starting to get embarrassing."

Ele ducked her head and chuckled, slipping around the desk and wrapping her arms around herself.

"I'm not trying to," she promised. "I suppose I'm just too quiet."

"I'm probably too loud," he said. "Or...not paying attention."

"Maybe," Ele shrugged amiably. She canted her head. "What are you running from?"

"Oh," he gestured toward the door, and that furrow returned to his forehead. "There's a knight out there who wants to kill me."

Ele's eyebrows went up.

"Kill you? Why?"

"I danced with the princess. And then I tried to get a drink of punch." He sighed, setting his lute gently on the floor and leaning it against the mantel. "Apparently, I'm not allowed."

Ele pulled her arms in tighter, then took a quick breath.

"That's Sir Roderick."

"Hm. Nice fellow," Amber muttered.

"You're afraid of him?" Ele wondered.

"Ha. Well," Amber shot her a glance and sat down on the rug. "I can't really count someone who threatens to cut off my fingers as a *friend*, can I?"

"What?" Ele yelped. "Roderick...Roderick said that?"

"I don't know if it was Roderick," Amber said. "I only just got here. I barely remember the way to my rooms, I don't know anyone—and I would rather not make any mortal enemies *just* yet."

24

"You know *me*," Ele corrected quietly. He looked up at her.

"Just a little," he said. "What's your name?"

"I'm...I'm Ele," she said.

"Oh, well—" Amber sat up and held out his right hand to her. "My name's Amberian, son of Caspell of Nerrinton. I'm called Amber."

Ele hesitated, then stepped fully into the firelight and stretched out her right hand. He caught her fingers. His were warm, and soft. Again, he gave her that smile—a smile that had faded in the wake of his mood, but now shone back bright as day.

He held onto her a moment, gazing up at her. She watched the firelight play across all the colors in his eyes.

He let go.

"Nerrinton?" Ele repeated. "That's very far south, isn't it? Close to the ocean?"

"Mhm," he nodded, settling back against the stone of the mantel. "It's always hot there—it's wonderful. Big city, busy all the time. My parents are merchants. Well...My father started the business, but then he died and his brother married my mother."

"Oh," Ele nodded, cautiously settling down onto her knees a few feet from him. "Have you moved in here all right? To your rooms? How are they?"

"They're fine," he assured her, folding his arms and stretching his legs out in front of him. "Much better than any I've had before. Someone named...Roger showed me the way. I tried to take your advice and memorize the halls," he shot her a twinkling glance. "But I know I'll get lost at least once, especially in the dark." He shifted toward her. "So, what do you do here? You're too well-dressed to be a kitchen maid or anything like that. Are you a lady's maid? You help the queen?"

"When she needs me," Ele hid a smile.

"No wonder you know everything," he remarked.

Just outside, a sprightly whistle-and-pipe tune began to play, and the whole hall thudded with a hundred sets of footsteps, in time with the music. Amber groaned.

"I wanted to at least *watch* the dancing," he complained. "But now if I show my face that knight will pound it in."

Ele giggled, and covered her mouth with her hand.

"It isn't funny at all," he muttered. She choked on her laughter.

25

"You're missing the party too," Amber noted. "Why?"

"I just..." Ele lowered her hand and swallowed hard. "I wasn't in the mood. To be around a lot of people."

"But you like dancing," he lifted his eyebrows.

"Yes—"

"Then let's dance."

Ele mentally staggered.

"What—?"

"Yes, come on," he said, hopping to his feet. He clapped his hands once, then held them out to her. She stared at him.

"Come on," he beckoned with his fingers.

"I only know line dances—" Ele protested.

"I'll show you a dance we did all the time in Nerrinton," he cut in. "You'll pick it up right away—promise."

"I'm..." Ele started, her heart hammering. He just waited, then looked slyly at her sideways and wiggled his fingers. She heaved a sigh, rolled her eyes, and tried not to smile as she got up and grasped his hands.

"All right, this is a quick tune, but we can do it," he said, setting his stance. "First, it's three fast steps this way..." He led her thus. "And then three fast steps back. Then we do that again."

Ele battled to keep up, biting the side of her cheek.

"Then we twirl under," he went on, and whirled her into a bridge-like spin, and they faced each other again. "Then this way three steps, that way three steps—"

Ele stumbled.

"I'm actually rubbish at dancing." She caught her balance and blushed. "I can never pick it up—"

"Nonsense, you're fine," he said. "All right, the three steps is the pattern, remember that. We do that one way, then the other way, and then something in the middle, repeating. First the under twirl, then the spin, and then we come in and do the three steps a different way."

"What different way—?"

"Three steps first. Go." They hopped three steps one way, then three steps back, and then he spun her around by her hands so the whole room whirled. She accidentally giggled. He beamed.

"All right, three steps—go!"

They danced one way, then the other—

And he stepped in, slid his right arm around her waist and pulled her against his chest. Their faces were suddenly inches apart. She looked up at him—she saw flecks of gold in his eyes. Her heart caught—

The next moment, he tugged her into a dizzying spin, and then they danced their six steps that way. Ele couldn't breathe.

"All right, and then we start over!" Amber said, leaping back and gripping her hands again. "Three steps this way!"

They did this again and again, faster each time, it seemed—and yet, before Ele knew it, here feet were flying. And she was laughing. Laughing so hard she thought she might break a rib. Around and around they spun, across that library rug, rushing by the mantel fire, sending mad shadows flashing upon the faces of the book-covered walls.

Finally, the music burst to its end, like a firecracker, and Ele and Amber collapsed to the floor, panting through their laughter.

"Well..." Amber managed. "I might need a while to recover from that one."

"A year at least," Ele answered. Amber fell backward, laughing full-out, pressing both hands to his heart. Ele managed to stay sitting up, her skirt thrown haphazardly across her legs.

"Yes. At least," Amber said, swiping at his eyes. "Especially with no food in me."

"What?" Ele asked, brushing her own tears away. "You haven't eaten?"

"No," he said. "Not all day."

"Oh, no," Ele clambered to her feet, clearing her throat. "That isn't good—you'll be ill."

"Ha, don't worry about me. This would *not* be the first time I went a whole day without food."

"Well, you shouldn't!" Ele insisted, smoothing her hair. "Not while you live here." She started toward the door.

"Where are you going?" Amber wondered, propping himself up on his arms.

"I haven't eaten, either," she told him. "We'll have a picnic."

"Inside?"

"Why not?" she grinned at him. He grinned back. She found the door in the far corner—far opposite the one Amber had entered—pulled it open and stuck her head out into the cool, dark corridor.

"Hattie," she called in a sharp whisper. "Hattie!"

Clattering issued from the end of the hall, a door opened—light spilled out. Then, the plump maid came bustling down the hall toward her, her face pinched with alarm.

"Your Highness?" she hissed back. "What are you doing in the library?"

"Is there any food left?" Ele asked. Hattie came to a stop, and squeezed her fingers together.

"Erm—there is one little roast hen, erm...some little potatoes, some carrots, bread sauce, sweet onions—"

"Oh, good!" Ele cried. "Bring all of that, prepared for two. Along with some water. And some tea as well."

"Two, miss?" Hattie jumped.

"Yes, the minstrel and I will be eating together in the library."

Hattie's mouth pursed so tightly it almost vanished.

"He hasn't eaten the entirety of the day, and he is near collapse. I thought I would keep him company, seeing that he is a complete stranger here, and lonely for his home. Would you like to join us, Hattie?" Elle invited. "I'm certain you'd like to sit down for a while—you've been working so hard. Betsy too, she can come—"

The tension vanished from Hattie's face.

"No, thank you, ma'am—maybe in a little while...But yes, I'll get that for you, straightaway!"

"Thank you, Hattie," Ele said sincerely, and the maid turned and bustled away. Ele shut the door again, swung around and strode back to the fireplace where Amber sat cross-legged. He watched her with narrowed eyes, and a small smile.

"What?" she asked lightly, coming to sit just in front of him, parallel to the fireplace, in the same fashion.

"You're more important than I thought," Amber noted, studying her. "Giving orders to other servants? What are you, the...Mistress of the Robes?"

Ele sighed, smiled a little, then rolled her eyes at the ceiling.

"No," she admitted. "I'm Oralia's sister."

She pulled her gaze down to meet his. The mirth faded from Amber's features. He stared at her.

"Her...*elder* sister," Ele added.

"Oh..." Amber's eyebrows came together. "I..."

Ele waited, not moving.

"I've really put my foot in it, haven't I?" he said.

"What?" Ele said. "What do you mean?"

"I'm..." he shook his head, baffled.

A knock came at the door. He twitched.

"Stay there," Ele told him. She got up, hurried to the door, and opened it.

"Here you are, miss," Hattie entered, smiling, carrying a wide tray of steaming food. Betsy, a much younger kitchen maid with frayed blonde hair, entered after her, bearing a tray with the tea and the water.

"Where would you like them?" Hattie asked.

"Just on the floor, there," Ele pointed. "Like mother and I do when it's cold out."

"Yes, miss," Hattie said, lowering the platter down to the rug with a clatter. Betsy bent and carefully did the same.

"Hattie, Betsy, may I present Amberian, the new court musician," Ele said, gesturing to him. "Amber, this is Hattie and Betsy. They work in the kitchens. And Hattie is the greatest cook in the realm."

"Oh, tut, tut," Hattie waved her off, clearly pleased. "We certainly already know who this young man is."

"Yes, we heard him singing," Betsy murmured, her face going red.

"And a lovely voice it is, too," Hattie declared, tipping toward him. "We are so happy to have you with us, Amberian."

"Thank you, ma'am," Amber answered brightly. "The pleasure is mine, truly. And thank you for the food."

"My princess' command is my delight," Hattie declared. "Eat quickly! Don't let it get cold!"

"Thank you, Hattie; Betsy," Ele dipped her head to them as they scurried out. As soon as the door had shut, Ele sat down with a huff, facing Amber, and took a deep breath of the delicious, rich, steaming scent of the roasted hen and vegetables.

"So, you were saying," she prompted Amber, snatching up a long fork and a carving knife.

"I was saying," Amber said. "That...I've only been here a day and I've danced with two princesses."

"You're liked by the royal family," Ele said, stabbing into the hen and deftly sawing it in half. "Isn't that a good thing?"

"That knight will kill me," Amber muttered. "Sir Rodback."

"Roderick," Ele shot him a glance.

"Yes, him."

"Ha," Ele snorted. "Roderick doesn't care what I do."

"He doesn't? Why not?" Amber asked. She lifted her eyes to his for a moment—he gazed at her softly.

"Here," she said, pushing half of the hen toward him. "Eat."

"Is there...another fork?"

"No," she set the utensils down. "No need." And she took hold of a greasy piece of meat with her fingers, tore it off, and put it in her mouth.

"Ha. All right," Amber chuckled, and followed suit.

Together, they ate with their fingers, not bothering to divide the food into separate portions. The hen, as usual with Hattie's cooking, melted in Ele's mouth, and the potatoes, carrots and onions had been glazed in honey, and roasted to utter perfection. In between ravenous bites, Ele and Amber talked about dancing, and about his mother's cooking, which he said nearly rivaled this.

After they had cleaned the plate, Ele poured some water into a bowl and they washed their fingers, and dried them on a towel Hattie had put on the tray. Then, they drank their tea while leaning back against the warm mantel, each of them on one side of it. At last, in a moment of silence, Ele glanced up, and sighed.

"The hall has gone quiet," she observed.

"Mm," Amber acknowledged drowsily.

"Are you tired?"

"Mm," he said again, stretching his legs.

"Come, then," Ele said, setting her tea down. "I'll walk you back to your quarters."

Amber glanced over at her.

"Are you supposed to do that?"

She looked at him.

"Would you rather get lost?"

"*No.*"

"Thought not," she said, and got to her feet, her skirts rustling. "Come on. I'll clean this later."

Amber groaned and stood up, then gestured to the door.

"Lead the way."

Together they left the library and wound through the dark, hushed stone hallways, flickering in and out of the moonlight that sneaked in through the occasional window. They turned a corner—

"Watch out for the—"

"Oof!" Amber tripped down the single stair. He lashed out and grabbed her—she grabbed him back.

"—stair," she finished, gripping his jerkin as he regained his balance.

"Why in the—" he started loudly.

"Ssh!" she giggled. "People are trying to sleep."

"You need to tell me sooner about the stairs," he hissed, dusting himself off.

"I tried!" she insisted. "Shh! Come on." She reached down and grasped his hand. In spite of his loss of footing, his fingers wrapped around hers in instant trust. Her heart warmed. She tugged on him, and together they pattered down the final stretch of corridor.

"All right—this is your room, isn't it?" Ele gestured to a low door.

"Yes," he answered breathlessly. "Thank you."

"You're welcome. Get some sleep!"

Amber passed around her and opened the door.

"Thank you for the evening," he said. "I enjoyed myself."

"Yes," she answered. "I'm...I'm glad you've come to Tirincashel."

"So am I!" he agreed. He reached out, his hand blundered into her arm, and he squeezed her fingers. "Goodnight!"

"Goodnight!" she replied. And with that, he ducked inside, and shut the door behind him.

CHAPTER FOUR

"THIS PRINCESS HAD A SISTER"

Ele suppressed a yawn as she pushed the door of the family common room open, preparing herself to tiptoe past her parents' chamber door to avoid waking them. But when she crossed the threshold, she had to blink to adjust—a fire blazed in the hearth, and all the lamps and candles burned. Mother and Father, dressed for bed, sat in their chairs across from her. Oralia stood by the fireplace, arms crossed tightly, still in her ball gown.

"What's the matter?" Ele asked, stepping into the room and searching their faces.

"Oh, Ele, we'd given up looking for you!" Mother cried, hopping up from her chair. Father did the same.

"What's wrong?" Ele wondered.

"I saw you."

Oralia bit out her words. Ele turned to her.

"What?"

"I saw you," Oralia said again through her teeth, glaring at the rug. "With the minstrel. In the library."

Ele stood still, absorbing that.

Then, very slowly, like silver cooling into a mold, something settled down within her bones. She canted her head.

"Oh. You were there? I'm sorry you were so shy—you could have come through the door and eaten with us. We would have been happy to have you."

Oralia's wide blue eyes met Ele's. Then, a tremor passed through her whole body.

"You...You were eating with a servant!"

"I eat with servants all the time," Ele said plainly, glancing over at her parents. "I have breakfast every morning with Hattie, and tea with John in

32

the stables three hours past noon. Unless he's busy at the forge. Everyone knows that."

"You danced with him!" Ele shrieked.

"So did you," Ele countered calmly.

"Ele," Father interjected, holding up a hand. He looked at her. "Where were you this evening? Why did you never come to eat?"

"I was on my way," Ele replied. "But I was waylaid in the hall by Sir Roderick—who wanted to feign paying court to me to make Oralia jealous."

Mother's eyes flashed.

"That is not true!" Oralia yelped.

"Were you *there*, also?" Ele shot back. "Listening to our conversation from some corner somewhere?"

Oralia's face flamed. Ele shook her head.

"I know precisely where you were—you were sitting right next to Amberian in the hall while he sang."

"Why would Sir Roderick say this to you?" the king frowned.

"He didn't, at first," Ele said. "But it became clear very quickly."

"Roderick had no business talking to you about me," Oralia sputtered. "What I do is none of his concern."

"Oh, no?" Ele retorted. "Not after you've paid him so much attention he honestly believes himself bound to you—only to watch you throw yourself at a minstrel?"

"What are you talking about?" Mother cried.

"It's true, isn't it Oralia?" Ele prodded. "You told me you'd fallen madly in love with this minstrel—that you want him to write songs about you. That I can *have* Roderick back if I wish."

Both parents' gazes flashed to Oralia.

"That is a lie!" Oralia shouted.

"If it is, the lie is yours," Ele answered. "You told me those things yourself."

Another terrible tremor seized Oralia's body, and she pointed violently at Ele.

"You're the one buried in scandal, not me!" she yelped. "*I* wasn't alone in a dark room with a piece-of-dirt minstrel, flirting and eating with my fingers like some peasant! I don't even *touch* people who are beneath me, let alone—"

"STOP." Ele threw up a hand, silencing her. Mother and Father went very still. Watching their eldest.

Fire burned through Ele's whole chest and flowed down through her arms. She took a deep breath.

"I have had enough," Ele said, slowly—in a low, deadly tone. "I have held my tongue for a very long time, but I will not stand for this, not anymore." She leveled a severe gaze upon Oralia as she lowered her hand. "Today, I've come of age. And the simple fact is that now *everyone* in Tirin, except Mother and Father, is beneath me. Including you."

Oralia's mouth fell open. Ele lifted a finger.

"No, be quiet. I've heard everything you've said and I know what you're thinking of saying. It's time for you to listen to me."

Oralia's mouth worked and she whirled expectantly toward her parents. But the king and queen waited with thoughtful, solemn features, their eyes fixed on Ele. Oralia blinked, and spun back toward her sister.

"There are several reasons I did not come to the feast," Ele stated, lowering her arm. "Firstly: the dress you gave me, with no formality, no graciousness, no presentation and no dedication—the one you left on my bed as if it were yesterday's wash—was unfinished, unflattering and completely inappropriate for my ceremony. You were given the task of designing and fashioning a dignified gown for this occasion, yet you threw down something you would not wear yourself. I had nothing suitable in which to appear. Secondly," Again she raised a swift finger when Oralia opened her mouth. "It is clear you designed all the festivities and food with yourself in mind, as if it were your own birthday instead. All of your favorite dishes were served, your favorite dances were played. And you conspired to have Amberian brought because you saw him at the fair and *you* wanted him."

"I did *not*—" Oralia tried, her face red.

"I said be quiet," Ele snapped. She lowered her arm once more, forcibly keeping her fingers relaxed instead of closing them to fists. "Third: Sir Roderick paid court to me all through the winter, whilst you were away visiting Aunt and Uncle. And as soon as you returned, and saw how fond he was of me, you *dared* to insinuate yourself between us, manipulating and twisting him until now he can see no one but you—and you do not even love him! He was just a prize to you—a prize of which you have now grown tired, and so you set your sights upon a minstrel, driving Roderick to act despicably out of jealousy."

"I'm a princess!" Oralia said shrilly, wrapping her arms around herself. "I can do what I like!"

"I will be *queen!*" Ele thundered. "And you shall *not* do what you like."

Ele started toward her. Oralia took three steps back until she bumped the mantel. Ele gritted her teeth.

"You have long been old enough to know better, Oralia, yet you act as if you're a child," she bit out, trying not to shiver. "You are selfish and heartless, and if I were less civilized and did not love you I would have your head."

Oralia gasped. Tears tumbled down her cheeks.

"Do *not* cry," Ele warned. "You always cry, and expect all of us to relent. But I will not—I will *not* endure this any longer." She drew herself up. "Since I will be queen, the law of Tirin states that I may marry whoever I like—the first man I meet on the street, if I wish, since it will not diminish my position. I may also strengthen my household by bestowing love and kindness upon my servants and subjects in whatever manner I deem good. *You* on the other hand, have *one* task: you must marry a man of nobility, who brings prosperity to the kingdom and yourself. I do not care who you marry at all, aside from that." Her voice hardened. "But upon my word, Oralia, you will no longer act like a spoiled little girl. You will not speak to the minstrel except in passing, and you are to cease all contact with Sir Roderick, to spare him from any more of your deceit." Ele stepped back. A slight tremor traveled down her spine, but she bit down on her resolve. "And from now on, you will address me as Your Royal Highness, until I give you permission to use my given name."

Oralia stared at her, stunned. Their parents said nothing.

"Is that understood?" Ele lifted an eyebrow. Oralia said nothing.

"*Is* that understood?" Ele repeated.

"Yes," Oralia breathed. Ele waited.

"Yes...Your Royal Highness," Oralia said, barely audibly. Ele nodded.

"Good. Now, I am very tired." She turned, and started toward her room. "If you want to discuss further, we can talk at breakfast. Goodnight Mother. Goodnight, Father." And Ele left them behind, passing into the coolness of her chamber and shutting the door, feeling as if her legs had turned to water.

Ele lay on her side on top of her covers, her knees curled up to her chest, facing the window. Moonlight poured in through the diamond-shaped panes, casting the rug and furniture in silver. A while ago, a single tear had escaped her guard, and trickled down her nose.

A latch behind her clicked. The door creaked open. Soft footsteps entered—footsteps Ele would know anywhere.

She sighed. It shuddered her frame.

"Oh, Mumma..." she moaned, squeezing her eyes shut. Her mother eased down onto the bed behind her and lay down, facing the ceiling. Her shoulder pressed against Ele's back. For a while, they were both silent, listening to the vast quiet in the depths of the castle.

"Before Oralia went to the fair with Father," Mother finally said. "I spoke with her about Sir Roderick."

Ele choked, blinking back more tears. Her brow twisted.

"I told her how much she had hurt you, by doing what she did," Mother went on. "I told her that she must make amends somehow. So she proposed that she would be in command of your birthday, and that I ought to leave all the arrangements to her. That she would make it a wonderful day for you."

Ele clumsily swiped at her face. Mother let out a long sigh. It sounded like wind through rowan trees.

"That is why I could not better control what happened in that dining hall, with both your sister and Roderick. And the poor minstrel. I saw Roderick go speak to him, but I do not know what he said. I doubt it was friendly." Mother shifted slightly on the bed. "And it is also why I could not believe, even as I watched it unfold, how badly your sister behaved."

"You are not angry with me?" Ele asked, tears running onto her fingers. Mother rolled over onto her side, wrapped her warm, strong left arm around Ele, and rested her chin on Ele's temple.

"You behaved like a woman, and a queen," she said, squeezing her. "Father and I will uphold what you said, and we will speak to her, also. We love you both, but we will not tolerate that kind of behavior from either of our girls. The two of you are too dear to be thrown away in such a fashion." Mother's voice lowered further. "I have spoken to Oralia again and again, but she has clearly never heeded what I say. You are different.

36

You, as her sister...Perhaps she will listen to you."

Ele swallowed hard. Mother laid a soft kiss on her cheek.

"I love you, dearest. And I am proud of you. We will all talk in the morning. Sleep well." And with one more kiss, Mother slipped off the other side of the bed, opened the door and departed, shutting it behind her.

Ele lay there for some time, staring at the windowsill. Gradually, however, a chill settled in the room, and her muscles began to ache. So she wearily sat up, tugged at her covers, and slid beneath them, burying herself down into the bed, vowing not to rise until long after the cock had crowed.

CHAPTER FIVE

"WHO CALLED UPON A WITCH"

Oralia stood next to her tall, restless black horse, her shawl wrapped tightly around her and bound around her head. The wind whipped the dead leaves in rustling circles around her feet—she shivered and gritted her teeth. They felt like rats...or bits of snakeskin...

This afternoon, as the kingdom had prepared for the feast, summer had flown high through the skies and covered the fields in gilded heat. The birds sang, the brooks danced, the crops waved in luscious, rippling health.

But here, in these woods, a deathly autumn reigned.

Oralia stood upon the gray dirt of a path bordered by withered grass. Bare, gnarled trees hunched next to the crooked road, their branches clicking together like dry teeth. Behind her waited darkness—darkness through which she'd ridden at the height of speed, hoping desperately she remembered the way. Moonlight now filtered down through the hollow trees, casting shivering shadows across the clearing before her. It smelt of frost.

Her horse nickered nervously behind her, shuffling backward.

"Silence," she muttered, staring at the clearing. Slowly, she stepped out, to the edge of the empty space, and stopped. She clutched her shawl closer, and drew a deep breath.

"Gwiddon. Gwiddon. Gwiddon," she said, as loud as she could muster.

"Gwiddon, come to me. Come to me when I call."

For a long moment, nothing happened. She held her breath. And waited.

The wind overhead lulled to silence. The trees fell still. The brittle leaves lay motionless upon the dirt. Oralia's knuckles turned white.

A light flickered.

A light, directly across from her, in the shadows of the wood. She stayed still, her eyes fixed on it.

Very slowly, the light brightened. A sullen, reddish light with golden edges, like the eye of a dragon. Another light soon joined it, winking in the blackness. Another. Another.

The outline of a house.

A peak-roofed cottage, with two windows in front, and a door. Through these hooded windows burnt the sullen light she had first glimpsed. It illuminated the pathway leading up to the door.

The pathway flanked by lights on posts.

Or rather...

Skulls on pikes.

Slack-jawed skulls, alight from within with snarling flame, their white edges blackened by the smoke. And as the light grew, like some hellish dawn, it became apparent that the walls of the cottage had not been fashioned out of anything as ordinary as wood.

For that which formed the frame and walls, the peak and shingles, the lintel and posts of that house were bones. Bones of men, women, children and beasts.

Silence waited. The house waited.

Waited for Oralia.

She stood, frozen to the ground, for several minutes. But the eyes of the burning skulls seemed to watch her. And the longer she stood, the wickeder their grins became.

She bit the inside of her cheek, braced herself and strode forward.

"Oh, stop it," she muttered. "You've come this far."

She passed between the flaming pikes, ignoring their low, cackling crackle, and their stinging heat. She drew up to the front door, lifted her hand...

And knocked three times upon the wide brow of a particularly white-washed head.

The door creaked open. Oralia made a face, pushed on the leg bones near the latch, and shoved the door out of her way. She stepped inside.

A fire writhed in the stone hearth to her right. Worn furs covered the floors. Odds and ends dangled from the ceiling—beads, strings of glass, feathers, chimes and finger bones. Untidy stacks of strangely-shaped chests and boxes leaned against the walls. Dozens of colored candles dripped wax down across the mantelpiece, creating a slowly-rolling waterfall. It all reeked of burnt hair. Shadow hung throughout the tiny room like drapery.

And next to the fireplace, facing Oralia, sat the witch.

She crouched upon a red, tattered, tall-backed armchair. She wore rags that had been patched many times over, and a headscarf that did not fully conceal her wiry gray hair. Her long chin and hooked nose jutted and almost met each other. Her wrinkled face sagged, and her brow frowned with dark and heavy fierceness. Her tiny, silvery eyes caught every bit of light, and glittered against the darkness, fixing on Oralia. Her claw-like hands rested on her ragged lap, wrapped round and round with bandage. One forefinger lifted, and tapped against her bony knee.

"Oralia of Tirincashel," Gwiddon declared, her voice soft as two dead branches rubbing together. "Have you finally come to regret the beauty and charm I granted you as a child, as recompense for misleading the king's men for me? Have you come back so I can roast you on a spit?"

"No, Gwiddon," Oralia managed.

"There can be no other reason," Gwiddon replied, an eyebrow arching. "For you know that I warned you, thrice, never to come here again, or that is exactly what would happen to you."

"I've come," Oralia went on, taking fistfuls of her shawl. "Because I want to strike a bargain."

"And why would I bargain with *you*?" Gwiddon leaned forward, and bared her sharp, yellow teeth. "Granddaughter of Heathlane Witch-Burner? Last time, I granted you a splendid boon—I made you the fairest maiden in the land, and gave you the power to make every citizen of your kingdom love you. This time you are trying my patience."

"Hear me out," Oralia persisted. "If you help me succeed in my plan, then I will be queen. And I swear I will cease the hunt for you and your kind. You will no longer be troubled by anyone in my kingdom."

Gwiddon watched her a moment, then slowly sat back. The chair squeaked.

"*You* will be queen?" she repeated. The edge of her mouth curled up. "But you are the younger of two daughters."

"I know," Oralia rolled her eyes. "I've been reminded of that quite often, recently."

"Then it's a poison you need," Gwiddon assumed.

"No!" Oralia shot back. "Why would I want to *poison* her? That is

40

terribly risky and I *know* someone would find me out. At the very least, people would start to suspect something and I'd lose their trust, and then I'd be unable to command my soldiers to leave you alone. Besides," Oralia lifted her chin. "I could certainly have managed some silly *poison* on my own."

"Then what do you want from me?" Gwiddon tilted her head. Oralia took one step toward her.

"I want you to do the opposite of what you did for me," she said, her voice low. "You made me beautiful and charming—I want you to make her ugly and repulsive. Worse than that. I want you to make her terrifying. So she'll be driven out of the castle. So no one will recognize her or even want to remember her. But..." Oralia leaned on one foot, then the other "I...I don't want her to come back. Like that. You know...in case she's...angry. So...I don't want her to remember anything. At all. Not her name, not Tirin, not who I am, nothing."

Gwiddon studied her, a small, eerie smile on her thin lips.

"I once learned a curse such as this," Gwiddon paused, and gnashed her teeth. "But even I have not the power to cast such a hateful spell."

"It isn't *hateful*," Oralia corrected. "It's *fair*. Ele deserves every bit of this." She sniffed. "She is spiteful, spoiled and overbearing. So we'll make it so she can't fool anyone anymore. Let everybody finally know what she's really like on the inside—let it show on the outside."

Gwiddon said nothing. Oralia shifted impatiently.

"If you know the curse, and you know how to cast it, why can't you cast it?" she demanded.

"I told you, I do not have the power," Gwiddon replied, smiling. "But—"

"But *you* do." Gwiddon's eyes blazed. Oralia stopped.

"I do?"

Gwiddon nodded.

"I can see that. Quite clearly. However..." Slowly, she arose from her chair, and paced toward Oralia like a rolling fog. Oralia fought to hold her ground. Ice passed over the backs of her hands as she clutched her shawl.

"This sort of spell has depths and twists that few others possess," Gwiddon hissed, looming over her. "Layers and levels to build the curse, and layers and levels to break it."

"Break it?" Oralia frowned. "No—I need one that can't be broken."

41

"There is no such thing, little princess," Gwiddon canted her head so far she looked like a fiendish owl. "All spells can be undone. This one will undo with all manner of violence—and if it breaks, the life of she who casts it shall be snuffed out."

Oralia swallowed hard.

"How...How can it be broken?"

"Do you want it, then?" Gwiddon twitched her head far to the other side.

"I don't know—I haven't learned enough—"

"It is all I have," Gwiddon snarled, clenching her fists before her. "Take it and strike the bargain, or prepare yourself for my spit."

Oralia sucked in a deep breath.

"I will take it."

Gwiddon spun around and made for a pile of chests behind her tall chair. She opened one and shuffled through several crisp, brown papers. Finally, she drew something out with both hands, and faced Oralia.

"This," she said, holding a small scroll the size of her palm. "You must not read the words until you are standing before her, and when you do, you must read them aloud, in the clearest voice as ever you can muster. The curse should take effect immediately. Stand clear when it does." She held out the little scroll to Oralia. Oralia stared at it. Then up into Gwiddon's eyes.

"What breaks the curse?"

Gwiddon grinned. A devilish, delighted grin. She leaned forward. Her stench nearly drowned Oralia. And she whispered in her ear.

Gwiddon withdrew. Oralia stood there, baffled.

"But...how is that even possible, if the curse does what it should?"

Gwiddon's grin remained.

"Then you should be free of worry, should you not?" She held her hand out, palm up. "We have a bargain, Princess of Tirin. One I shall remember well."

Oralia gulped again, squeezed the scroll...

And slapped Gwiddon's hand.

The striking of the bargain shook the night.

Amber lashed awake.

He slapped his hands down onto his straw mattress and gripped fistfuls.

He stared up at the white-washed ceiling—crisscrossed with moonlight—

"Where am I?" he gulped, breaking out in a cold sweat.

He sat up too fast. His head spun. Twitched toward his right...

A low door. His lute leaning in the corner.

He let out a labored sigh and covered his face with his hand. Now he remembered.

"*Aaaah!*"

He threw himself out of bed, his bare feet striking the thin rug. He whirled around to face the window, the thrill of that tearing female scream turning his blood to ice.

Outside his window stood the broad, moonlit courtyard of Tirincashel. Directly across from him, on the second story, was the tall, elegant window where Princess Ele had first leaned out to listen to him sing.

Clattering bashed through that wing of the castle.

Amber leaped onto his low bed and shoved his own small window open, staring as lamplight flickered against the panes in those corridors, as if carried by people who were running.

Shouts.

Thrashing.

The skidding of a heavy piece of furniture across stone.

"*Aaaaaarrggghhh!*"

Amber's hand closed tight on the sill. A man howled that time. And then—

A shriek. An animal shriek, like a banshee. It ripped the night in half.

Ele's window burst.

Amber jerked back—

Shattering jingling spilled loudly into the courtyard—glittering glass rained like water. And out from the window—

A long, lithe, powerful creature sprang, clawed its way up to the roof and into the moonlight where, for just a moment it perched, looking like a long band of silver.

Then, with a furious hiss, it vanished down the other side of the castle.

And Amber stayed planted where he stood, hardly breathing, even as all of Tirincashel awoke and began to wail.

Pather the Huntsman died that very night. Rumor quickly rippled through the castle—rumor that Princess Oralia had entered Princess Eleanora's chambers to speak to her sister, only to cry out in terror at what she beheld. Pather had been the first to come to her aid. Two other house servants, and the king and queen, had witnessed his entry into the Princess' chamber. But Pather had hardly opened the door when he was stricken in the chest by the lash of some wicked sort of tail—a great tail that left behind three long, silvery spines. Spines that apparently carried poison.

In panic, the king and queen had rushed into their daughter's chamber—but found the furnishings demolished, and Princess Eleanora gone. And as Pather slumped against the doorframe, rasping, he only managed to utter two words:

"Blue...asp."

As the sun rose, a deathly pall settled over all of Tirin. Amber stood at his window, watching the light glisten across the strewn glass, unable to think of any tune to hum, his lute forgotten in the corner.

CHAPTER SIX

"AND BID THE MINSTREL COME"

One Year Later

Amber shrugged into his jacket and faced his chamber window, halfway listening to the low voices of the footmen as they discussed the state of the roads. He sighed, pushed the window further open, then rested his arms on the sill.

Early morning light filled the courtyard, and gleamed across the flawless black edges of the royal carriage as it stood, with six bay horses hitched to it, awaiting the king and queen. The driver had mounted, and held the reins. The green-clad footmen waited next to the red carpet that led back to the large double doors. Amber lifted his eyes, and gazed across at Princess Ele's window. The only window in the castle that had been boarded up.

With a groan, the double doors swung open. The king and queen, garbed in fine-but-functional black travel garments—and the queen wearing a black headdress—strode out, saying nothing. The queen held her husband's arm, and never once did her vibrant green eyes lift to meet anyone else's. The king gazed ahead of him, distantly, and his handsome face sagged with a long lack of smiling.

The footman opened the door. Another footmen set down the steps. The king helped his wife climb into the carriage, and then he climbed in after her. One man removed the steps, the other slammed the door with a bang. Then, the servants hopped onto the back of the carriage, the driver slapped the reins against the backs of the bays, and with a clattering, clacking racket—surrounded by silence—the king and queen departed Tirincashel.

Amber stood outside the throne room, his lute gripped in his left hand, frowning at the seam between the doors. He had been waiting there for twenty minutes now, but no one had come to let him in. He ground his teeth.

Five minutes later, he straightened up, took a breath and stepped back. He turned toward the side corridor and started that direction—

The door squeaked open.

"The princess will see you now."

Amber halted mid-stride. Tried not to roll his eyes. Turned back around and paced past the guard with a brief nod. He entered the throne room, and the door banged shut behind him with a mighty echo.

He walked halfway to the throne, his footsteps tapping, then stopped in the middle of the floor and bowed at the waist.

He stood in the oldest part of the castle, now. In antiquity, it had been a mead hall, and more recent builders had reinforced that architecture with stone. Late afternoon light poured in from skylights, attempting to banish the gloom of dark ages past. But it still bore a rough-hewn floor; twisted, ugly, multi-faced wooden carvings on the pillars that flanked the hall; a square fire pit in the center, and a low dais at the far end, upon which sat two ancient, fur-draped wooden thrones.

And Oralia, dressed in lavish emerald, with her golden hair washing over her shoulders and down to her knees, a silver circlet on her head, sat upon the one belonging to the king.

She pinned him with her blue stare the instant he straightened from his bow, and a small smile crossed her lips. Amber looked back at her, and waited.

"It has been a few days since you have played, Amberian of the Lute," she remarked.

"No one's called for me, madam," he replied.

"You played for my mother," she countered.

"She always called for me," Amber answered.

"Why?" Oralia asked.

"Because it's been difficult for her to sleep these past few months," Amber said.

46

"That is why I called you here," Oralia declared. Amber looked at her.

"Because you can't sleep?"

"No—because I want you to play," Oralia lifted her chin, then waved to him. "Go on. Sit in front of me and play."

"With respect madam, I can't."

Her eyes flashed.

"What? Why not?"

Amber shrugged.

"I can't."

"Are you defying me?" she asked, confused.

"No, madam," he shook his head once. "Just stating a fact."

"Oh, stop calling me *madam*," she huffed, getting up from the throne, hopping down the steps and coming up to him. She looked earnestly up into his eyes, reached out and took hold of his right hand. "I've missed you, Amber. I've hardly seen you. Where have you been? What have you been up to?"

"I wrote Princess Eleanora's funeral music," he answered. "You wouldn't remember, though, since you didn't come to the ceremony."

"I was far too distraught," Oralia insisted, sniffing. "Besides, there was nothing to bury, and no grave to decorate. It was pointless."

"And then I've been staying up most nights with the queen, playing all of her favorite songs, and all of Princess Eleanora's," Amber continued. "So the queen allowed me to sleep during the days. It's become a habit."

"That's no excuse," Oralia protested, her eyes even more vivid. "Don't you think I needed consoling, too?"

Amber glanced down at her. His brow furrowed.

"You seem happy to me."

She studied him for a moment, then laughed, shook her head, and swung his hand back and forth.

"There is no point in being agonized *forever*," she said. "Which is *why*...I have a surprise for you." She let go of him, skipped up the steps, turned and plopped down in the throne. She crossed her legs and sat up coyly, perching her fingers on her knee. "A surprise that will fill the whole kingdom with joy—we'll all have a reason to celebrate again. We can *finally* get all these dirty palls and mourning banners taken down and put away, and hang bright colors, and have a feast and a dance—"

"What are we celebrating?" Amber cut in. Oralia beamed at him.

47

"I'm going to marry you."

The words hung in the air.

Amber's pulse slowed to nothing.

Slowly, he looked at her sideways. His lips parted.

"What?"

"I'm going to marry you," she repeated, with more delight than before, if that were possible. She put her hand on her heart. "It will be terribly romantic—the princess with hair like spun gold, marrying the minstrel with a voice like...like gold." She sighed, and gazed at him, a faraway smile on her face. "They'll write stories about it for years."

"But you're going to be the queen!" Amber burst out. It was the only thing he could think of.

"Exactly!" she cried, springing off the throne again and dancing toward him. "Which means I can marry whoever I want! It's in the law!"

"But..." Amber tried, feeling the heat drain out of his head. "What if I...What if I'm not ready to get married?"

"Oh, tosh," Oralia twirled around and then cocked her head at him. "It isn't as if you really have a choice."

He stared at her. He was certain his heart had stopped now. She laughed and grabbed his hand again.

"Oh, come now, it'll be fun! We'll travel and see the whole world, you'll sing in front of all kinds of nobles and royalty—and you'll get that chance because you'll be *my* prince," she poked him in the chest. "And then when *I'm* inconsolable, you can sing to *me* as I go to sleep. I'll only let Mother borrow you if she asks nicely, and we're not busy." She winked at him, then leaned up and kissed him on the lips.

Amber mentally jerked backward—he only saved himself from physically twitching with a threadbare shred of will. Oralia hopped back, swung around the fire pit, then tried the queen's chair this time.

"As soon as Mumma and Papa come home from visiting Aunt and Uncle, we'll have the wedding. That should be enough time—they'll be gone a month and a half at least. I'll be able to have the whole castle dusted and scrubbed, Ele's room gutted and that window bricked up, and all the invitations sent out by then. Oh, I'll need to order the livestock we'll need to fatten up in the meantime." She snapped her fingers rapidly, her mind clearly racing. "What else, what else?"

"I'll...leave you to it, then?" Amber managed. "You clearly have a lot of work to do."

"Don't think you'll get out of all the decisions," she warned, pointing playfully at him. "Oh, and pack up your things—I'll have Roger move you into the family wing so we're closer together." She winked again. "And I'll have you fitted for new clothes—those are ugly and faded."

"Yes, madam."

She didn't correct him this time, just gave a long, contented sigh. Weakly, he bowed at the waist again, then turned and left the throne room.

He hurried down the halls, back toward his chambers, his strides lengthening and quickening every moment. At last, he arrived, opened his door, entered and threw the bolt behind him. Panting, a cold sweat standing out on his forehead, he began to pack up his belongings, just as the princess had commanded.

But he would *not* be moving into the family wing.

CHAPTER SEVEN

"THE MINSTREL FLED"

Amber let out a long sigh as some of the tension released his shoulders. He stood in the middle of the wall-bordered road on the crest of a hill, his lute strapped to his back, his small leather bag hanging over one shoulder. He gazed back at Tirincashel, its towers and walls touched by the soft, purplish twilight. The banners hung limp, for no wind stirred, and he could hear the bustle of the servants within as they went round, shutting the windows for the night, tugging the animals inside, and preparing the evening meal. Birds twittered as they flitted across the walls, searching for a place to roost amongst the parapets. Beyond Tirincashel, in the village below, a church bell rang out, sending its lonesome notes meandering down through the green valley. The hearth fires of the cottages sent tendrils of smoke wandering up into the air, and the farewells of the people in the market square echoed as they closed up shop, and headed to their homes.

He had strode out of the castle gates not long ago, putting as much purpose into his step as possible. Gareth, one of the guards at the bridge, had called out in a friendly voice, asking where he was headed.

"The princess wants heather," Amber had lied. "I have to go get it for her."

Gareth had laughed, waved him on, and warned him to be back before dark.

However, Amber had no intention of coming back at all.

He turned again to the castle, his attention pulled back to it one last time. He could just glimpse Ele's boarded-up window from here. An ache ran through him. A dulled, familiar ache.

He sighed again, turned around and faced the west, where the road wandered up country toward the moor, and Thornbind Wood beyond.

His footsteps crunched on gravel as twilight gave way to night. He had hoped to come to an inn to spend the night, but apparently not many folk had inclination to travel this way. He glanced up. The moon shone full, as well as the stars, so brightly that most of the hilly countryside bathed in muted white, contrasted by deep shadows. The air here smelt damp and fresh, and wilder than in town. Dew had settled on the grass, and gleamed like pearls. And ahead of him loomed the dark, tangled wall of Thornbind Wood

He only knew its name because of a large map that hung in a corridor in Tirincashel. The inked drawing had caught his attention because so many roads seemed to lead into the wood, but all of them narrowed and petered into nothing. And in amongst the illustrations of the trees had been drawn thin, nasty-looking wolves, elves—and witches.

Amber paused, frowning up at a leaning wooden sign that waited as the only gatekeeper to the entrance of the forest. He stepped closer, but the writing had faded off a long time ago.

He heaved a deep breath, glanced behind him at the empty hills, and took off his bag.

"I'll spend the night out here, thank you," he muttered. "Rather die of damp than get *eaten*." He took off his lute, too, left the road, sat down by the wall and leaned back against it, setting his lute in his lap. He pulled it close, laid his head against the wet stone, and let his eyes drift shut as a lonesome breeze wandered across the moor, and danced through the knotted hair of the forest at his left hand.

He felt it before he heard anything.

He blinked his eyes open. Stared straight ahead at the moss-covered wall on the opposite side of the road.

He sat utterly still for several moments, curling his fingers through the grass as he studied the faintest of stirrings traveling toward him through the earth.

"Horses."

Quite a few of them, if experience had taught him anything. But they were still some distance off—otherwise, he'd be able to hear their hooves. All he had to do was get up, climb over the wall and hide on the other side, and they'd never—

"Oh-oh-oh!" he gasped, leaping to his feet and swinging around.

They came.

It had to be thirty hooded horsemen, their cloaks billowing out behind them, racing toward him at break-neck speed—and their horse's hooves had been tied with cloth, to muffle the shoes.

Highwaymen.

Amber's heart banged hard. He swung his lute over one shoulder, his pack over the other, and glanced at the wall—

Too high.

Faced the blackness of the wood.

Winced.

A shout went up from the highwaymen.

"Heigh ho!" he roared. "We've got one!"

Amber ran.

He pelted headlong past the leaning sign, his lute close, his pack banging against his side. His feet thudded on the dirt—the hooves shook the ground right behind him—

And he dived into the forest.

Darkness swallowed him, shattered by shards of moonlight slicing through the skeletal trees. Horses huffed like mighty bellows behind him— whips lashed their flanks.

"He's a runner! Hahaha!" one brigand crowed.

"It's a fast one, lads!" the leader cheered. "C'mon, boy, pick up your feet!"

Amber's heart raced—gasps tore through his chest. He couldn't see anything—wind roared past his head—

A whip kissed his ear.

Snap!

He yelped, jerking sideways, throwing a hand to his head—

He tripped. Flung forward—

Twisted mid-air, desperately scrabbling to get his lute on *top* of him—!

His back slammed into the dirt. The back of his head slapped the road.

"Gah!"

Pain snapped through his back. He tried to pull in a breath—

Nothing. *Nothing—*

His vision blurred.

The thunder of hooves surrounded him, swam all around him. Then, worn, leather boots struck the earth right next to his nose. Amber fought to scramble to his feet, but his head spun sideways...

A man leered down at him. Blearily, Amber could make out half of his craggy, bearded face in the moonlight, shadowed by a wide-brimmed hat. The man grinned. His two gold teeth and his hoop earring glinted.

"We've got a musician, eh?" he growled, his grin broadening. "Well, he won't have much in his pockets then, will he?" He cast a look up at his fellows. A rumble of laughter passed through their ranks.

"The lute looks quite fine, though," the leader observed, canting his head. "I'd imagine we'd fetch a nice price for it, if we don't decide to keep it for our own amusement."

"You cannot have it," Amber gritted, tasting blood on his tongue. He lifted his head off the ground, and stared the thief right in the eye. He gripped the lute's neck so hard the strings cut his palms. The other highwaymen laughed now. They sounded like a pack of gnashing wolves.

"It's already mine," the leader chuckled. "Give it to me, or I'll cut your hands off *before* I rope you up in that tree." He jerked his thumb toward a gnarled oak beside the road. "I..."

The leader paused. Amber's breath caught.

The men and horses had gone still.

"Thhhhht....thhhhhht...thhhhhhttt...thhhhhhttt..."

A deep, throaty...almost purring...ticking...clicking...

Hissing.

In the *tree.*

The hair stood up on the back of Amber's neck.

The sound pulsed through the forest, echoing over their heads, pulling through their bones.

A chilling shiver raced across Amber's skin. He turned his stiffened neck and looked to the right...and *up...*

A tail.

A long, shining tail wrapped around the trunk of the tree like a bracelet of silver around a forearm. Straight, foot-long spines lined this tail like thorns, their tips dark with venom. The tail thickened as it ascended, muscular and sleek...

It moved.

The horses shrieked and threw their heads.

The tail thrashed loose of the tree, and the dark creature it belonged to dropped from its perch and hit the ground.

The men howled as their mounts pulled the reins loose. Two horses went tearing off into the wood.

The creature charged and raced round them like a whirlwind, binding them all close together. A gnashing, chesty, seething snarl slithered with fiendish speed as the tail flashed in the moonlight. Then—

"Agh!"

The tail backhanded one of the highwaymen—silver spines went through his chest—his eyes stared wide at the sky for an instant before he toppled backward. His horse barreled off through the shrubs.

Amber curled up tight on the ground, wrapping his arms around his lute, clamping his jaw. More horses tore loose—then the men started clawing their way onto their saddles.

Thwack!

The tail smacked a man off of his horse and into a tree. He fell like a rag, filled with spines. Amber yelped and covered his head.

The men without horses turned to the entrance of the wood, and with wild eyes, raced toward it, screaming all the way.

The creature whipped after them at a pace Amber couldn't track. They all vanished into darkness—

The men suddenly wailed.

Bodies crashed to the ground, into brush, onto stone—

Went still.

The hammer of hoof beats faded away.

Silence.

The barest breeze tickled the twigs far overhead. The old oak creaked.

Amber lay there for a full minute, trying to unlock his chest.

"Gaaaahhhh...!" He breathed in dust, and coughed. His whole

body quivered.

Shakily, he managed to sit up, feeling a line of blood trickle down his chin, and sweat break out on his forehead. He swiped at his mouth with his dirty sleeve and swallowed, frantically straining his hearing.

But he heard nothing. Saw nothing.

Nothing but the footprints and hoof prints in the dirt...

The giant, snake-like trails through the dust...

And the highwayman across the way, pinned to the tree with three finger-width needles, his eyes wide, his jaw slack.

Amber scrabbled to his feet, holding his lute in an iron grip.

He had to get out of here.

"Your Royal Highness?"

Oralia, her hands braced on the long table, looked up from the dozens of bolts of colorful silks and satins. She frowned across the parlor at the skinny, blond page who stood in the doorway. The fire in the hearth only lit the sitting room dimly, and she couldn't make out his features.

"Didn't you tell him he can come in?" she asked impatiently. "I don't care how late it is—I cannot sleep until I've picked out the right fabric, and he must help me."

"Madam..." the page cleared his throat and took one step inside. "The minstrel is not here."

Oralia straightened up and frowned harder.

"What do you mean, he's not here?" she demanded. "You didn't bring him with you? Didn't you understand what I said?"

The page clasped his hands in front of him, his wide eyes forcibly fixed on hers.

"Madam...he is not in Tirincashel," he answered, his voice trembling. "His effects are gone from his room, and he is nowhere to be found on the grounds."

"What? Where else would he be? Is he in the village?" Oralia pressed, coming around the table. The page almost flinched.

"No, madam," he said. "Gareth the sentry says..."

"What does he say?" Oralia strode closer to the boy, who took a step back.

"He says he saw the minstrel, several hours ago, leave the castle to go onto the moor searching for some heather for you. And he..." the page swallowed. "He has not come back."

Oralia stared at him.

Her hands closed to fists. She lifted her chin, and stared blankly past the page, into the hall.

Suddenly, she shoved past him, out into the stone corridor, and marched toward her room, her skirts trailing behind her. She raced up the stairs, turned, pushed the door of her chambers open, barreled in and slammed it behind her. The tapestry hooks trembled, and the candles on the mantle wobbled.

For a long time, she stood in the center of her room, her fists clenched so hard it hurt. Then, she lifted her eyes to the curved, circular mirror hanging beside her fireplace.

She reached over, snatched a silver brush off her vanity and threw it at the mirror.

It *smashed*. Glass showered over the rug. The brush thudded to the floor.

"Guard!" she roared.

The door burst open—she whirled around. The armored man almost toppled into the room.

"My lady, what is—"

"Get me Sir Roderick," Oralia barked. "*Now!*"

"Yes, Your Highness," the guard huffed, and dashed away.

Oralia stayed planted in place, her blood hot, until she heard familiar footsteps in the corridor. The next instant, Roderick, dressed in only trousers and a loose green shirt, swung around the doorframe, panting.

"What?" he asked, worriedly running his gaze across her and the rest of the room. "What is it? What's wrong?"

Oralia lifted her chin.

"The minstrel is gone," she said. "I want him back."

Roderick instantly straightened, his brow furrowing.

"What?"

"Didn't you hear me?" Oralia gave him a look. "He's gone! Left the castle, lying that he went to get heather for me, and he has not come back."

"Wh..." Roderick stammered, off balance. "Why should that matter so much? To you?"

"Because!" Oralia threw up her hands. "He left without my leave, without asking permission, and without being discharged! He is my *servant*, and he has disrespected and disregarded me as acting queen and I demand that he be brought back here to face the consequences!" Tears stung Oralia's eyes, and her throat suddenly felt thick. She pressed a hand over her eyes.

Calloused fingers teased that hand. She squeezed her eyes shut, sniffing hard, and let him take hold of her hand in both of his. Tears ran down her cheeks.

"My lady," Roderick murmured. "My dearest lady, don't cry."

She blinked her eyes open, and looked up at Roderick, who gazed softly down at her. He smiled in a quiet, boyish way, and dipped his head toward her.

"I will find him," Roderick said firmly. "And I will bring him back."

"Would you?" Oralia brushed at her tears. Roderick lifted her hand that he held, and pressed his lips to the backs of her fingers.

"I swear I will. And I'll leave tonight."

"Thank you, Roderick," Oralia managed a smile, stepped in, and kissed his lips. He leaned into her, deepening it—

She broke it, and stepped back.

"If you must go into the woods, take only a few men with you," she warned.

"Wh...Why?" he blinked, fighting to regain his balance.

"Because I said so," Oralia answered, briefly touching his cheek. "It's for the best—Please trust me."

"I do," he said, eyes locked with hers.

"Go," she urged.

He watched her just one more moment, then took a crisp breath, nodded, and hurried away.

For a long moment, Oralia stayed where she was, her fists closing again. Then, she raised herself up.

"Guard!"

"Yes, Your Highness?" the same guard stumbled closer again, his face red from running.

"Get someone to clean this up," she said flatly, gesturing to the glass all over the floor. "I'm going back down to see about my fabric."

CHAPTER EIGHT

"HE BEHELD A STRAND OF SMOKE"

Amber paused in the center of the leaf-strewn, narrow road, and as his rustling feet stilled, silence sank down around him. He shivered, and pulled his pack closer to him.

He had gone deeper into Thornbind Wood.

After the chaos with the highwaymen, he had considered just heading straight back out of the forest, the way he had come. It took him about half a second to realize that the creature had gone that way too—and it hadn't come back.

So he had turned, and, by the light of the slivered moon, dashed down the winding road, his feet crashing through fallen leaves, trees flashing past, until he had put enough distance between himself and the scene of pandemonium that his pounding heart had slowed, and he'd allowed himself to walk.

Now the dawn lifted the skies—but not as much as he had hoped. This forest seemed to live in a perpetual autumn; a very few brown leaves clinging to the branches of the black-barked, gnarled trees. Mist hung like cobwebs in an empty house, circling the trunks of the nearby trees, and turning those in the distance to phantasms. The air felt cool and close—musty and still.

He peered ahead, squinting, trying to see through the thick fog. The road had waned swiftly; now it merely resembled a trail. One which would have grown over, had anything in this wood been alive. Amber fought to calm his uneven breathing and just listen.

Nothing. Not even a breeze moved now. Not even...

Wait.

He tilted his head, frowning hard.

It was muffled, but familiar. It sounded like the rustling of leaves. A great number of leaves—like a gust through a cottonwood in full summertime. But that couldn't be. No wind disturbed the fog or the branches, and all the branches were naked.

Then it had to be—

He turned to the right, set his jaw, and left the path.

His feet sank into dead underbrush and black, rotting leaves. His shoes swished as he worked his way down a slight hill, maneuvering between the twisted trees, keeping his lute close. The mist closed in tighter and thicker around him with every step. Then, finally...

He slowed to a stop, and almost smiled.

Just below him, vapor rising from its surface, flowed a dark, languid stream. It rushed and rustled, just like leaves, and brighter.

Amber took three more steps forward and lighted on a broad stone, studying the slow-moving water. It had a narrow bed. With two steps, he could ford it. But he could glimpse absolutely nothing past that—the fog stood opaque as a wall.

Gingerly, he bent his knees and squatted down, running his eyes across the surface. He stretched out his hand, then gradually lowered it, until his palm rested atop the silvery surface.

Icy liquid licked his skin. The murmuring water diverted briefly to oblige his intrusion, and flowed on. Nothing else happened.

Amber let out a breath he didn't know he'd been holding.

He reached out both hands, scooped up a handful of water, brought it to his mouth and drank.

It tasted clean, if a bit metallic, and felt immensely good in his mouth and throat after all his racing through these dry woods.

He took five more swallows, then washed his face, and ran his hands through his hair. Cold droplets ran down his neck. He put his pack down on the stone next to him, opened it and reached inside, searching for his canteen. He'd fill it now, then get back to the road. It had to lead out of here somehow. If it did come to a dead end, he would turn around and go straight out the way he had come, beast or no beast. He was getting hungry, and his back and feet ached so badly he—

He stopped.

Frowned ahead of him.

The fog on the other side of the stream had parted.

And through it, he could just see a break in the woods. And a clearing beyond that.

And beyond that...

He stood up, his heart jolting.

It looked like the edge of a stone tower. A tower with a chimney.

And smoke rolled upward from it.

Amber picked up his pack and lute, slung them over his shoulder, and plunged his foot into the stream.

Stones slithered underneath his shoe. He shuddered as chills raced up his legs, but he wallowed through, splashed up onto the muddy bank, and hurried up and out, leaving a wet trail behind him.

Amber charged up the hill, never taking his eyes from that parting in the woods, praying that the heavy fog wouldn't come around in front and seal him inside it again. He picked up his pace, kicking through the leaves, until...

He passed between two trees, and stepped into the clearing.

Deep, pale grass muted his footfalls. He slowed to a halt, his fingers closing around his pack strap.

A wide lawn spread before him, sloping up and away from him in a gentle hill. And atop that hill stood a castle.

Weathered and stocky, built of pale stone, it had two square-topped towers: one at the fore, to the far left of the castle, one at the rear, to the far right. From Amber's view, thick green vines covered the entirety of the left half of the structure—climbing up to the parapets and winding around the whole of the front tower. Small, dark windows peered dourly out at him from the main wall. No banners flew. No one moved atop the walls.

But that strand of white smoke lifted into the sky, like a silk ribbon, from the chimney of that fore tower.

"All right..." he whispered. "Might as well look."

He started forward, hiking up the hill toward the main gate, which stood off-center, further toward the right of the face. Ivy hung in its arch, draping down over the beaten wood like a curtain.

Once he had reached it, he hesitated there at its feet, glancing up at the silent, settled fortress, then down at the welcome stones.

Shrubbery grew before the threshold, thick and thorny. He leaned closer, studying its leaves.

It looked like a tangle of sickly roses and thistles. He shook his head. Nobody had used this door in years. He adjusted his pack and turned toward his left, marching across the front of the castle toward the tower. There had to be another way inside.

He rounded the corner, eyeing the virtual thicket of thorns that clung to the side, then turned right again, following the sharp angle of the wall. Attached to the back of the castle stood a short structure that looked like a kitchen, for behind it, a sharp iron fence gave a rectangular border to what had to have been a chicken yard. Now it waited, its dirt floor empty, its little coop quiet and motionless. He passed the hen yard, turned right again, and followed the length of the back wall, searching it for an opening.

Something caught his attention. He shot a glance out, to his left...

Slowed and stopped. Tilted his head.

Upon first blush, it just looked like a mess of shrubs, knotted dead vines and hunched, naked trees. But as he studied, there seemed to be an arrangement to them, beneath all that overgrowth and rot. It almost looked like...

"A garden."

A breeze touched his hair, floated past him, and disturbed the strands of gray, draping ivy. It carried the scent of dew, like morning. For a moment, it banished the must and murk. Just for a moment.

Amber sighed, turned back toward the castle, and kept pacing the length of it. He could smell the burning peat in that hearth up there, and whenever he strained his neck to see, he could catch the edges of that smoke, still wafting upward. He held out his hand and ran his fingertips along the rough, cold wall, lengthening his stride...

There.

He rounded an indentation and stopped in front of a low, round-top door. The grass near the welcome stones had been worn away to dirt...

He hesitated. Took a deep breath—it quavered.

He reached out, grasped the icy handle, and tugged on it. The door creaked open.

Straight ahead, down a short corridor, waited daylight. He stepped inside, leaving the door open behind him.

His shuffling footsteps echoed in the stone space. He sensed a closed door on his left, and one on his right, as he passed them. After just a few steps, he entered a tall, square courtyard.

A covered well stood in the center, with no bucket. Beyond that, he could see the tall, arched corridor that led to the main gate. At that end of the courtyard, a door led off to the left, and one to the right. Weeds poked up between the smooth cobbles of the floor.

He wandered out to the center, by the well, and glanced down inside. The bottom of the well was dirt. He then cast upward and around. The courtyard walls were two levels high—this main floor, and one above it. A line of windows encircled the courtyard, but all stood shuttered. He turned and faced where he had come, and ran his eyes up and down the tower that stood in the rear right of the castle. But no smoke trickled from its chimney. He shifted, and faced the front again, but couldn't see the fore tower. He'd have to cross the courtyard and take the right hand door.

"If it'll open..." he muttered. He started across, trying to keep his breath and feet quiet so he could listen. He drew close to the door—

It hung open.

He glanced over his shoulder at the one directly across the way. It was shut, and thistles grew in front of it. He swallowed, and pushed through the half-open door.

The squeaking hinge resounded through a very large, empty room— one whose two high front windows allowed a bleak light to tumble down onto plain flagstone. To his left, against the castle's front, a curved, high wall enclosed a broad, winding staircase. Ahead of him stood giant double doors, carved with a scene of knights at a banquet. And to his right, he could see a little green door crouching, almost as if it didn't want to be noticed. It gapped open, but it was pitch dark beyond. And Amber knew that his answer to the smoke lay up at least three flights of steps.

He crossed the wide space, leaving footprints in the dust, swung around and glanced up the curving staircase. A little way up, he could see daylight again. So he started climbing, past the empty hooks that used to hold torches, his steps thudding on stone. He took great care where he put his feet—castle stairs were purposefully built unevenly to cause intruders to trip, fall down and break their necks. He rolled his eyes.

"Wouldn't *that* be nice." He passed a narrow window, taking a brief look out onto the bleak front yard before continuing upward. The stairwell darkened—he slowed down and put his hand against the wall, wincing as it became harder and harder to see...

Finally, it lightened again. He stepped onto a landing, then turned right, where the stairwell opened up into a small room. A wide, tattered red rug covered the wooden floor. Otherwise, nothing at all decorated the space. Light wandered in from little windows behind him, showing him a wide gap in the wall straight ahead. He headed through it, and found himself in a dim crossroads of corridors. One wide one headed straight on, into darkness. One to his right looked narrower, and darker. But the one to the left appeared broad, and at the far right end of it, light poured in through a large window, revealing the foot of another staircase. Amber paused a moment, re-orienting himself—

And realized that this staircase had to lead to the smoking tower.

He hurried toward it, his feet sounding even louder in the absolute, dusty silence. He passed three closed doors—one on his right and two on his left. He hopped up the first three steps...

Stopped.

The stairwell was dark.

"Door must be shut..." he mused. Setting his jaw, and pressing his hand to the wall, he started up.

All too soon, he could see nothing. He carefully lifted one foot before the other, groping ahead with his free hand so as not to bash his face on the door when he came to it. It seemed to go on forever...

There.

His hand met wood. He let go of the wall and slid his palms all over the new surface, searching...

Found it. A metal handle.

"Please open..." He gripped it, pushed it...

It released, swinging away from him.

At the end of a long corridor, he could see the bright outline of a door that clearly led outside. His brow knotting, he walked all the way toward it, reached it...

And realized that a little offshoot led to his right, as well. Up a set of stairs, he could see another door outlined in daylight. His frown deepened. If these stairs only led to the outside, then where was the *smoke* coming—

He bit his tongue.

An unmistakable *crackle* had just issued from somewhere to his right.

The crackle of embers in a fire. His heart pounding, he quickly searched through the dark...

Near the floor. A line of dim, gold light.

A doorway. To an *inside* room.

He fumbled, and found the handle. Worked it—it freed with a *clack*. He pushed on it—

"Oh!"

He stumbled, then jerked back. His mouth fell open.

That rich, sweet smell of burning peat bog flooded his senses, along with the bright dance of flames in the white-marble hearth across the room. The scent of spiced oranges and cloves joined the peat. Bright, ornate scarlet carpet lay across the floor, covering it entirely. To his left stood a gold-gilded, round table encircled by four plush red chairs. Tea for one, in silver setting, laid out with cakes and sandwiches, sat before one of these chairs—and the teapot steamed. To his right, on the wall, hung a huge, finely-crafted tapestry of a lush rose garden and a young, dark-haired woman in rags, standing with her back to him. And next to the right of the hearth stood a four-poster bed draped with thick maroon curtains and covered over with cloud-like white comforters and gold pillows. A delicate glass lamp flickered atop a little bedside table. A shiny cauldron hung from a spit above the fire, and four wooden bowls sat upon a stone near the hearth. A short washing stand, with pitcher and basin and towels, also stood beside. And off to the left of the hearth opened a wide window, overlooking the front yard, and through it had grown countless branches of roses that crawled across the wall above the fireplace, seeking the warmth of the chimney. But the vines did not bloom, and he could see their large thorns from here.

Amber stood frozen for several minutes, unable to pull in a breath, or let go his death grip on the door handle. But nothing moved except the happy flames, and the steam from the spout of the teapot.

"Hello?" he called hoarsely. "I'm...not trying to bother anyone, but..."

He trailed off. Waited. No one answered.

He stepped inside, letting the door drift shut behind him. He crept toward the window, and halted in front of it, gazing for the first time out and over Thornbind Wood.

The thickest fog still held it fast, the sky and earthy mist meeting in the near distance. He could not see the road on which he'd been traveling, the stream he had crossed, or the edge of the wide, black forest.

His stomach growled. At the same time, a full, airborne taste of some kind of creamed chicken soup filled his mouth and nose. His head came around and he found the cauldron on the hearth—and heard it bubbling.

He approached it, bending closer, and took another deep breath even as he saw the soup inside boil and steam. A ladle sat inside. His stomach growled again.

He took off his sack and plopped it down, then removed his lute and rested it gently against the side of the fireplace. Then, he grabbed one of the wooden bowls, snatched up the ladle, and dipped himself four spoonfuls of thick, creamy soup. He let go the ladle. It clacked back into the cauldron. Holding the bowl in both hands, he eagerly made his way over to the table where he sat down in one of the chairs, poured himself some tea with cream, and began to eat.

He drank down all of the delicious soup—it flooded his whole aching body with warmth—and he devoured the sandwiches and cakes on the tea tray. He also downed three cups of tea, until the pot sat empty. Then, with a heavy sigh, he flopped back in the chair...

And realized that the bed seemed much more appealing than the chair at the moment.

His entire frame suddenly heavy, he dragged himself out of the chair, pulled off his shoes, trousers and tunic and tossed them down, tugged back the thick blankets and tumbled into bed in his underclothes. He pulled the covers over himself, sinking down into the luxurious softness of the pillows and mattress. His eyes drifted shut immediately, as he absently thought to himself that if the masters of the house somehow materialized and wanted him to move, they would have to wake him first. He wished them luck with that.

"Your Highness?"

Oralia didn't turn toward the new voice right away—she stood with arms folded, facing the dressmaker's mannequin, studying the dress that hung upon it in the new morning light.

It looked like spun fire—fantastic golds, reds and oranges bloomed into a full, layered skirt and streamed from the shoulders and the sleeves in feathery strands. The haggard seamstress stood beside it, her lips pursed, staring at Oralia.

Oralia ignored her.

"Your Highness." The call came again, and she reluctantly turned toward the end of the grand hall, where Sir Roderick now strode toward her, his left hand on the butt of his sword.

"Where did you come from?" Oralia wondered. "You're dirty."

"Myself and three others have been searching the highways, just as you asked," Roderick answered, a little out of breath. Oralia's attention sharpened.

"Where is he?"

"We didn't find him," Roderick said. "But we found something else."

Oralia bit back her instinctive reply and forced herself to ask the right question.

"What did you find?"

Roderick sighed, and gazed at her solemnly, his blue eyes bright in the morning sun.

"At the edge of Thornbind," he said, his voice low. "Several highwaymen, all slaughtered."

"Good," Oralia said shortly. "We all need fewer of that kind, don't we?"

Roderick shook his head.

"They weren't killed by the sword or bow."

Oralia's eyes narrowed.

"What, then?"

Roderick hesitated.

"What is it?" Oralia demanded.

"They were struck with...with poison spines," Roderick almost whispered. "Just as the huntsman Pather was when he came to Princess Eleanora's aid."

Oralia went completely still. Roderick swallowed, glanced around the room, and leaned closer to her.

"I believe that the same beast who killed your sister and the huntsman now resides in that part of the woods."

Oralia said nothing. Her gaze unfocused, and she stared off, past Roderick. Her thumb rubbed against her opposite arm.

"What should we do?" Roderick asked.

Oralia paced away from him, into a beam of sun on the floor. She stood in its center, and then lifted her face to the fullness of the light.

"I want you to find where it's living," she said. "If you would, please, Roderick. And when you do, come back to me and tell me what it looks like."

"Do you want me to kill it?"

Roderick's words hung in the air. Oralia drew in a breath.

"Not yet," she finally answered. "Just tell me what it's doing. But take those same men with you—just a few. Everybody knows there's magic of all kinds in Thornbind. It's an ugly place, and it's better not to attract a lot of attention." She turned her head, and gazed at the knight. "Thank you, Roderick. You are so brave."

He inadvertently smiled, then bowed at the waist.

"Anything for you, Princess," he breathed, then turned and left the hall. As soon as the door shut behind him, Oralia turned on the seamstress.

"The hem is too long," she snapped, pointing at the dress. "I'll not be tripping up the aisle, thank you. Fix it at once."

"Yes, Your Highness."

CHAPTER NINE

"AND CAME UPON A BEAST"

Amber *stretched*. His legs swished beneath smooth sheets. He blinked his eyes open, and gazed drowsily up at the red curtains above his head. He sighed, rubbing his face, grimly recalling what had happened with the highwaymen, and how he'd found himself wandering into a strange castle and up a lot of stairs...

He frowned. Then, slowly, he sat up.

He felt different.

When he had tumbled into bed hours earlier, he had been grungy, sweaty and dusty from falling and running down that dirty road. But now, his whole body felt refreshed, as if he'd bathed in hot water with soap and dried with a soft towel before climbing beneath the comforters. The underclothes he wore also felt clean.

He twisted, searching the room—

His clothes lay folded on the chair by the fire. The fire that still crackled and danced just as merrily as it had before he fell asleep.

"All...right...?" he muttered, unsettled. He glanced out the window.

Clouds still covered the sky, but he could sense it was late afternoon. He had slept all day.

Swallowing, he shoved the covers out of the way and got up. He grabbed his clothes and pulled them on, as well as his shoes. He glanced over at his lute and pack, a twinge running through him, but he decided to leave both of them for the moment. *Someone* was here. Someone else. And he had to find him or her. If for no other reason than to thank him for the food and the bed.

And to ask him why in the world he was being so sneaky.

He headed to the door, hoping he could remember the way down. He left the cozy room, turned left twice and made himself slow down, because it instantly got quite a bit darker. He ran one hand along the wall and held the other out to feel for the door. When he found it, he pulled it open, and then he maneuvered his way down the curling staircase until he reached that long corridor with the window. From where he stood, he could see one set of footsteps in the dust.

One.

His own, when he'd come up here in the first place.

A quiet shudder ran down his spine.

He started forward again, very carefully, listening with all his might. His footsteps creaked on the wooden floor.

He looked ahead, to his right. That was the door he'd come through that morning. If he headed down those stairs, perhaps—

He stopped. Turned and stared at the door directly to his left.

He'd heard something—a low rustle. Then a clank.

Amber stood just as he was for several minutes, straining. But he didn't hear anything else.

He pushed through the door.

The hinges creaked loudly. Ahead, a little window illuminated a small room, and a staircase. It looked like a servant's staircase. He made for it, and headed down.

This stairway curled even tighter than the others, and the steps were especially narrow. He had to move gingerly or he knew he'd slip and fall. Down below, some other light source managed to creep up this way, showing him the edges of the stairs at least. Finally, he emerged onto a landing. To his right, the stairs kept plunging downward, into the dark. Ahead of him stood an open door that led to a kitchen.

Or rather...

What *had* been a kitchen.

He stopped on the threshold, his brow furrowing. Windows to his right revealed the hen yard, and accompanied a little door he had not noticed from outside. Another door across to his left hung open to a much larger, dark room...

But no fire burnt in the thick stone oven. Dust coated the wide baking table in the center of the room. All the counters lay empty, the open shelves bare. No torches or lamps lived here, either.

"Hello?" he called. The tones of his voice danced between the wooden shelves and echoed out into that wider room. No other voice returned.

"Oooh," he breathed out tightly, closing his hands. He stepped over the threshold, listening to the sound of his steps on the stone. He eyed the dusty brass kettle atop the stove, and canted his head. Why had everything else been taken, but not this?

His toe hit something.

It skittered away across the hard floor.

He jumped back—

A tinder box.

Quickly, he snatched it up. He had one of his own in his pack, but like an idiot, he'd forgotten to bring it down with him. Now, if he could just find a lamp or a torch—

He whipped around, his heart rate skyrocketing.

A sound.

A rustling, heavy, sweeping sound.

Kssssssssssshhhhht...

Clenching the tinder box, he inched back toward the door through which he had come.

He leaned around the frame, peering down into the dark. He held his breath.

Silence.

He braced his hand on the wall and glanced back into the kitchen, his jaw clamping. No lamps, no torches, not even any candles—

His hand bumped iron.

He twitched it back, his heart slamming into his ribs again.

The handle of a torch clanked in its sconce.

"Aha. Good," he sighed shakily. He snatched it up, carried it back into the kitchen and set it down on the table, the flammable end sticking out over the edge. He lifted the tinder box, opened it, took out the flint and struck the side with it, sending sparks flaring toward the torch.

The next second, flames burst to life, heating his hands. He snatched up the dancing torch, stuffed the tinder box in his pocket, and faced the dark again.

He stepped through the door and down the first few steps, holding the torch down lower so he could spy where to put his feet. Every ten stairs he stopped, halting his breathing, trying to catch that noise again.

70

Nothing came.

Down and down he paced, until the darkness pressed in thick, and the air smelled moldy and wet and—something else. The torch illuminated just a short way ahead of him. He bit back a shiver, and kept going.

Finally, he strode out onto even ground. Biting the inside of his lip, he lifted his torch over his head and looked up.

A huge room, the edges in shadow. Low ceiling. Earthy floor. And a strange, rank odor that almost smelled like...

"Fish?" He took a step forward—

Crunch.

He recoiled, jabbing the torch at his feet—

Piles of white fish skeletons carpeted the ground. He backpedaled, sucking in a full breath of that horrid stench—

"Thhhhht....thhhhht...thhhhhttt..."

He went rigid. His knuckles turned white.

Something moved in the shadow.

A long, lithe, powerful form. It scuttled forward through the bones, slithering between the rancid piles, speeding toward him—

Amber's heel hit the bottom step. He reeled—

It swooped toward him—and reared up like a threatened cobra.

A tail—ten feet long, covered in flashing spines, lashed feverishly through the skeletons as it lifted the creature's upper body, towering over Amber.

The upper body of a woman.

And yet—nothing like a woman.

In size, shape and curve, it followed. But her entire figure was covered over with bluish, silvery scales, and spines laced up her back. She spread her arms wide, looming over him as low in her throat a deep, thudding hiss vibrated her whole frame. Amber thrust the flame toward her...

The shaking torch lit a vivid fiend.

A human head—ears, eyes, nose and mouth—but broad fans,

anchored behind her pointed ears, flared out—just like those of blue asps. And scales layered these features, too. Her shining silver eyes fixed on him, her dark brow snarled and she opened her mouth—

Her teeth—razor sharp and bone-white—gleamed in the dark.

And she let out an inhuman, grating, scraping howl—

And lunged at him.

He whirled around and charged up the stairs—she slammed into the stone right behind him. The torch bounced in his sweaty fingers. He clawed his way up, up, up, as fast as his feet would move. The beast slapped the walls with her bare hands, her fury of hissing like the chatter of teeth and the swarm of bees.

Then, for one horrid instant of blackness—the torch went out.

The next second, he burst out into the kitchen, threw down the useless torch and pelted out into that large room—a room that yawned far to his right. He ignored it, making for the sliver of light to his left...

He flung that door open and, in a blink, recognized one of the rooms he had been in before, and those stairs!

He bolted toward them, and hauled himself up and up and around and around, until he flung himself into the landing, out into the corridor, up the stairs, down the hall, and through the door of his room.

He slammed the door shut and threw the bar across it, then lunged at one of the chairs, grabbed it and propped it up under the handle, hard. Then, his pulse raging in his ears, he retreated, his attention captive to that door.

Any second, it would rattle. Any second, she'd slam her shoulder into it, and the wood would shiver.

He shot a glance at the window—

"No good," he rasped. That entire way was covered in rose vines. He would shred himself before he touched the ground.

He took three steps back toward his bed and reflexively gripped the wooden post, struggling to calm his breathing. He waited, his mind flying.

Nothing happened.

He stood there for several minutes, his head hurting from listening so hard. But nothing came winding and sliding up the corridor. Nothing hissed outside the wooden barrier.

Nothing.

A listless wind murmured outside, wandering through the leaves of the thorny vines by the window.

Gradually, Amber loosed his hold on the post, and dared to take a few steps back toward the door. He edged close, leaning his head toward it...

Outside, the hallway sounded hollow. He could only hear that wistful breeze muttering against the opening that led to the top of his tower.

"Gah," he gushed, slapping his hands over his face. He dragged his fingers down his cheeks, then swiped the sweat from his brow. He backed up, sat down heavily in the chair, and remained there for a very long time.

Night fell uneasily, crouching closer and closer to Amber's window until blackness covered the entire view as completely as a shutter. But the fire in the hearth burnt brighter, filling the room with light and warmth. And before long, Amber noticed a rich, different smell.

He climbed out of his chair, frowning, and crept back toward that little cauldron and peered inside...

To see a different kind of stew bubbling there.

It had a reddish broth—tomato, perhaps—and all kinds of vegetables kept it company.

Amber stared. He hardly breathed for several minutes.

Yet the stew continued to bubble pleasantly, and his mouth started to water.

So, he grabbed one of the bowls, ladled himself a good portion and, trying not to drip, went back to the table...

To see the tray filled with sandwiches and cakes, and a trail of steam issuing from the teapot.

He clenched the soup bowl so hard it almost shook loose of his grip. Some soup sloshed over the side—

"Ow!" he yelped, nearly dropping the bowl, and stuck his burnt finger in his mouth. He gaped at the tea setting for a full ten minutes—but though the tea innocently steamed, nothing else stirred. So he eased toward it, set his soup down and sat down himself, and began to eat.

The food tasted even more delicious than before. He ate it all and drank it all, attempting not to scald himself. But when he had finished, the silence weighed on him. And that *door*, with the chair still propped up against it, stood before him in surly half shadow. He glared at it, shoved his chair back and got up. He sat down by the fireplace and leaned against it, taking up his lute. He plucked aimlessly on the strings, resolving to ignore that frowning door and the dark that lingered on the other side.

Eventually, his aimless plucking grew a tune—the tune of an old song he had not sung in a while. He wondered if he could remember all the words. Re-settling himself, he lowered his head to concentrate, and began to sing.

> " *There is a legend only told by old folk in the inns*
> *Of a happy castle, long ago—filled with laughing kin*
> *A fairer folk you ne'er would see now in any land*
> *Fairest of them all by far was princess Airinlee*
> *Her eyes of blue, no star shone brighter in the sky at night*
> *None is worthy, ever worthy, but a pure and gentle knight."*

"Aha...I remember now..." Amber lifted his head and grinned to himself. He plucked more swiftly and more loudly, embellishing the melody as he kept going.

> *"Alas a curse fell on this place and put them all to sleep*
> *A fairy witch was slighted and her peace she could not keep*
> *Now all the court does slumber in the places where they stood*
> *And Arinlee lies tower-high behind an open door.*
> *Her eyes of blue, they close now softly as she lies on high*
> *None is worthy, ever worthy, but a pure and gentle knight.*
> *Now a mighty wall of thorns has grown around the castle wall*
> *None can breach it, many try, but meet their deaths do all*
> *So there she sleeps, centuries long, the fair maid Airenlee*
> *And none can reach her, thus to kiss her, thus to set her free.*
> *Her eyes of blue, asleep like death, behind that thorny height*
> *None is worthy, ever worthy, but a pure and gentle..."*

Amber stopped. He lifted his hand off the strings, then pressed his palm to them, silencing them.
Another sound. Like...
A sigh.
He lowered his lute to the carpet and gingerly got to his feet. He tiptoed across the room, grabbed the chair and eased it away from the door. Clenching his teeth to keep them from rattling, he worked the handle—begged the hinges to be quiet—and pulled open the door.

Outside and to his left, he could sense that the door to the roof hung slightly ajar. He twisted around and looked to his window.

The clouds had parted, just a little, and the full moon bled down through them.

He slipped out, and padded toward that outside opening. He paused behind the door itself, and inched his head around the wood to see.

His breath left him.

All the way across the roof, near the foot of the opposite tower, stood a person. Full in the waning white moonlight. Her face tilted toward the shrouded sky.

The light shimmered against her smooth, fine scales, making them look like liquid silver, and it softened the slender curves of her body. The fans near her face had calmed, and rested against the sides of her neck. Her large eyes reflected a luminous shine as she gazed, unblinking, at the moon. Watching it withdraw behind the clouds. The black shadow of the tower fell across her long, sweeping tail. Thus, from where Amber stood, he could have mistaken her for a pale young woman dressed in blues and whites.

Except for the bearing of her features.

Her gaze—vacant. Barren as a waterless sea. Her mouth— incapable of speech, of smiling or frowning. Her expression blank, and immovable. She stared, without pondering. No thought lived behind those eyes, or flickered at the corners of those lips.

A silver serpent. Still and silent as ice. Inhuman as stone.

Her attention drifted downward, and she stared out into the lightless forest. She started forward.

Amber twitched back—but she made for the front wall, her powerful tail steadily slithering, propelling her, the spines tamed and lying flat. She leaned down, walking with her hands, until she braced herself up on the parapet, and canted her head, gauging the downward angle.

Then, without another moment of calculation, she plunged over the edge.

Amber gasped, grabbing the door as the end of her tail waved against the dark...

And then she was gone, down the side of the castle and into the night.

Amber stayed where he was for several minutes, the night air touching his face. He gazed at the place where she'd disappeared, letting the

75

side of his head rest against the door.

Finally, he pulled back, shut the door, and returned to his room. He barred the door again, but not as violently. And as he undressed for bed, he did not prop the chair against it.

CHAPTER TEN

"A BALM APPEARED"

Clink.

Amber jerked. He grabbed the bedcovers, heart pounding as he fought against the shadows to recognize some part of the ceiling. He couldn't.

He thrashed onto his right side —

Found the side of the fireplace. And beyond that, the vine-draped window. Moonlight poured in, turning the leaves to silver and the stones to alabaster. The fire burnt low in the hearth—so low, he could hardly hear it crackling. He tried to calm his breathing, tried to swallow. His throat felt dry.

"All right...all right...the tower in the castle..." he whispered, squeezing his eyes shut for a moment before opening them again. "But what..." He stopped.

There, on the mantel, stood a bottle.

A bottle that had not been there before.

For a long moment, he gawped at it. Moonlight glinted off of its smooth shoulders. It looked about as tall as his hand; plain, slightly-transparent green glass, with a cork in the top. Dark liquid filled it. And it had a label he could not read from here.

Slowly, he pushed the covers off and stood up. He shuffled across the soft rug until he stood eye-level with that bottle. He tipped his head, frowning hard, and read the black-ink label on the side.

Snakesalve
balm for scar and skin

"Snakesalve?" Amber reached out to touch it.

A shriek.

He leaped back, tripped and almost fell. The wailing echoes fled like ravens across the outer yard and over the trees.

He hurried to the window, his footsteps thudding. He put his hands out to lean forward—stopped himself just short of plunging his fingers down through a tangle of thorns. He bared his teeth at the wicked plants, then lifted his attention to the edges of the moonlit yard.

He couldn't see anything. Nothing but the bare, open space and the woods beyond. He knew the sound had come from out there, not very far away. Probably just the distance to the stream...

Again!

A ripping howl, like a cornered cat.

Low rolling thuds. Slashing through dry underbrush.

A sharp, guttural, mammal growl.

Amber absently took hold of a leaf and squeezed it hard between his fingers.

Rippling thrashing amongst low bushes.

A violent *crash* against a tree trunk.

Amber twitched. The uppermost branches of one of the trees out there shuddered.

Silence fell.

He sucked in a breath. Held it.

Nothing.

Nothing moved. No more snarls, no more howling.

Amber started breathing again, unsteadily, his teeth clamping. He took half a step back.

Wait—

Something appeared, at the corner of the yard. Sliding out of the dark.

He stepped forward again. Leaned halfway out the window.

It was her.

The creature—the snake.

She crawled full on her belly, her long tail trailing behind her, writhing weakly as she clawed her way across the withered grass. She stretched forward, one hand at a time, taking fistfuls of plants and tugging the rest of her body along.

She paused once, her head hanging, her shoulders heaving. Then, she rallied, hissing in her throat, and scrambled onward, upward.

Amber's fingers found that leaf again, and plucked it loose. He watched, transfixed, as she struggled up the hill, furiously slapping the earth with her tail, leaving spines in her wake, grunting, spitting and keening with every advance.

Finally, she achieved the edge of the castle, and rounded his tower. He couldn't see her anymore.

He took three steps back, eyeing the edge of those menacing woods, and bit his lip. But no other sounds drifted out of Thornbind, and no menacing hisses issued from the chambers below.

All fell back to quiet, leaving Amber alone with the embers of the fire, and the bottle of Snakesalve winking at him.

He sneaked out into the corridor, taking deep breaths of the dawn fog that trickled in through the open outside door ahead of him. After what he had seen at the window, it had taken great effort to make himself get back into bed. He had slept fitfully all the rest of the night, twitching awake each time the smallest twig snapped somewhere far out in the forest. As some odd result, he did not feel nearly as clean or refreshed as he left his room and warily headed to the stairs. He hadn't eaten, either, and his stomach felt hollow and tense.

He made his way down the winding stair, swished through the dust, turned right and found the next set of stairs. Down he went again, listening. Every noise he made amplified a thousand times, resounding against the barren stone. He winced every time he set his heel down. At last, he reached the main floor, and paused in the middle of the large room, quieting his breath.

Nothing.

He made himself turn to the left and step through the huge doors into the towering, shadowed chamber. He glanced through it, but could only make out a dark dais at the farthest end, the outlines of what could be fire pits and hearths, and something else—something like faintly-gleaming ribs that rested against the wall and stretched up into the blackness. He kept moving, his footsteps tapping too loudly...

Stopped at the threshold of the kitchen.

The door that led to the hen yard hung open. The table stood askew. And all along the flagstones trailed a ragged wake of blood.

It stood out clearly in the pale morning light that entered through the windows: fresh blood, accompanied by bright scarlet palm prints. Left by hands the size of a woman's.

Amber gulped, sick to his stomach all at once. The trail led to the door over there—the door that opened to the downward spiral and the pit of bones. And he still couldn't hear anything.

For a very long time, he stood there, staring at the dark doorway. He stepped back.

His gaze caught on the blood again. So much blood.

A deep, quiet pang traveled down behind his breastbone.

He crossed the floor, scouring it—found the torch and picked it up. He reached in his pocket, grabbed the tinderbox and lit the torch, ignoring how badly his fingers trembled. The flame sputtered as he turned and faced the shadow. He gritted his teeth, took three sharp breaths, and stepped through.

Amber moved very carefully, setting each foot upon each step with as much silence as he could manage. He kept one hand on the stone wall even as he lowered the wavering torch, studying the persistent red stain that marred the stairs. It seemed to take forever—much longer than before—and the fish carcasses reeked now, making his throat snap shut so that he had to snort to make himself keep breathing.

The last step approached. He ventured out onto the even, bone-strewn ground. Lifting the torch, his heart hammering against his ribs, he peered down the long chamber.

Save for the fish skeletons, it was empty.

He frowned, his eyes flashing. He swept the torch to his right...

The blood trail continued on that way...

Through a wide door that hung open. It doubtlessly led to some kind of larder...

Or dungeon.

He gulped again, but ventured toward it, his heels crackling over the bones. He stepped through...

And let out a minute sigh.

Not a dungeon. A wine cellar.

Large barrels, all standing, lined this smaller room. The floor smoothed out beneath his feet—paved. He lowered his torch again...

Blood here, too. A lot of it.

"Kttthhhht. Kttthhhhht. Kttthhhht."

Amber jolted. The deadly hissing thudded through the barrels and vibrated through the floor.

But, somehow, it seemed fainter. And a strained gasp separated each spit.

He stood frozen for several moments, holding his breath.

"Ktthhhht...Kttthhhht....Ktthhhhh....hhhhttthhh..."

The hissing faded off.

Rustling issued from between the barrels. A distressed grunt. Amber pushed the torch closer toward the barrels...

A glimmer of scales.

He stepped nearer. Three steps nearer. Lifted the torch...

There she was.

He could hardly make out her shape. Her long tail wrapped so completely around her, every spine flared, forming a tight, poisonous hedge around her upper body. She lay on her right side, her arms wrapped around her chest, her shoulders hunched, her gleaming eyes peering just over her tail, through the forest of spines.

Staring right at him.

She breathed uneasily. Long shivers traveled from her head all the way down and around the length of her tightly-spiraled body.

"Tht. Tht. Tht," she clicked. Her tail curled tighter, like a closing fist. Amber took another step closer...

His toe slipped. He glanced down.

A puddle of blood. He had stepped in a puddle of blood.

That pang ran through him again, and he edged even closer, pushing the torch nearer...

Now he could see them: dark lacerations on her arm, her head. But he had no doubt that she was hiding the worst ones underneath that muscular tail and all of those venomous needles.

"You're hurt."

81

His voice rang through the room—much too loudly. She flinched, pulling even tauter than he had thought possible.

"*Thhhht! Thhhht...*" she spat, finishing it with an almost cat-like, waning growl. Amber didn't pull back. Instead, he very, *very* carefully knelt down near one of the barrels. She stared at him over her spiny tail, her eyes narrowing to slits, tremors racing through her frame. She shifted painfully, snapping out another sound like a cornered cat. Amber managed to draw in another breath.

"Can you understand me?" he asked, more quietly. "Do you...Do you understand anything I'm saying?"

Her silver gaze flicked from him to the torch, back to him, then to the torch again.

"I'm not going to hurt you," he said, leaning toward her. "I just want to—"

Her attention fixed on the torch—

She *hissed* violently, showing all her teeth—

And flung out her tail.

Amber threw himself onto his back, almost dropping the torch—

Her tail slammed into a barrel, knocked it sideways, split it open—

Amber wrenched himself into a sitting position...

She seethed and writhed like a boiling pot, the end of her tail feverishly slapping the stones and the flinders of the empty barrel...

A long, keening groan pulled through her body. The slapping slackened, then ceased. The tension melted from her length, her tail unwound...

And she tipped onto her back. Her head lolled, her arms loosed, and she let out a gurgling sigh. Her right arm, limp, slid to the floor. All the spines relaxed, and slowly laid down.

She stopped moving.

Amber scrambled onto his hand and knees, holding the torch as steady as he could. He crawled to her, his heartbeat raging as he eyed that vicious tail, ready to scald it with his torch if it so much as shifted...

His gaze fell on her upper body. He stopped.

All the scales there were slick with blood. Her chest, her belly, her throat, her face, her arms. Long, successive gouges punctured and slashed across her skin.

She had been mauled by something huge, with long, curved claws.

82

Perhaps a lion. Or a bear.

Amber scooted even nearer, blood seeping through the knees of his trousers. Her silver eyes had closed. Her lips parted. He couldn't tell if she was breathing.

His free hand closed to a fist.

For a very long time, he did not move. He gritted his teeth, and glanced sideways at that long, evil tail. His eyes found her again.

He stretched out his right hand. Lowered it. Rested his shaking fingers on the base of her throat.

Cool. Smooth.

He waited.

And then, the barest flutter touched his fingertips. Something like a pulse.

Her throat spasmed three times—like the throat of a bird. And her eyes rolled beneath delicate lids.

Amber sucked in a gasp.

"I'll be right back."

He jumped to his feet, turned around and raced out of the wine cellar.

Amber took the stairs back down from his tower at a reckless speed, his breath rasping in his ears. He gripped the bottle of Snakesalve in his left hand and steadied himself with his right, realizing that if he *dropped* this bottle...

He hurried out of the stairway, back across to the large chamber, through the kitchen and into the winding stairwell. There, he snatched the burning torch out of its rack and headed down the stairs, without hesitation
this time.

He strode across the fish bones, the torchlight bouncing wildly.

He entered the wine cellar, splishing through blood. He set the torch down on top of one of the barrels, so that it burned above her head as he knelt. He pressed his fingers to her throat again.

Again, that flutter. But fainter.

He pulled the cork from the bottle with a *pop*, and set the cork aside. He tipped the bottle and poured some of the thick, molasses-like salve into his palm. It felt ice cold, and tingled against his skin.

Amber grimaced, and took three sharp, bracing breaths, just knowing that he was about to get cracked over the head with that tail and the spines were going to shoot straight through his brain...

He reached out and rubbed the salve across a long gash on her upper chest. The salve glittered as he spread it. Amber's hand stopped.

Her throat spasmed weakly again. Otherwise, she stayed still.

Biting his tongue, he scooted closer, poured more salve, and set in to work.

He gently smoothed it over every bleeding tear. Papery scales came away on his fingers. Blood soon mixed with the salve on his hands, but as he watched, the salve on the wounds congealed, sealing around the ripped skin. He concentrated first on the damage done to her chest, belly and throat, then moved to her slender, muscular arms. The knuckles of her hands had been flayed, with black fur imbedded under her sharp, black claws. Amber's brow twisted as he softly held her right hand in his left, studying it. It had been a bear, after all.

Delicately, with his fingertips, he spread the salve across each torn knuckle, occasionally glancing up to her motionless face. But she did not stir.

Finally, after he had finished with both arms, he edged uneasily closer, bending over her, running his gaze over her face, where two long lines of open flesh crossed her cheek and nose—and one gash crossed the upper lid of her right eye. He dipped the very last bit of salve into his left palm, took some onto the fingertips of his right hand, and touched her face.

He grimaced, waiting for that tail to crackle behind him. Waiting for her icy eyes to fly open...

They didn't. He slowly traced those wounds, watched the salve seal them...

And gazed at her in the firelight.

He lowered his sticky hand, and rested it on her throat.

That little flutter remained. But the rest of her seemed to be made of stone. Feeling sick to his stomach again, Amber straightened his stiff back and sat down cross-legged. He sighed, closing his cold, slick fingers.

"Don't die," he murmured, absently realizing that his trousers were now soaked in her blood.

CHAPTER ELEVEN

"A SONG WAS FINISHED"

Amber lay in bed, listlessly gazing at the window, watching the dim afternoon sunlight and breeze play across the rustling leaves of the rose vines, and studying the elaborate woven pattern on the red rug in front of the hearth.

He had sat down in that damp, bloody pit for several hours, watching the snake beast breathe shallowly. She never moved. Finally, pain began darting around in Amber's legs and lower back, and the blood on his hands caked and cracked. He made himself climb to his feet, take the torch, and, with a lingering look back down at her, he had hobbled up the stairs, all the way back up to his tower—though he left the extinguished torch in its rack at the head of the cellar steps.

Upon his entry to his tower room, he had found a wash basin, towels and pitcher on the table. The tea tray had vanished.

Magic, then. It had to be magic. All of it. He wearily kicked himself for taking so long to figure that out.

Now, he turned over onto his back in bed and rubbed his face. Stripping off his bloody clothes, bathing all the grime off his skin and falling into bed had felt infinitely wonderful, and sleeping buried in those warm blankets and pillows for several hours had eased the penetrating aches in his bones.

Gradually, the smell of a creamy chicken stew teased his senses.

He sat up, pushed off the covers, got up, and found his clothes folded neatly on the chair. And clean.

"Sure," he muttered, rubbing his face again. "Now it makes sense." He dressed himself, then moved to the stew, ladled himself out a bowl full and ate, seated by the fire, pondering. As he drained the last bit, his gaze had unfocused almost completely. He paused, the bowl at his lips.

Then, with decision, he got up, ladled a new bowl full, and headed for the door.

He trailed down, down, through the halls, the great room, the kitchen—he lit the torch, and carried it with him down the winding stair, careful not to spill and burn himself.

It stank even worse as he descended. He bit the inside of his cheek, half wondering, stopping each time he wondered too far...

He picked his way through the bones, grimacing, and into the wine cellar.

"Hello," he called, biting back his nerves. "It's just me. Just me."

No sound came in reply. He stepped nearer, holding the torch higher...

She lay on her back still. She looked exactly the same—a long, dully- gleaming form amid shadows upon black stone. Except...

Her eyes were open.

Just slitted open. But he could see the glint of silver between her lids. And she was breathing.

"I brought you food," he said, forcing his voice to stay even. "It's some kind of cream chicken broth. I ate a bowl of it already—it's good. And...not poisoned."

She did not respond. He risked coming even nearer, bent his knees, and set the bowl next to her arm. He straightened up, and swallowed.

"I have no idea if you can understand me," he admitted. "And I'm too afraid to try to feed you myself."

Nothing happened for a long moment. Then, she swallowed.

"Do you...do you want it?" Amber asked, brow furrowing. He picked the bowl up again, and edged closer...

She shifted her shoulder, and then the end of that deadly tail hissed slowly across the floor.

Amber set down the bowl with a clack and backed up. The tail went still. She blinked languidly, and her throat smasmed once more. Her right eyelid was still swollen almost shut. The sealed patches of snakesalve glistened across her body. Amber gritted his teeth.

"All right, Silver," he said softly. "I'll leave you alone. But you've...You've got to put something in your stomach or gullet or whatever it is if you're going to live."

She did not move. He eased forward again, wincing, and pushed the bowl toward her hand. It scraped across the stone and bumped her knuckles. She did nothing. He waited. Waited for several long moments, only taking half breaths, watching her in the flickering flame. The only thing she did was blink once in a while. And her throat throbbed occasionally. Nothing else. So, finally, Amber got up and reluctantly left her there.

The rest of the afternoon, Amber wandered through the lower portion of the castle. He hung up the torch, stepped out of the stairwell into the kitchen, then, instead of going through the door into the vast chamber, he turned to his left and passed into a wide, dim, dusty hallway. Across from him stood a line of low doors, all shut. He stepped toward the one right in front of him, reached out, grasped the latch, worked it and pulled—

"*No!*" a witchy, wooden voice barked—

—and the door pulled out of his hand and snapped shut again.

Amber leaped backward, slapping a hand to his heart. He stared, wide-eyed at the door...

But it remained as it was.

He eyed it sideways, and set his teeth. He grabbed the handle again and *pulled*—

"*No!*" the rusty voice shrieked, and slammed shut with even more force than before.

"*What* on *earth...?*" Amber gaped. "I wonder if..." He moved to his left, to the next door, grabbed it and pulled it open—

"*No!*" it clipped angrily, slapping closed and wrenching Amber's fingers. He stood there for a while, staring at it...

Then grinned.

He grabbed the handle with both hands, braced his left foot against the door post, worked the latch and *pulled* with all the strength in his shoulders and back.

"*Nnnnnnnnnnnnnnn...*" the door squeaked desperately as it gapped open. "*Nnnno!*"

It yanked out of his hand and crashed shut with a thunderous *bang*.

Amber burst out laughing. He wagged a finger at the door.

"I *will* get you open. Just wait."

Deep inside its frame, the door seemed to growl. Amber's grin widened.

He moved down the line of doors, some on his left now, as well as his right, testing all of them—and every single one clapped shut with a resounding *"No!"* so cranky and cat-like that it amused him to no end. Finally, he ran out of doors to torment and found the end of the hall. Hoping that *this* door didn't snarl at him, he gripped the latch and tugged...

It moaned, but otherwise acted perfectly respectable as it swung open...

To reveal a short passage open to the outside air. To his left, out the tall cobbled hallway waited the gray, dusty grounds. To his right opened the broad courtyard. But in the wall straight ahead of him stood another door. He crossed the passage, studied the broad, iron-bound door, and grasped the handle. This one he had to push open, and it did not want to budge. He was forced to lay his shoulder into it before it gave way into the room beyond.

He stepped in, his feet sweeping through dust. Pensive light poured in from a window to his left, and another to his right. A large, tattered rug lay on the floor. An iron chandelier hung from the ceiling, and a small fireplace stood lifeless in the far left hand corner. Otherwise, the place was empty. It must have once been a kind of sitting room. Straight ahead was another door, a narrower one, but this one hung open. He stepped toward it, tilting his head...

And paused after he had crossed the threshold, gazing up and through an enormous room whose walls—when not interrupted by windows—were covered with wooden shelves.

Empty shelves.

He stood in a beam of listless sunlight, glancing slowly up and down, listening as even his slightest movement echoed through the empty.

A library. With no books. Not a one. Not even a stray scrap of paper, or a bookmark left behind.

Just a hollow room, gutted and lifeless. Its purpose robbed.

Amber suddenly wondered if he'd ever seen a sadder place.

That deep, aching pang ran its thumb along the inside of his breastbone again, and he pressed his fingers to his heart, the skin around his eyes tightening. Then he ran his hand through his curls, turned and left the library, shut the door behind him, and headed with swift purpose through the corridors, up the stairs and to his tower.

Twang.

Amber sighed and set his lute down on the rug, then rubbed his eyes. He glanced to his right, through the window, wondering at how thin the morning light looked—almost like the light of a winter day, rather than midsummer. He climbed to his feet, hesitated, and bit his lip. His door glared back at him.

He had slept last night, but not well. He had thrown the covers off and stared in exasperation at the ceiling more than once. When dawn had finally come, he had climbed out, dressed, and drank down the chicken broth he had found in the cauldron. After that, he had diddled on his lute, but he had kept biting the side of his cheek and making mistakes until he had given up.

Now, he huffed, strode across the room, and opened the door. Keeping his teeth set, he made his way down the passage, down the stairs through the dusty hall, down and down, his footsteps battering through the silence. Through the grand chamber, into the kitchen...

He paused at the top of the cellar stairs, his hand pausing by the lifeless torch. He listened.

Nothing.

He lit the torch.

The scent of burning oil snapped through the air in front of his face.

He blinked against the sudden brightness, took the torch down with a *clack*, and started down the stairs.

He took a deep breath, and then held it as long as he could as he descended to avoid that stench of fish. Grimacing, he hurried through the bone room, his feet crunching, and stepped through into the wine cellar.

He slowed down, and paused.

It stank in here now, worse than the fish. The pieces of the broken barrel spread all over the sticky floor. He peered past them, wincing.

There.

She rested on her right side in the filth, facing him, her arms loosely crossed over her chest. Her long tail lay in a lifeless curl, her spines flat.

She watched him. She breathed shallowly. And the bowl of cream chicken soup sat on the stones in front of her, as full as when he had left it there yesterday.

Amber heaved another sigh.

"You didn't listen to me, did you?" he muttered. "You lost too much blood—you need to eat." He stepped forward and crouched down, glancing at the soup. "This is ice cold now. It's no good." He lifted his head and met her eyes.

She gazed back at him. Unmoving. Then, she blinked—very slowly.

Her eyes were green. Deep green, with flecks of silver. And empty as the sky—though the right one could barely open.

Amber's eyebrows drew together as he opened his mouth, but words died on his lips.

"All right," he finally said. "All right, something else."

He got up, turned around, and left.

He charged up the stairs, put the torch back, and marched all the way back up to his tower. He fished out another bowl and ladled the hot broth into it, then snatched up his lute and threw it over his shoulder. Then, he went back down.

All the way back down, less careful on the stairs, and moving fast enough through the bone room to avoid choking.

Her eyes immediately found the fire he carried, and dully followed it as he came closer than before. Gingerly, he set the torch down on a barrel, then rested the new bowl on the floor near her. He pulled the old bowl away and set it aside.

She eyed the torch for a long time, without moving her head, but it flickered steadily and did nothing else. Finally, her attention wandered down to the new bowl. Amber held his breath again, and waited.

She took a breath, released it...

And her gaze found his. She did not move.

"Come on," he urged. "You need to eat. Do you...Do you *want* to die?"

She blinked again. Slight tension appeared on her brow. But she did not reach for the bowl.

Amber stayed still, studying that change on her face. Then, he reached around, pulled his lute free, and sat down cross-legged, ignoring the stickiness of the dirty floor.

"Ahem," he said, tuning his instrument with several quick strums and a few quick twists of the keys. "All right, hm...All right." He adjusted the way he was sitting, took a breath and fought not to gag.

"If a gold coin lies down
In the shaft of a well
And deep water hides it
Its worth can you tell?
If the shadows conceal it and moss makes its bed
Is this gold valued less than upon a king's head?"

The strumming of the lute filled the black, horrid room—and Amber's voice flooded the shadows. Out of the corner of his eye, he saw her shift the slightest bit, and her gaze sharpened. But he avoided looking at her, watching his fingers instead.

"So mark well my words now
Remember this tune
Lest the world tries a falsehood
To lead you untrue
No matter the depths of the black water cold
The coin is still worth—"

"—all its true weight in gold."

The faint female voice cut through the chord.

The lute almost fell out of Amber's hands. His heart *banged*, and his head flew up...

He stared at her.

She stared back. The skin around her eyes tightened, and she shifted her shoulder, pulling her arms harder around herself.

"What?" Amber breathed. Her lips tightened. She did not answer.

"You...You understand me, then?"

A shiver raced down the length of her body, and her tail curled around behind her.

"You can speak," Amber whispered. "Are you...What's your name?"

She said nothing, and did not move.

"I'm Amber," he said. "Amberian. I'm from Nerrinton. It's a...port city in the south. Have you ever heard of it?"

She watched him, her gaze intensifying. Still, she stayed silent. Amber swallowed, and shifted a little.

"I'm not going to hurt you," he said quietly, raising his eyebrows. "I honestly wouldn't know how, even if I wanted to. And besides..." he paused. "I think you were the one who saved me from those highwaymen at the entrance to the forest, weren't you? So..." he took a slow breath. "That wouldn't be a very good way to repay a debt."

She did frown now—hard. It startled Amber—such a suddenly human expression made with reptilian features. Her lips parted. She took a low breath.

"You aren't going to kill me."

Monotone. Cold.

Almost a question.

"Well..." Amber swallowed. "Are *you* going to kill *me?*"

She blinked. Her gaze trailed down to the soup bowl, then focused up on his lute—the face of which looked like melted butter in the firelight. Her attention wandered up, and eventually found his eyes. Rested there for a very long time.

"No."

She breathed the word, but he heard it. He took a deep breath of the rancid air, then heaved out a sigh.

"Good. Then...We can be friends."

This didn't seem to register, but Amber hadn't expected it to. He reached up and set his lute on top of one of the barrels, then scooted a little closer. She blinked rapidly, but didn't twitch.

"I want you to eat this," Amber said firmly, pointing to the bowl. "Then we're going to get you up and out of this place. The air here is making me sick."

Her lips parted again, but she didn't speak.

"I'm not moving until you eat something," Amber insisted.

93

She stayed still as a stone for a full minute, staring at him. Amber folded his arms and waited.

She stirred. Just an inch. She shuffled her shoulder back, the skin around her eyes tensing again. She pushed off, raising herself just a little onto her right elbow, letting out a deep, painful growl. Now she rested forward on both elbows, her fists clenched, her face hovering over the bowl.

"Go on," Amber pushed. She stared down at the soup, drawing in a few low breaths to smell it. Finally, she dipped her face down and began sucking the soup loudly, taking long swallows. The fans around her face fluttered absently. Once in a while, she would glance up at him with just that one good eye, like a wary cat, but Amber stayed very still.

Then, abruptly, she lifted her head, the soup running down her chin and dribbling to the floor. She did not lick her lips—only made a thick grunt, and scooted stiffly back from the bowl. Amber sighed and scrubbed his hand through his hair.

"Well, all right—that's about half of it, I suppose. We're getting you out of here now." He got to his feet and dusted his hands off on his trousers. "Come on."

"*Thhhhtththththt!*" She bared her fangs, and gave him a sideways, savage look—her teeth glistened in the torchlight.

An icy thrill shot through all of Amber's veins. He clenched his fists.

"Look, I promised not to hurt you," Amber retorted, his heart bashing against his ribs. "But if I leave you down here, you *will* die. And I'd be breaking a promise. So, come with me."

She let out a low, trailing whine through her nose—like a cornered feline, and then gnashed her teeth. The tip of her tail tapped restlessly against the stone.

And her left fist trembled.

Amber gently knelt back down. He slowly moved the bowl out of the way, then tilted toward her, ignoring the spasms in his chest.

"I know it hurts," he said earnestly, watching her face. "One time, when I was only about five years old, I was playing in a tree and I fell out, and then I crashed all the way down the hill through a thicket of wild rosebushes. I'd never seen that much blood—I thought I was going to die. I'd also bit the inside of my cheek, so I was bleeding from my mouth, too. My father came and found me, and my mother had to cover me with bandages and salve, and I had to lie in bed for a week. See?" He rolled up his sleeve, and showed her his left arm, where dozens of thin scars crisscrossed his dark skin. Her glance flickered across them...

Then lifted to his face.

"But my mother had me lay in the sun," Amber continued quietly. "And she fed me six times a day—even though my mouth hurt. And a lot sooner than I wanted to, she made me get up and start walking, so that I wouldn't get stiff and cold." He paused, waiting for that to sink in. "This is not a good place to be, down here. You have to come up."

Her tail had gone still, and her mouth had closed—but her hand still quivered.

"Come on," Amber murmured. "Come with me." And he reached out, and touched her fist.

She sucked in a sharp breath—jumped—

Amber bit down hard.

She didn't pull back.

She stared at his hand, eyes wide, brow furrowed. The sinews in *her* hand stood out like wires. She did not move.

Then...

Very, very slowly...

Her hand relaxed. Her fingers loosened from their fist, and hesitantly stretched out, as if feeling through the darkness. Ever so slightly, she tipped her wrist, allowing Amber's fingertips to ghost toward the corner of her hand, between her forefinger and thumb.

Her skin felt soft, but like ice, riddled with a maze of torn edges and slick Snakesalve. She kept turning her hand, inch by inch...

And Amber, his pulse racing, slipped his fingers forward until they lay gently in her open palm.

Her throat flickered, and her breathing quickened.

Then, her fingers suddenly closed around his.

She pulled in a deep, desperate breath, wrenched herself into a half upright position, and took hold of his wrist with her other hand.

Amber twitched—

She pulled him toward her, then pressed his palm to her throat...

And let out a long, shuddering sigh—as if a delicious wave had washed through her whole body.

All at once, Amber could *feel* his own heat pouring into her—her throat instantly lost its chill. He scrabbled to get his feet under him.

"Yes—that's it," he urged her. "It's even warmer upstairs. Come on."

He took hold of her right wrist with his left hand, and tugged on her. She grunted sharply, but kept hold of him and lifted up. Amber, bent almost double, took three strenuous steps backward—she held on, grimacing, her long tail dragging behind. Amber started to sweat.

"You're going to have to help me," he gritted. "You're too heavy to carry."

She broke out in shivers, and her head came up—her good eye searched his, bright and lost. He tried to smile at her.

"Come on."

She hesitated.

Then, her hands clamped down.

"Aaaah!" she cried as she forced her body upward even further, and her tail slithered forward. Amber gasped in relief as he was able to straighten up—her head raised to almost the height of his shoulder.

"Right, right—that's it, Silver. Come on," he muttered even as she leaned hard on him. He shuffled back toward the door, his shoes and her tail scraping loudly against the filthy stones.

They passed through the door, and into the dark bone room. The stench flooded his throat as his heels crunched and her tail swished and clattered. Her breath came in short, tight spurts, her fingers like iron around his. She sagged a little, and he had to bend again to keep hold of her. The light from the torch in the wine cellar faded so he could just barely see her. The stairwell would be pitch black.

His foot struck the bottom step. He winced, carefully stepping up and back, drawing her with him. Shivering, Silver glanced urgently up and past him, and let out a piercing whine.

"I know, it's a lot of stairs," Amber panted. "But it's the only way out."

She swallowed three times, then tried to tug on him to lift herself.

Amber staggered and almost fell off the step.

"Wait, wait, wait." He caught his balance. "Let me...Let me get a better hold on you."

He pried her hands off of him—her eyes went wide—reached forward and caught her under her arms. She snatched at the shoulders of his shirt and gripped them hard, and laid the weight of her whole upper body upon his arms.

"This...this isn't ideal," Amber struggled. "I wish I could...I could stand beside you and lift you that way, but I think you have spines on your back..."

"*Thnk, thnk, thnk,*" Silver clucked in her throat, and Amber nodded. "Thought so," he sighed. "All right, fine."

He started up and back again, one stair at a time, grinding his teeth as he pulled her. He could feel her body undulating as she writhed up the steps—he had to fight to keep from staggering sideways with each awkward twist of her tail.

In no time at all, darkness swallowed them. Amber had to slide each foot backward until his heel hit the front of the next stair, then heave the weight of her upper body as he stepped up. They inched up the staircase, winding around the spiral with agonizing effort, both of them hissing and rasping through their teeth. Her claws dug through his shirt and into the skin of his shoulders, but that didn't compare with the pain in his back.

Then her arms started to tremble, and she began to keen softly every time he lifted her.

"Halfway there," Amber breathed, sweat trailing down his face—even though he had no idea if that was true or not. He'd never bothered to count the steps.

Up, up, and round and round, bumping their shoulders on the damp walls, stumbling on the uneven edges. Silver's icy cold began to soak into Amber's arms and chest, and he could feel the strength draining out of her.

"Almost," he kept saying. "Almost, almost..."

Then...

Light. Gray light.

He smelled fresh air—a breeze brushed the back of his sweaty neck.

"Feel that?" he rasped. "Just a few more steps and we'll be there."

Her head lolled forward, her hands weakening on his shoulders. He adjusted his grip on her, his back muscles screaming, and hefted her up one, two, three, four, five...

Ten steps. Ten steps, and then they suddenly found the landing. Amber's shoulder thudded against the iron sconce that used to hold the torch. Bright air flooded across them from the door to his left. The kitchen door.

"In here," Amber said through his teeth, and hauled her just those few more feet, across the threshold, and into the dusty room.

But it didn't look the same.

The morning sun had broken through the clouds, and now streamed in through the wide window, creating a large, golden pool on the flagstones.

Silver saw it. Her eyes fixed on it. She let go of him.

Amber lowered her to the floor, letting out a few grunts of his own, and after her hands slapped to the ground she crawled forward, past the wake of blood she had left just the other day, and into the light.

Amber hopped out of the way of the lash of her clumsy tail, then watched as she found the center of the beam and stretched herself out on her back in anguished relief. Her face twisted, her tail curled up and beside her, her chest heaved as she took deep breaths that exhaled in soft cries. She lay her head back, sighing over and over, her arms drawn up next to her head...

Until at last she relaxed, letting her arms float down to her sides, her eyes drifting closed, the tension melting from her long frame.

And finally, Amber could really see her.

Rivers of sapphire and silver coursed across her scales, shifting hue and tone with every gentle curve of her body. She would have been quite captivating to look at—in an icy, poisonous way—if much of her was not caked in blackish, crusted blood, and almost every surface not broken and lacerated. Many of her scales had turned white and hung loose. Many others were jagged, interrupted by the sickly-greenish seal of the Snakesalve. In a few other places, the color had paled, and her skin seemed to sag. She was also clearly missing about half of the spines on her tail.

Amber sank to the floor, swiping the sweat off his forehead, and leaned back against the wall. He would have to go back down there one last time to retrieve the torch, the bowls and his lute—but after that, he would shut and bar the door and never set foot in that hell again.

Chapter Twelve

"And the Doors Opened"

Amber took several deep, hungry breaths of noonday air, closing his eyes as the cool wind blew through his hair and clothes. He stood just outside the back kitchen door, letting the rot and reek wash out of his lungs. Finally, he opened his eyes, and glanced up at the sky.

Thin gray clouds trailed across the blue, sometimes obstructing the sun, making the day moody and low. He looked down at his clothes and made a face at the stains—but he didn't feel like going back inside and sleeping or bathing. So he started out toward the tall tangle of underbrush and thicket behind the castle.

He approached the nearest broad-facing hedge and peered through thick, colorless ivy and rose leaves, then watched as the wind rustled through them. Frowning, he maneuvered a hand inside, hoping he wouldn't get stung by a thorn...

His fingers met stone. A wall, then.

He trailed on to his right, carefully keeping his hand beneath the leaves of the ivy, until his fingers pushed through into a gap. He paused, looking up. The top of the hedge dipped down here, for just a few feet. This must be the opening.

He faced it and began tearing at the ivy—noisily ripping it down and pushing it aside, which wasn't difficult. The plants were weak, and the thicker branches beneath seemed to be dead, and he could snap them easily.

Finally, he had torn a hole wide enough for him to see through, and found a rotten wooden gate hanging slack on its hinges. He stepped through the mess of vines on the ground, grabbed the edge of the gate with both hands and wrenched it toward him.

It gave way with a painful groan, and as it came, it shoved the broken ivy out of the way, making a clear path for Amber. He leaned forward, and peered through.

A huge garden—bordered by towering, low-hanging trees, filled with rolling vines that had gotten out of hand years ago. The roses and ivy had overflowed, sweeping over and across any landscaping and climbing up to join hands with the beeches and oaks, creating strange and haunting shapes—like a shroud covering a corpse. It smelled like dust and dried leaves.

Nothing bloomed. Midsummer flourished in the rest of the world, but here...

Leaves the color of slate rattling like dry bones in the wind. Snarls of old thorns twisting and winding around each other.

The garden was sick.

Sleeping.

Hiding.

Amber stepped inside.

The wind suddenly shivered the branches, and the rose leaves chattered.

He stopped and listened for a moment, the wind rushing all around him, then picked his way forward, frowning warily down at the thorns. Dead underbrush crackled and crunched beneath his feet. He crept between the larger heaps of vines, guessing that there might be statues or stonework underneath them.

He stopped several paces in, and looked up to his left, where a particularly tall tower of vines stood...

And he thought he could glimpse a slender gray hand beneath.

The breeze muttered around it, and stirred the brush around his feet.

"I'll come back to you." He gave that figure a pointed look. He kept on, his gaze sweeping beyond that, into the shadows, trying to find the corners.

His attention landed on what had to be a building. A small shed, perhaps, backed up against a section of the wall, closely guarded by an ancient, tilted apple tree. Amber forged toward it, baring his teeth in a wince as he gingerly moved a few thick strands of rose vines out of his way. At last, he stood in front of the stone shed, equally as draped in vegetation, but with a door that looked just as rotten as the front gate.

He kicked a pile of dead leaves out of the way, grabbed the rusty handle and *tugged*.

Crack!

It popped off in his hand.

"Well...That's helpful," he muttered, tossing it down. He stuck his hand through the hole left behind in the wood, grabbed it, set his stance, and pulled.

The door broke in half. Amber staggered, then bit his lip and tore the door down, piling the useless timber off to the side.

"Hope nobody lives here," he joked, straightening up and venturing to the threshold.

The vines had invaded the rafters, but several implements still hung from their hooks: a rake, shears, a hatchet, a pitchfork, a shovel, and some waxed rope.

"Aha!" he crowed, stepping inside and grabbing the hatchet down. He fingered the blade. "Sharp enough," he decided, then took it back outside.

He ventured back toward the furthest edge of the garden, hacking swiftly at any thick branches that impeded him. The hatchet swung easily in his hand, and sliced through most limbs without any trouble.

He then came across something else—something that resembled a very short tower hidden by a curtain of ivy. He pulled in another experimental breath, and noticed that the air had become musty.

Amber set his hatchet down, gripped the ivy and tore it loose, throwing it to the side, until he uncovered a small roof, two iron posts, and a low, circular wall of stone.

"A well," he panted, swiping his sleeve across his forehead. He hopped up to it and leaned his upper body down on the top of the wall, staring down into the depths.

Light twinkled and winked down there. The scent of water filled his mouth. He twisted and glanced up.

Just overhead, a metal bucket on a chain dangled from its winding bar. He straightened a little, grabbed the winding bar and began to work it.

It screeched and whined, but it relented, and the bucket lowered down into the shadows.

Amber grinned when he heard it splash, and when it sank and filled, he began winding it back up. It took some effort, and the metal workings howled, but after a few moments he was able to grab the wet handle of the bucket and pull it over to set it on the wall.

Clear, ice-cold water filled the bucket. Amber dipped his fingers in, then scooped out some water and sipped it loudly. Then, he splashed the rest all over his face.

It smelled and tasted and felt exactly like the water from the river he had drank from a few days ago, when he had crossed to the castle. Maybe this well tapped into it.

Amber cleared his throat, pushed his wet curls out of his face, and turned around toward the garden. It didn't take long to find what he was looking for.

A low rose bush draped in ivy and bind weed stood beside the well. He grabbed handfuls of the twists of vine and began to work.

All the rest of the afternoon, he ripped the stubborn entanglements away from the little rose bush, stacking the brush in the center of an ever-increasing clear space. Once he got the ivy and bind-weed clear, he took the hatchet back and hung it up, then retrieved the shears and the rake. He raked all the dead leaves away from the base of the bush and piled them with the other weeds, then trimmed the bush with the shears, shaping it back into a reasonable form. Loosening the mean curls of thorns made him grimace, but he managed not to stick himself too badly. After that was done, he took those tools back and got the shovel. He roughed up the ground all around the rosebush, turning over rich, black earth. He put the shovel away, grabbed the bucket of water, splashed his face, then knelt down and carefully poured the water all around the base of the rosebush, pausing every once in a while to let it soak in.

As the afternoon light waned into twilight, he straightened. His back aching again, he tucked the bucket against his side and grinned down at his handiwork. Then he sighed, looked around...

"One finished..." he said. "Seven-hundred more to go."

The wind answered him—whispering through the vines again. But it didn't sound as dry and thin as before. And the touch of it refreshed him.

Strangely, he couldn't keep a smile from his face. The garden hadn't wanted to be disturbed, but once he had disturbed it, it hadn't bitten him. And the more often he came to it, and the more he rustled and tugged on it, the more awake it would become. He knew it.

And for some reason, he wanted to do that.

Evening drew its cloak over the castle, and Amber wearily came inside and pulled the kitchen door shut behind him. He held a bowl of cold water in his blistered hand—he'd drawn it from the well.

He stopped just inside the threshold, gazing down at Silver.

She'd turned over on her belly, probably when the beam of sun had vanished, her arms wrapped tightly around her, her head ducked low, her eyes squeezed shut. By the fading light, he watched her slow breathing rise and fall.

Carefully, he stepped around her, then bent down and set the bowl of water down by her head. She shivered slightly.

Amber stood up, and made his way back through the vast, dark room, to the staircase, and all the way back up and to his tower.

When he pushed the door open, the smell of fresh tea, melted cheese on toast, and a beef stew overwhelmed him—as did the sight of a bright, dancing fire in the hearth, a ready washbasin, and a turned-down bed. He strode right to the fire, dipped into the cauldron, and ladled a generous helping of stew into a bowl. Then, he set that on the table, turned to the bed and pulled off the top feather-stuffed blanket. He folded it up tightly and tucked it under one arm, then picked up the bowl of soup, and headed back out the door and down the stairs.

His whole body ached by the time he reached the kitchen again, but he ignored it. He set the soup down next to the water bowl and unfurled the thick blanket. It swished as he draped it over Silver, and he tucked it in around her shoulders. For a moment, his hand lingered on the blanket, just above her shoulder blades.

"Don't die," he said. Then, he dragged himself to his feet, and stumbled back up to his tower.

Amber hummed a blithe fishing tune as he trotted down the winding staircase, passing through the beams of sun that flashed through the narrow windows. In spite of his hard work and sweat, the exercise yesterday had felt good, and after eating and washing his face and hair and pulling off his clothes, he had tumbled into bed and slept at least ten hours. He had awoken refreshed—his blisters seemed to have disappeared—put on his clean clothes and eaten the breakfast laid out on the table for him.

Now, he hopped out of the stairwell, into the great, dusty entrance hall, and toward the kitchen door. He slowed as he approached it, an uncomfortable sensation settling down in his gut.

He hesitated, then pushed on the door.

She sat, her tail coiled casually around her, on top of the blanket, her upper body facing him but her head tilted up and to the side, the sun washing over it. At his sound, her good eye blinked open, and she turned to him. Her bright glance caught him, and the fans around her face flared in interest. They turned almost an emerald color as the sun shone through them. The rest of her looked just as tattered as before—perhaps even a little less colorful—but she was sitting up.

Amber's grip on the door handle relaxed, and he smiled.

"Are you feeling better?"

Silver said nothing, but she glanced down at the two bowls—the two *empty* bowls.

"You liked the soup, then?" Amber ventured inside. "I know that water was good—I felt like drinking a whole bucket-full. It came from the well in the garden."

She just watched him, but not the way she had before. Just bright. And curious. And calm.

"Are you still hungry?" Amber asked.

She stared silently at him, some of that reptilian blankness abruptly clouding her gaze.

"Look, you can understand me," Amber said, stepping closer— and her attention instantly sharpened. "So even if you don't want to say anything, you need to nod or shake your head, so I know you heard."

A small line appeared between her eyebrows.

"So this means no," Amber shook his head. "And this means yes." He nodded. "Understand?"

She frowned harder, her gaze piercing him. Then, very slowly, she nodded.

Amber grinned again.

Her eyebrows went up in surprise.

"Good!" Amber said. "So, are you still hungry?"

She blinked, and shook her head.

"All right, then," he said, drawing himself up. "I'm going to look through the castle a little bit more, and you can rest here. I'll bring you food at noonday. Is that all right?"

She studied him again, then nodded again. He couldn't help but smile at her odd expression.

"Good," he replied. Then he turned and left the kitchen again, feeling her glance following him.

He stepped out into that same hallway he remembered from before: the one with all of the screeching doors. He stopped.

Tilting his head to the side, he narrowed his eyes at the long line of shut doors, then stepped up to that very first one he had encountered. He stretched out a hand, grasped the cold brass handle...

Worked the latch, and pulled.

With a quaking sigh, it let go, and swung toward him—though its whimper hurt the air.

Amber let go of it and gaped. The door hung open, making no motion to slam shut. A room waited beyond.

A window stood exactly opposite the door—it looked out upon the courtyard. From it came drab light, for dust covered the panes of glass. Amber risked walking carefully inside, halfway sure the door was going to crush him against the frame. It didn't.

The room was empty. Off to his right, a stove stood, its pipe broken off. No rugs, no tables, chairs or lamps. Just dust.

"Hm," he mused. He turned and walked out, but left the door open.

He tried the next door.

"Siiighhhh..." it breathed, and grudgingly gapped, its rusty hinges wheezing. This room looked almost exactly the same. Not one stick of furniture, nothing hung on the walls. Just one window, facing the courtyard. Amber left that room as well, casting a mystified glance across the door that had, for some reason, lost all its hostility.

He worked his way down the line, and every single door now swung open for him. All of them moaned, as if in terrible pain, but they did not fight him. All the rooms were completely empty, but he left the doors open. Finally, he reached he last door, and tugged on it.

This one truly did sound as if he was breaking it. Its hinges howled, and the very wood wailed. Once he had pushed it back against the outside wall, and the squeal had died away, he tipped inside.

This room was bigger, with a taller ceiling. A low, wide, empty fireplace waited off to his right, and a few shelves stood nailed to the walls—all vacant. A straw-stuffed mattress lay on the floor, against the wall, near the hearth.

And something leaned against the opposite wall—something draped in a white cloth.

Amber started toward it, cocking his head. It looked like something tall and flat, and circular. He squatted down in front of it, then reached up to pull off the cloth.

"What is it?"

Amber bumped it—it squeaked and slid toward his feet. He lashed out and grabbed the edges of it, and his head whipped up.

Silver had slipped in just past the threshold—and spoken.

When he saw her, she shrank back. Her fins flattened and her arms curled toward her chest.

Amber laughed.

"Ha—you scared me."

She ducked her head and moved to leave.

"No, it's all right," Amber called. "Come look."

"Come?" Silver repeated, her eye glimmering vividly again.

"Yes," Amber said. "I think it's a mirror."

She hesitated, but Amber returned his attention to the cloth, and pulled it loose.

A mirror in a pewter frame glittered at him. He took the cloth and dusted off the surface.

He had never seen such a clear reflection in his life—and the surface was not curved as almost all other mirrors were. He lifted it.

"It's very light," he commented, sensing Silver slither partway inside. He lifted his head and looked around the room. "Aha," he noted, standing up. "There's a hook..." He lifted the mirror up over the mantel and hung it there. Then, he dusted off his hands and assessed the way it looked.

"Is it supposed to be there?" Silver murmured.

"*Yes.*"

Fire blazed to life in the hearth, drowning the room in light.

Amber leaped back, almost crashing into Silver—Silver hissed and flashed back against the far wall.

A face bloomed to life inside the mirror. A face white as the moon, with eyes like pools of stars, and hair like vines trailing through ocean waves.

Amber felt all the heat drain out of his head.

"What...?" he croaked. "Who are you?"

"*Thk, thk, thk,*" Silver clicked menacingly.

The mirror did not answer.

"Are you..." Amber tried again, his heart beating far too quickly. "Do you live here?"

"*Yes,*" the mirror answered—a voice like the winter wind.

"What is your name?" Amber demanded. The mirror said nothing—her fathomless eyes fixed on him—and on nothing. At the same time.

"Do you *have* a name?" Amber pressed.

"*No.*" The mirror face blinked slowly.

"You aren't...a person?" Amber frowned.

"*No,*" came the breathed reply.

"You're just...the mirror."

"*Yes.*"

"Where did you come from?" Amber asked. The mirror said nothing.

Silver's glottal clicking had stopped. Amber felt her slip cautiously away from the wall, and draw nearer to his right shoulder.

"Were you born here?" Silver asked, her voice low, her words formed carefully.

"Yes," the mirror replied.

Amber, startled, glanced over at Silver—and light dawned in his mind. He faced the mirror.

"Can you only answer questions with 'yes' or 'no'?"

"Yes," the mirror said—and smiled.

"You give advice?" Amber guessed.

"No," said the mirror.

"You tell the truth?" Silver asked.

"Yes."

Amber, struck by the way Silver kept speaking, studied her for a moment—before his thoughts caught on an idea.

"You know about what's going on in the kingdom?" he asked, stepping toward the mirror.

"Yes."

Amber's heartbeat picked up speed again.

"Is the princess Oralia looking for me?"

"Yes."

He swallowed.

"Does she know where I am?"

"No."

"Will she find me?"

The mirror said nothing. Amber sighed.

"All right, she can't tell the future, either."

"What is...Oralia?" Silver asked, inching up closer to him. He turned to her.

"A princess. She rules at Tirincashel. Well, her parents do. She isn't of age yet, but...Since her older sister died, she'll be queen."

"Why is she looking for you?" Silver frowned again.

"She wants to marry me," Amber sighed once more, running a hand through his hair.

"You ran away?" Silver guessed.

"Yes," the mirror said. Silver glanced back and forth between the mirror and Amber.

"Believe me, she is not a lady that *anyone* should marry," Amber assured her. Silver's expression became vaguely perplexed. Amber turned back to the mirror.

"Do you know her?" he asked the mirror, pointing at Silver.

"Yes."

"Do you know her name?" he wondered eagerly.

"No."

"Hm," Amber grunted, folding his arms. He faced Silver again—she waited uncertainly, watching the mirror.

"Is it all right if I call you Silver, then? Is Silver a good name?"

"Yes," said the mirror. Silver blinked, that right eyelid still not opening all the way, then frowned intently at Amber.

"Name..." she repeated. "My name..."

"Do you remember your name?" Amber questioned, taking a step toward her. Her eye unfocused, her gaze drifting down. Then, she shook her head.

"All right, well, then Silver it is," he smiled at her.

"And you...are Amber," Silver ventured.

" *Yes,"* the mirror grinned. Amber chuckled, and held out his hand.

"An honor to meet you, Lady Silver."

Her fins flickered, and her lips parted as she stared at his hand. Amber just waited.

Gingerly, Silver stretched out her right hand, and set her fingertips in his palm. Amber took another half step closer, slid his hand up and closed his fingers around hers, holding on gently. Roughened, scaly, and chill. He didn't let go. Instead, he squeezed once. She lifted her head, and met his eyes.

"Amber," she said again—and the fire crackled in the hearth like quiet laughter.

CHAPTER THIRTEEN

"THE STONE SPOKE"

Amber straightened, setting the shears down, and gathered up the fresh broom that he had just cut. He then grabbed the short limb he had hacked off earlier, sat down on a stone and began binding the broom to the limb with the waxed rope he had found in the shed. Morning sun warmed him, and the breezes tousled his hair. He sat just outside the garden gate, facing the sunny towers of the castle.

He had asked Silver to come out with him while he did this chore, but she had backed away from him and shook her head harder than she ever had, so he left her alone. Occasionally, though, as he wrapped the rope around the broom, he caught sight of her peering out one of the windows at him. He smiled to himself and kept working.

Finally he finished. He stomped through the weedy garden and put the hatchet and shears away, then drew a full bucket of water and unhooked the bucket from the chain. He then hauled it, and his new broom, back toward the kitchen.

He pushed through the squeaky door, scraping his shoes off on the threshold, and looked up to see Silver hesitating in the opposite doorway.

"Hello," he greeted her. "Could you help me?"

She stiffened, and her head tilted far to the right.

"Can you pick up that blanket and put it on the table?" Amber asked, nodding toward it. "I'm going to clean the floor."

Silver still hesitated, but Amber strode in and set the broom and bucket on the counter. Then, he bent and started opening each one of the cupboards beneath the counter.

"Nothing, nothing, nothing..." he muttered as he moved down the line. "Noth...Ha!" He reached in and grabbed a thick parcel wrapped in wax paper and string, and a wooden box. He pulled them out and opened the box...

Rose perfume wafted up, and he took a deep breath of it.

"Soap!" he cried in triumph. He reached in and pulled out one of the white balls, and marveled at it. "It looks like...*Castilian* soap...!"

He turned around to see Silver laying the wadded-up blanket on the baking table.

"Thank you," he said brightly. He then untied the parcel and revealed a stack of white linen towels. "Perfect." He took one of the soaps over to the bucket, rolled up his sleeves, got the soap wet and started foaming up the water.

"Oooh, that's cold..." he gritted. When a layer of suds coated the surface, he dropped the soap down in the bucket, set the bucket on the floor, dipped his broom in and began to scrub the dried blood off the stones.

The broom hadn't had time to dry out after it was cut, and so pieces came loose, but it worked well enough. He soaked the floor, and briskly swept and scraped the stains off of it and out the door. Silver drew back from the splashing, but lingered in the corner.

With a brisk *swish-swish-swish,* dust went the way of the blood as well, and as he worked, Amber uncovered a beautiful, colorful pattern in the floor beneath all the grit. The stones shone in the morning light like river rocks, and Amber hummed merrily all the while. The water in the bucket had turned black by the time he reached the far corner where Silver was.

"Almost...done..." he declared, sweating again. He dipped the broom one last time, then grabbed the bucket and took them both outside. He hung the broom on a hook on the outside of the chicken coop in the full sun, then fished the soap out of the bottom of the bucket and dumped out the dirty water. He then trooped all the way back out to the well, filled the bucket again, dropped the soap in again and frothed it up. After that, he dragged it back to the kitchen.

Silver had come to the door to watch him—she backed up a great deal to let him in.

"Here," he set the bucket on the counter again, snatched up on of the towels and dunked it in the water. He squeezed it out a bit, then held the dripping rag out to her.

She stared at it.

"Wash!" he urged.

She opened her hand, and he set the rag in it. He grabbed another rag, dipped it in the water, and started washing his own face and neck and arms. He felt her watching him.

And in a moment, she began to dab at her face.

"Here, come closer," Amber instructed, stepping to the side to make room. "Use this water. I know it's cold, but you'll feel better."

She slithered up to his left side, still studying him intently as he kept washing his own face.

"Here, get it wet and wash that off of yourself," Amber pointed at her front, where blood and dirt caked her scales. "Don't get soap in your eyes."

Silver warily dipped the rag in again, and squeezed it out with both hands, just as he had. Then, she lowered her head and methodically began to clean the grime off of her chest, stomach and arms. It did not come away easily, and she was very ginger around her long cuts. Her mouth tightened, and stayed that way.

Amber stepped around behind her, eyeing her tail—but it didn't move, so he stepped over it, took a fresh towel and dried himself, observing Silver as he did.

Loose gray scales flaked off, fell, and clicked against the floor as she cleaned, and the rag turned rust-colored. Amber's own hands stilled, and silence settled through him as his eyes traced all the lashes that marred her skin. He leaned on the counter, his humming fading away, and listened to the soft *scrape-scrape-scrape* as she worked.

Eventually, she sighed, and set the dirty rag on the counter, her shoulders sagging.

"You've done most of it," Amber said—quieter than he'd meant. "But you've..." He stepped up and reached past her, and dunked his own rag in the water. "Turn to me," he said.

Surprised, she did so.

Amber hooked his finger under her chin, squeezed out the rag, and brought it up to wipe firmly but cautiously across her face.

And she let him.

Part of him, deep down, suffered a flash of astonishment. But she only gazed steadily up at him with her good left eye. And Amber watched what he was doing.

He washed off the dried soup from her chin, and the crusted blood and dirt from the entire right side of her face. Her eyelids drifted shut. Amber avoided the two long cuts that started at the back of her right jaw and ended at the bridge of her nose—and he was especially gentle around her wounded eye.

"All right," Amber dipped the rag one last time and rubbed it against her throat, taking off one last smudge. "Much better."

She opened her eye, looked up at him, and swallowed. He smiled at her, and tossed the dirty rags into the bucket.

"I'm going to wash these out," Amber sighed. "Then hang them to dry, and then I'll bring food down. Are you hungry?"

She kept gazing at him—something quiet and open in her eyes—but she nodded. He grinned.

"Good, I am too. Then we can go out into the garden."

She pulled her arms up and wrapped them around her chest, and dipped her head. Amber frowned.

"You don't want to go out to the garden?"

She paused, then shook her head.

"All right, you don't have to," he allowed, curious. "I'll...do this, then go get the soup."

She didn't look at him as he picked up the bucket and carried it out—but he took a breath, put on a cheerful expression and made himself start humming again, and the tension eased from her frame.

Amber splashed himself in the face with cool well-water, took a drink from the bucket, then sighed and looked around at the garden. He had been working for several hours—most of the afternoon—pruning away the ivy from the rose bushes that surrounded the well.

He had brought a bowl of lentil soup down from his tower for Silver—he'd moved the blanket off the table and set it there—but she hadn't seemed to want to even approach it while he was in the room. So he'd taken his own meal outside and eaten there, then started to work on the binding vines.

He had made some progress, stacking the refuse near the gate and wearing a path between it and the well. Now, he eyed that pinnacle of ivy standing in the center of the garden—the one in which he'd thought he'd seen a hand.

Picking up his shears, he started for it.

He felt through the curtain of vines and found a wide pedestal, and noisily climbed up on top of it. Once he had set his feet, he set to chopping the plants off the statue.

They fell off like locks of shorn hair, tumbling down around his feet. After cutting through the thick strands, he set the shears down and just started pulling and tearing. And the more he uncovered, the more interested he became.

It was a beautiful statue, made of snow-white marble. A woman, life-sized, clothed in a flowing robe. Barefoot. She had rolls of curly hair, bound back by a circlet. Her body faced the castle, but her head faced away from him. In her left hand, she held what looked like a fat tea-kettle by the handle. Her right arm was stretched out, pointing the direction she gazed: due north. Amber halted, following the point of her finger.

From here, he could glimpse the very edges of the gray northern mountains—the Giant's Shoes. Amber assessed the statue's placid face, but she gave him no hints.

"Hm," he grunted, then bent and started clearing away the mess from around her skirts.

When he finally did, he realized with a wince that he had been stepping all over the barest tips of what looked like lilies trying to come up. The pedestal was actually a planter. He quickly hopped down, hoping he hadn't crushed too many...

And stared at the kettle in the statue's hand.

"Brilliant idea," he snapped his fingers. He turned on his heel, and hurried back up to the kitchen.

Silver quickly ducked back from the window when she saw him coming, but he just charged inside.

"Hullo," he said quickly, and snatched the copper kettle off the stove. "I'm going to use this to water, instead of that heavy bucket."

Silver said nothing, just watched him, as he hurried back out and went to the well. He filled the kettle and carried it back to the pedestal planter, trying not to splash too much.

He cleared the dead leaves away from the lilies with one hand, then poured the water generously all over them, until the kettle was empty. He set it down on the stone with a *clink*.

The statue moved.

Amber yelped and fell onto his back.

And the statue *spoke*.

"*Follow the path by the river's edge*
Then up to the bee-wolf's stony ledge
Between two men that stand alone
To Reola Curse-Breaker's hidden home."

The statue's grating voice stopped.

Amber took fistfuls of grass, his mouth hanging open—unable to breathe. He stayed completely still for several moments, but nothing else happened.

He sucked in air, his heartbeat clamoring inside his ribcage and pounding through his head. He managed to sit up, eyes still fixed on the statue.

But it didn't stir. It remained as immutable as it had seemed before, turned slightly golden by the deep afternoon light.

"All right..." he muttered, then nodded firmly. "Time to go inside."

He climbed to his feet, inched toward the pedestal, and snatched the kettle off of it. It clanged loudly against his side as he quickly turned and left the garden and charged back up to the kitchen.

Amber's brow furrowed as he adjusted his grip on the dinner tray and glanced through the huge room that had the silver ribs against the wall. It stood empty. The kitchen had been empty, too.

The outside light had dimmed to twilight, and shadows hung in all the corners of the castle. He was having a hard time maneuvering—and he couldn't find Silver. However, with all the eerie, talking inanimate objects lurking in this place...

He didn't feel like shouting.

Frowning harder, he made his way down the corridor of formerly-stubborn doors, his lute bumping against his back. He peeked into each room, but found nothing.

Finally, though, he glimpsed light spilling from the far door, and he could hear a fire snapping. He picked up his pace, and stepped across the threshold.

The face in the mirror above the mantel, still shining like the moon, had closed its eyes, its viney hair drifting silently around its head. A bright, healthy fire burned in the hearth, and Silver lay upon the mattress off to the left, on her belly and facing the fire, propped up on her elbows.

At the sound of his footsteps, she sat up and twisted to face him—and the reptilian alertness on her face instantly melted away.

"Are you hungry?" Amber asked, starting forward. Silver nodded. He came up to her side and set the tray down with a sigh, then pulled off his lute and leaned it against the side of the mantel.

"All right, then, we have what looks like potato soup, tea, biscuits, toast and eggs."

Silver leaned over the tray and took deep sniffs while Amber portioned out the meal between the two of them, and poured tea into two cups. Silver reached toward a piece of toast—then stopped. Pulled back.

"What?" Amber asked, picking up his own piece of toast and taking a bite. Silver's glance flickered, and she looked away.

"Look, you don't have to be formal around me," Amber assured her, taking another bite. "I eat with my fingers all the time."

She still wasn't sure, but Amber pretended not to notice, and kept eating. Soon, out of the corner of his eye, he saw her pick up a piece of toast. She gnawed on it like—well, like an animal. But she also watched him carefully—and so he showed nothing on his face, and concentrated on his own meal.

"I found a talking statue today," he told her, taking a drink of tea. "I cut all the ivy off of it and then I watered the plants around it, and it talked. I almost died."

Silver kept chewing, but she listened.

"I fell down, my heart stopped..." he said, picking up his soup bowl and spoon and starting to eat that. "I don't even remember what she said. Something about a bee-wolf and a curse...or something." He shook his head. "Things are going to have to stop popping out like that at me. I *hate* that."

Silver snorted. He looked up at her—she glanced at him for an instant before picking up her bowl, too. She took her spoon in her fist and puzzled at both objects. Amber didn't say anything about it, just kept eating his own soup.

"I have no idea what else is in that garden," Amber confessed. "Could be anything, underneath all the vines. Probably a few more statues, probably some walkways, probably other plants besides roses, if they've been able to grow at all with all those thorns around." He adjusted the way he was sitting and glimpsed Silver take a deliberate spoonful of soup and mimic him, though she dripped a little as she put it into her mouth. He kept talking, as casually as he could.

"My mother had a garden—a kitchen garden, in the courtyard behind our house. There were only two pathways, paved. We had vines on the wall, but they were something else. Maybe morning glory. It was too hot for ivy. She carried me on her back when I was a baby while she worked, and when I got big enough she'd give me little things to do, like pull up weeds or plant seedlings. Most of the time, I just wound up playing in the mud, but..." he chuckled and shrugged. "I liked it. And I liked being with her. And picking all her tomatoes."

Silver kept eating, and Amber kept talking. He told her all about the rose bush he had cleared out and trimmed yesterday, and the shed with the tools, and the rotten doors, and how big he thought the garden was.

"You'll have to come outside with me tomorrow."

Silver set her empty bowl down and shook her head. Amber flashed his eyebrows at her.

"You'll come eventually," he smirked. "You will."

She gave him a sideways look—narrowed her eyes—and the corner of her mouth did something.

Amber stopped moving.

But just as soon as he thought he knew what he saw, she scooted back from the tray and onto the mattress, and settled back down onto her belly, resting her chin on her overlapped hands.

Amber ate the rest of his food, and drank her tea as well, then pushed the tray away, grabbed his lute and sat back against the side of the hearth.

"Ahem," he said, strumming the strings and twisting the tuning keys. Silver's attention instantly caught on him. He glanced up at the dark ceiling and thought. Drawing a deep breath, he found the correct fingering, and began to play and sing.

"Lonesome as the wind that wanders o'er the moor
But not half as lost as he
Bound in bones that are not his own

The prince of Dallydanehall
Dallydanehall in the valley
The prince of Dallydanehall
Roams alone, quite alone."

Amber sensed the whole length of Silver's body relax even further as he plucked each chord and let his voice wash and weave through the room. She blinked slowly as he sang, breathing deeply.

"He fell afoul of dwarven goods
A dwarven treasure, crowns and chains
And jewels that outshine the brightest stars
The master caught him thus.

Body of beast but mind of man
A torment in his heart
He cannot free himself, you see
But might, by a lady's pity."

He sang the chorus again, then diddled out a little conclusion, and let the crackling fire fill the silence.

"What happened to him?"

Amber sucked in a breath to shake his thoughts and turned to her. Her silvery eyes reflected every spark of flame.

"Who?" Amber asked.

"The prince of Dallydanehall," Silver murmured. "What happened to him?"

"Well, from what I heard from the minstrel who wrote the song," Amber shifted to face her. "He was turned into a bear by a dwarf, and he's wandering somewhere in the woods. The minstrel wasn't sure how that spell could be broken, but it has something to do with a lady."

Silver frowned, and she turned to the fire.

"I'm not fond of bears."

"No, I wouldn't be either," Amber said. He moved his lute a little. "But...See, he isn't really a bear. He's a man. But being a bear makes it hard for him to get someone to break the spell. *Most* people aren't fond of bears. Which...was probably the dwarf's idea all along."

"Mm," Silver grunted, her gaze distant. Amber sat back again, and played another song without singing, listening as the ring of the strings flowed richly through the room.

In a few minutes, Silver sighed, and turned over onto her back and laid her head down. Amber kept playing, occasionally looking over until he saw that she had closed her eyes.

After he finished two more songs, he paused, and when he measured her breathing, he knew she was asleep.

Carefully, he stood up, put the lute strap over his shoulders, crouched down and picked up the tray, and quietly left the room, glancing back at her once before heading to his tower.

Chapter Fourteen

"And the Beast Laughed"

The snake opened her eyes. Gazed up with her one good eye, at the ceiling that was half covered by the morning light that leaned in from the courtyard. Took a deep breath.

The smell of him.

She blinked slowly, shifting minutely beneath the warm blanket that had once been on his bed. The familiar fire crackled by her head, and the mirror far above hummed a quiet tune, almost inaudibly. *He* could never hear it when it did—perhaps the notes stayed too low.

Him.

He had a smell that was good. A smell so foreign—not like grass or northern wind or fish or blood—yet like the scent of life. Perhaps a little like the fire in this hearth. Perhaps a little like rain. But sweeter. Stronger. Perhaps...

After all these weeks, she still could not name it.

But she remembered.

She remembered rising up, straightening her spine, atop the battlements of the castle, as the moonshine spilled across her. That bewildering scent had drawn her to the tower, piercing through clouds of ice and fog that filled her mind. It had clarified her way, intensified her vision, until what she saw and heard penetrated past mere flashes of survival, and had resolved into what she began to know as memory.

She had followed the scent that night, but had taken a wrong turning, and found herself out upon the rooftop. Confused, she had halted, and the clouds gathered back over her consciousness, covering her vision, returning her blood to frost...

Until a voice.

She hadn't known what it was. She had heard birds string notes together as they perched in the farthest reaches of the forest, before they flew away at the sight of her.

But this...

A voice.

Rich and soft. The notes flowed like breath, like pulse, like rivers...With a timbre that resonated through her chest.

It *hurt*.

Everything inside her had begun to ache—all the way down to her bones, the center of her gut, the joints in her fingers...

Yet with every note he sang, she rose higher and higher out of the murky depths that shrouded her mind...

Until at last, she could see the moon.

Truly see it. Its brilliant white face. The craters and canyons that marked it and mapped it. The silvery light that spilled like water down over the castle and all of the forest.

The world had filled with color at the smell of him.

The sound of him.

It hadn't lasted long.

When silence fell, the light and color had faded. The gloom had closed over her head, the ache vanished, and her mouth had watered for fish-flesh and blood.

But instead, that night had torn open.

And there *was* blood—but hers. Everywhere.

Rotten fish, and stone. Darkness.

And pain. Rolling, penetrating pain.

And as those long, fathomless depths stretched to uncounting, she had let go. No memory—only fog. No sensation. Only rocks, and cold.

Sinking.

Until a scent.

And a voice.

The *voice*.

And...

Words.

A collection of sounds, breathed through by that lilting, flowing song...

The nonsense and noise had suddenly coalesced, sharpened...

And she had *understood*.

And she saw him.

Looked up into vivid, coppery eyes framed by earnest black eyebrows and long lashes. Honey-colored skin, bright features, soft mouth; curls of black and gold and russet; with a beautiful wooden being cradled in his gentle hands that also had a voice—unmatched by his own, but at his fingers it rang like starlight.

"I'm not going to hurt you..."

Every movement he made had fascinated her. Otherworldly and incandescent, he sent the clouds in her head billowing away. Nothing in existence was clearer, brighter than he was. And as he spoke, and his words sank through her, that powerful ache had returned...

But this time, she called it to her. She opened herself, and embraced it.

Thus, the dark twistings of stabbing pain and fear had faded as gradual mornings rose and quiet evenings fell—and for the first time, she had begun to notice them, to truly *see* the days as they passed. She saw them because he came with the morning, *every* morning, and he departed as evening gave way to night. His voice, his being, his looks, pressed light into her mind with agonizing persistence, and she would have fled from it, if the brilliance and clarity he brought to the whole world around her had not been so completely captivating. Even with one damaged eye...

The myriad of colors in the afternoon light, the creamy brightness of the castle stones, the depth of the blue sky, the secretive murmur of the wind through the grasses; the crisp, diamond-like splash of water, the chuckle of the hearth, the taste of salty bullion and cooked carrots, the earthy, steamy breath of brewed tea...

When he sang, she could feel the blood flowing to regions of her heart that had somehow been empty—like hot springs bubbling up into a dry cavern. This hurt also, with a driving stabbing that panged through her chest—but the surges of strength that swept through her body at the same time made her hold her breath and soak in every note.

It was worse—and infinitely wonderful—when he touched her. *Warmth.*

It raced across her skin and pierced into her muscles and bones and sinew and heart. She could almost *feel* her wounds knitting together each time his gentle hand rested upon her arm, or persuaded some stain to leave her face, or brushed her fingers as he handed her a bowl of food or a piece of bread.

Daily, they ate breakfast together. Daily he talked about the castle, the forest, the grounds, his music. Daily, she became more and more acquainted with the dexterous capabilities of her own fingers and her mouth—and so daily she grew more skillful with complicated tools like spoons and teacups.

Also daily, he left the castle, and entered the garden.

Only at this time, every time, did she fill with panic.

She waited at the kitchen window, staring fixedly out at the garden gate, snatching glimpses of him as he moved back and forth from the shed to the well to the gate again, her tail swishing restlessly back and forth. She did not dare let him out of her sight while he was out there...

For whenever she did, she felt the shadows creeping back into her mind—the glassy Nothing, the murk and dark.

It made her heart beat faster—but *this* pulse drained her of her strength, and made her fists clench.

But she would *not* go outside.

The bear lived there. The bear, with his knife-teeth, and his dagger claws...

Every evening, though, *he* would come back inside, bring her hot food from his tower, and sit beside her and the mirror, and merrily tell her about what he had accomplished in the garden—though he grudgingly admitted he still could get no flowers to bloom. The two of them would chew on bits of spearmint he brought in, and she breathed it in deeply so that her head cleared. Eventually, her panic would subside into sleepy warmth as his voice filled the cavern in her heart.

And she would speak, too.

At first it took great effort to form anything at all with her tongue and lips and teeth—but she watched him, and understood him—and somehow, the more he spoke, the easier it became for her to translate her thoughts into coherent words. At first, it felt like water cracking through a frozen pipe. But every day, the water flowed more freely, and as she breathed his words in and out, words of her own sprang ready into her mouth—and when he would turn his eyes upon her, and listen to *her...*

Her thoughts would pour aloud into the safety of his silence.

He was called Amber.

Without being able to recall why or how she knew it, the realization eventually rose up within her that "amber" was a stone. A stone that almost lived, for it held both fire and sunrise in its warm, friendly depths. It did not sparkle with cut radiance, nor flash with refined, harsh edges. Instead, it glowed from within—softly. Without manipulation or design. Without the presumption of being like the fine and coveted stones that graced the crowns and throats of monarchs—therefore superior in its unassuming beauty. And in form and make, uncut and unsharpened, it was without similarity to any other stone on earth.

And he called her Silver.

A gleaming, precious metal that could be crafted into delicate jewelry, or woven into threads that adorned the clothing of nobles. But not as precious as gold. And it would tarnish.

But the way Amber said that name—pleasant upon his mouth, and in the air. Filled with warm regard, or earnest attention. The name sounded bright and young. Like a band of water shimmering through a valley, rather than a perishable, malleable metal.

So she called herself the name he had given her.

And in his absence, all through the steeping night, she lay beneath the blanket he had brought down for her. For, surrounded by his scent—the scent she still could not name—when the shadows and cold tried to creep near, they could not get past such a formidable shield.

Beneath such protection, night after night after night, her wounds stitched together, her heart beat stronger, and her mind slept deeper than she ever could remember.

Amber huffed and scrubbed the towel through his wet hair with both hands. Thunder rumbled over the rooftop of the castle as the rain poured down the battlements and drenched the yard. Sighing, he yanked the towel off his head and tossed it beside his sopping jerkin on the chair by the fire. He stood in his undershirt and trousers in the center of his tower, frowning sulkily out the thorn-covered window at the deluge. He had been happily pruning a monstrous tea rose near the entrance to the garden when a crack of thunder had nearly split his skull and the heavens had torn open to dump ice water all over him. He had barely managed to put all the tools away and get himself inside before he was drenched to the skin.

Now what would he do all afternoon?

"Amber?"

The voice resounded through the corridor just beneath his. Immediately, he padded across the rug in his bare feet, opened the door, and hurried out into the chilly hall. He headed down the stairs in the dark, no longer needing to feel his way, and hopped out into the dusty passage. His footsteps squeaked as he peered ahead through the dimness.

At the far end, near the turn of the corner to the left, he glimpsed a flash of a spiny tail. He picked up speed and trotted down the hall, then rounded the edge and found her.

Silver spun to face him, withdrawing her rattling tail toward herself and drawing up so she was nearly the height of a woman.

"Hello," Amber grinned, raking a hand through his messy hair. "Wondering where I was?"

"Yes," she answered, nodding. "I've never seen it rain like this. And the thunder has never been so—"

Just then, it snarled right over their heads and quaked through the walls. Both of them inadvertently ducked, and she slipped slightly closer to him. He glanced over at her. Her skin had lost a great deal of its lustre in this past week, and had faded to gray. Her expression now tensed, and her gaze flickered through the corridor.

"It makes me want to be underground," she muttered.

"No, it's all right," Amber assured her, making himself stand up straight. "We're safe here, in the castle. Thunder is just a bunch of shouting anyway. Does it scare you?"

She looked up at him, and shrugged one shoulder.

"It isn't pleasant."

"Well, come here," he touched her elbow and stepped past her, toward the shuttered window at the end of the hall. She turned and came with him, her tail gliding swiftly behind her as she kept near his shoulder.

"We can look out this window, and I'll bet we'll see clear sky to the east," he said. "Storms always move that way. It won't rain for long, especially if—"

Amber's stomach plunged.

Silver's hands clamped around his left arm—

He *shot* upward, swallowed in a gust of wind—

Blackness.

He staggered. His feet hit smooth wood.

He sucked in a gasp and he forced his eyes wide open.

Silver had crushed herself to his side, her face buried in his chest. Shaking all over, Amber battled to compose himself even as he cast a rapid glance all around them.

They stood in a small, square tower room. Two little windows allowed light in—one in the east wall, the other in the west wall. A few stacks of books stood stacked and covered in dust against the east wall. Otherwise, the room was empty.

"Silver," Amber said, reaching across to touch her shoulder. Her whole frame trembled. "Silver, look. It's all right."

She slowly lifted her head, and started breathing again as she looked around.

"Where are we?" she whispered.

"I don't know," Amber said, gently extracting himself from her grip and stepping forward. "It looks like...a *secret room*."

He turned around and grinned excitedly at her—and the ghosts plaguing her expression fled. She slid forward, clasping her hands together, casting about in interest.

"Secret for what reason?"

"Don't know," Amber admitted. "I have no idea who lived here before. Do you?"

Silver raised her eyebrows and shook her head.

"We must have stepped on something magic down below that sent us up here," Amber mused. Silver glanced past him.

"What are those?"

Amber spun back around.

"Books! I wonder which ones they are." He bent over and scooted a dusty stack out from the wall, sat down cross-legged next to it and grabbed the first book on the stack.

Silver swept toward him and lowered her body, leaning against his right side so she could see too.

"*Fairies: Endearing and Evil,*" Amber chuckled, knocking the cobwebs off and opening the cover to the first page. "Yiy! What is *that?*"

"I would kill it," Silver muttered, resting her chin on Amber's shoulder as she frowned at the illustration.

"I would too," Amber agreed, turning the next page so he could hide the drawing of the multi-legged, blue, nasty-toothed sprite that glared out at them. Page after page greeted them with all manner of strange pixies, some winsome and lovely, some grinning and naughty, some just plain sinister. Many had dozens of wings, some had far too many arms, and all boasted brilliant colors. Amber and Silver commented on all of the pictures, then set that book aside, and Amber grabbed the next.

"A Chronologie of Illustrious Swords," he read, hefting the thick gray volume. "Hm."

"Hm," Silver grunted too—and thus, Amber set it on top of the fairy book without opening it.

They worked their way through the pile of a dozen tomes, all bearing magical titles such as *A Complete Guide to Water Nymphs, The Compendium of Merlin, Enchanted Intelligence,* and *The Use of the Mushroom in Sleeping Draughts.*

Finally, Amber's dirty hands landed on the last one in the pile: a wide, emerald-bound book with silver edges.

"Florem," he read. And he flipped it open.

It exploded.

With a single *crack* like a firework, thousands of bluebells burst from its pages like a blown feather pillow. They hit Amber right in the face.

He crashed onto his back.

Flowers shot into the air and rained down all over them, covering the floor and showering their heads and shoulders.

"Ppppththhht!" Amber sputtered, spitting out petals and leaves—

And Silver burst out laughing.

She pointed and laughed at him as bluebells harmlessly battered her head and shoulders.

"What was *that?*" Amber cried. Silver just looked at him, shook her head and chortled louder, weakly toppling onto her elbow.

"It isn't funny—I'm allergic!" Amber scolded—which only made her writhe harder, and gasp helplessly. Amber grinned and scrambled to sit up.

"All right, let's see what *you*—" he grabbed the book, aimed the pages at her toward her and flung it open. " —think of it!"

Thousands of sweet alyssum erupted from the inner spine and buried her, making her fall on her back.

"Ppphh! Ppphh! Hahaha!" She swatted the white blossoms away to no avail, shaking her head again. Amber dropped the book and relentlessly scooped more flowers on top of her even as she sat up and started flinging them back at him.

Soon, they had both broken out into hysterical laughter, roaring and shouting at each other as they pelted each other with handfuls of brilliant petals.

That is, until Amber snatched Silver's right wrist just as she was about to smack him in the face with a fistful of alyssum.

"Wait—stop, stop, stop," he insisted. Silver lost her balance and nearly fell into him—

And Amber sneezed. And sneezed and sneezed and *sneezed.*

"Ugh!" he cried, let go of her and collapsed onto his back.

"Ha!" Silver crowed. "Do you surrender?"

"I give up," he sniffed, his eyes watering, as he waved her off. "You've killed me."

She slid up next to him, dipped down, and deftly reached out to smooth a flower out of his hair.

"Impossible," she declared quietly. For a moment, her fingers lingered in his curls. He gazed up at her, his eyes still watering, and smiled.

And she smiled back.

"You...want to go back down, then?" Silver asked, lifting up a bit.

"Yes," Amber said, sitting up—and he sneezed again, fiercely. "Somehow," he muttered stuffily, climbing to his feet. "I don't think that's what that book is supposed to do."

Silver giggled again—and the sound of it made Amber grin stupidly.

"Don't laugh at me, I'm dying," he admonished pathetically. Her laughter broke loose again, and she fell lightly against him, touching her forehead to his shoulder.

"Come on," he urged, casually tugging on her arm as she tried to control herself. "We have to figure out how to—"

He yelped as the floor vanished from beneath his feet.

In a flash, he stood solidly in the same corridor as before, Silver right in front of him, gripping the front of his shirt.

"All right," he muttered, his hands fluttering up to touch the backs of hers as he glanced up at the plain, dim ceiling. "So that's how you do it."

Silver chuckled weakly, and he glanced back down at her.

Alyssum and long stems of bluebells draped over her shoulders and over her head, and white petals stuck to her scales.

"You're a mess," he observed, brushing them off of her. She canted her head and smiled wryly.

"You should see yourself."

"Ha!" He ruffled his hair with both hands and white petals showered down. She dusted off his shirt too, and both of them kept chuckling until all the flowers had mostly fallen.

"Well," Amber cleared his throat. "After I wash all this flower dust off my face, I want tea. You?"

"Sounds fine," Silver replied—still smiling, but hiding it.

"Good!" Amber nodded. "I'll find you in the Mirror Room."

133

"On a hill, in the sun
A casket made of gold and glass
Hammer fell in dwarven forge
Hammering a coffin for a raven-haired lass

Hammers fell and tears ran down
Into beards as black as ink
Roughened hands gripped tools of brass
Hammering a coffin for a raven-haired lass

Billows heaved and fire burnt
Dwarven hands heaped wood and coal
Iron nails held wooden frame
Hammering a coffin for a raven-haired lass

Dwarven songs in hollow halls
Rang on anvils' backs
Sorrow, for the spell's been cast
Hammering a coffin for a raven-haired lass."

Thunder rumbled overhead, but with the upper level of the castle between her and the sky, the nearness of the warm hearth, and Amber's lute and voice filling the room, it seemed but an empty threat. Silver lay on her mattress, on top of the blanket, stretched out on her belly, her chin resting on her flattened hands. She gazed at Amber as he plucked absently at the strings, humming almost to himself. Awash in golden flamelight, he'd regained that quality of soft, vivid unreality that always left her speechless. He glanced over at her and smiled.

"You're quiet."

Silver took a breath, and tilted her head.

"The song is sad."

He chuckled.

"The song isn't finished."

Her eyebrows went up.

"You wrote it?"

"Yes," he nodded. "I did hear how the story ended, but I haven't worked out the rhymes for it yet."

"How did it end?" Silver asked, sitting up on her elbows.

"Well, to start with, the girl was a princess," Amber began, setting his lute down by the tea tray and folding his arms. "And her stepmother the queen was jealous of how pretty she was and tried to kill her. So the girl ran away into the woods, and lived with a handful of dwarf brothers. Eventually, though, the queen found her, disguised herself, and gave the princess an apple that had a sleeping spell on it. The princess ate it, and fell asleep so deeply that the dwarves thought she was dead. But they couldn't stand the idea of burying her, so they made her a glass coffin, and set her on a sunny hill. But *then*," Amber gave Silver a bright look. "A handsome prince came riding along, and he saw her. And he thought she looked so sweet, and he was so sad that she was dead before he could meet her, that he had the dwarves uncover her. And before he could help himself, he bent down and kissed her. And she woke up."

Silver jumped.

"She woke up? How?"

Amber shrugged.

"True love's kiss."

"True love?" Silver frowned. "How could they love each other if they've never met before?"

"Well," Amber canted his head. "Maybe they were always *meant* to love each other, no matter what. They just had to find each other."

Silver closed her fingers.

"And...what if they had never found each other?"

"But see, they *had* to," Amber said, facing her a little. "It was inevitable. That's the way it is with true love."

"And you know all about it, then?" Silver smiled crookedly—watching him.

"Of course. I'm an expert," Amber declared. Silver's brow furrowed, and cold settled in her gut.

"Oh? How did you...become an expert?"

Amber laughed.

"It's the only thing that anyone ever wants to hear a song about," he said. "The royalty, gentry, nobility, peasantry—all of them want a love story. So I have to travel from kingdom to kingdom collecting the best ones and writing songs about them." He stretched his legs, and yawned. "I've actually never stayed in a place this long without being commanded to. At Tirincashel I had to stay a whole year because the queen was so sad about her daughter's death that she couldn't sleep without my singing. But before that, I don't think I stayed anyplace more than two or three weeks. And how long have I been here?" he asked her suddenly. Startled, Silver shook her head—and her heart began beating faster.

"I'm not sure."

"Hm. I think it's been...Has it been a month? Longer?" He scratched his head. "I think it has. It doesn't feel like that long, but I think that's right."

"Are you going to leave?" Silver rasped. She felt him turn and look at her, but she stared down at her scarred, pale, scaly hands. "I...understand why you would want to." She murmured. "It is not exciting here, and you have no court to entertain. And...if you have stories you need to collect..." She trailed off, her throat thickening so much she couldn't speak. For a long time, she didn't dare lift her head—but when he didn't say anything, she finally wrenched her attention away from her ugly hands and looked up at him.

He was smiling at her, but with a bit of bewilderment behind his brilliant eyes.

"I'm not in a hurry," he said, keeping his smile, though his brow furrowed. "I have food, a warm bed, a garden, something to do during the day—an entire *castle* to keep me out of the rain—and someone to talk to."

Silver blinked, and painful warmth swelled through her.

"Seems to me that I'm faring about as well as a king," Amber surmised. He lifted one shoulder. "But, if I ever did need to leave, I'd take you along with me, you know."

Silver's heart stuttered.

"With you? Me?"

"Sure!" he said. "I'm not going to leave you here by yourself! But...if you were going to come with me, you'd actually have to *leave* the castle. You know—go outside."

Silver swallowed, a phantom ache running across all her scars.

But as his words sank in, they sent fire through her veins. Fire that drowned out the ache, and banished the cold in her gut.

"Come out to the garden when it stops raining," Amber suggested, tipping toward her. "I don't think there's anything to be afraid of—I haven't even heard any birds singing. Unless you're scared of talking statues."

Silver chuckled, fighting her nervousness, and Amber laughed quietly too.

Then, he reached out, and teased the edge of her fist with his fingertips.

"Come on," he murmured, smiling. "What do you say?"

Silver's fingers relaxed without her say-so. She opened her hand, and he slipped his in and gripped it.

Captured, she studied the facets of color in his eyes. And then, without realizing how or why or what she was doing...

She nodded.

"All right."

He grinned broadly, wagged her hand up and down until she laughed, and then reached for the tea tray.

"Do you want another one of these seed cakes? Because if you don't, I'm going to eat them both."

CHAPTER FIFTEEN

"AND THE CASTLE AWOKE"

The next day, however, it had still not stopped raining. The thunder had relented, but now the downpour just drenched the castle, so thick that it obstructed Amber's view of the forest from his window. It had been pleasant music to sleep to, but as the gray day dawned and the light hardly lifted—and a kind of damp chill crept into his tower—Amber started to resent it. He dressed and ate breakfast, then stood with his arms folded, chewing a piece of spearmint and glaring out the window. In other circumstances, he quite enjoyed the rain. A warm summer cloudburst had often cooled him as he walked on the road, and he'd sat underneath the spreading branches of an oak to listen to the whip and rush of it, and to breathe the fresh wind.

But there was nowhere to walk at the moment, and the water had cooled enough to be striking. And the entire storm tended much more toward gloom than freshness.

Amber let out a long, frustrated groan, spat the spearmint out the window and contemplated going back to bed. But he wasn't tired.

He surmised that Silver would be sleeping this morning, as she disliked damp and enjoyed the nearness of the fire best. So he groaned again, sat down by the hearth, and played on his lute and composed for at least two hours.

Until finally the tunes all started sounding the same, and his lyrics turned to nonsense.

He tossed his lute onto the bed, leaned over and snatched his shoes and put them on. Then, he got up, left his tower, trotted down the hallway and the stairs and strode out into the dusty corridor.

"Silver!" he called. He continued descending, absently trailing his fingers along a familiar path down the stone wall to his left as he spiraled down the stairs. He hopped out into the great, dim greeting room and paused.

"Silver!" he called again. His voice resounded through the emptiness. He frowned. He pushed into the kitchen, but it was empty, and he was sure she hadn't gone outside. So he turned and went into the huge feasting hall, glancing up at its vast, dark ceiling. He waited a moment for his eyes to adjust, and saw what he remembered before: a dais at the far end, two fire pits in a line, leading up to the dais; and the towering, silvery ribs against the wall to his right, stretching up into the void. He frowned harder, and cautiously approached them, his footsteps echoing as they would inside a cathedral.

As his vision grew more and more accustomed to the dimness, he could finally make out a huge, dusty cabinet at the base of these piled rows of towering ribs. And in the center of this cabinet sat some sort of keyboard—like on an accordion, only there were three of them, placed like stairs, one after the other—and they were quite a bit wider than an accordion. A bench sat before the keyboards, so that a person could sit and reach all the keys as well as the dozens of long, wooden pedals on the floor of the cabinet.

"This is an instrument," he breathed—and instantly he knew he had to try it. He climbed up on the bench, careful not to touch the pedals yet, and reached out toward the dusty, white keys.

He chose one in the very center of the center keyboard. He rested his finger on it for a moment, then set his jaw, and pressed *down*.

The pure, piercing middle tone shot up through the pipes and out into the hall like a cannon. Amber reeled back—

And all the torches burst into flame.

Sparkling light gusted through the hall, leaping up the looming walls—and the air instantly warmed. Amber stared, his breath caught in his throat...

But the torches just winked and twinkled back at him, as if they had been happily dancing in place just that way for a hundred years.

Amber grinned.

He reached out again, this time with both hands...

And pressed down on three keys.

The luminous chord jetted through the air, high in the ceiling this time, and three giant iron chandeliers lit up like Christmas wreathes. The wooden rafters bloomed into being, revealing carven faces in their beams, smiling placidly down upon the whole of the hall. This new light also showed three huge tapestries hanging on the far wall—all of knights and ladies feasting in a forest amongst elves and unicorns.

"Haha!" Amber cried in delight—and then really began to play.

He'd never touched an instrument like this before—but it was easy enough to decipher in which direction the notes proceeded from low to high. Very soon, he discovered how to make chords, and then began darting back and forth between them, running his fingers up and down first the middle keyboard, then the bottom one, then the top one—then two at a time. He experimented pressing his feet down on the pedals and found that they issued rumbling bass notes—so he gleefully incorporated those into his chords also...

Until he was composing. Composing music that sounded like a great, lusty autumn wind—bold, colorful and flurrying; deep-chested, whirling, rushing and laughing. And it was only after he had settled on a melody and theme that a great *bang* issued, and he looked to the left...

And saw what he was *really* doing.

Dozens of brooms and mops knocked a far door open and bustled out into the empty hall like a troupe of soldiers, followed by a row of rumbling buckets. The double doors heaved open to let them out...

Amber's hands froze on the keyboard.

The mops, brooms and buckets slowed to a halt, and tilted toward him, as if waiting.

He stared at them, but managed to make his quivering hands find the keys.

Immediately, the buckets, mops and brooms leaped into action again, and hurried out the door. Flabbergasted, Amber leaned back and craned his neck to see where they'd gone—but he didn't stop playing.

In no time at all, the cleaning tools returned, this time with water slopping over the edges of the buckets. And they all spread out across the reaches of the hall and began sweeping and mopping with more fury and vigor than any human servants ever could. The buckets of dirty water fairly flew out of the door and back again, the mops and brooms sloshing and slooshing and swirling like dancers at a ball until all the floor was spotless.

In no time at all, while the buckets and brooms and mops were putting themselves away, the floor had dried...

Amber, his heart pounding with adrenaline, and with a foolish grin on his face, varied his musical theme...

And all at once, with each throbbing, deep note he played, a long, ornate red rug appeared and unfurled—starting at the dais and whisking its whole length across the stones toward the great door. Two long, dark-wood dining tables jumped into existence, each nearly the length of the room, one on either side of the fire pits. Benches padded with blue velvet rolled up to flank them.

Two long swaths of brilliant cloth bloomed out of nothing high up in the rafters, and tumbled down like giant leaves, shimmering in the torchlight, and spread themselves smoothly out across the surface of each table, transforming into what looked like flawless sheets of gold.

Tears of delight filled Amber's eyes as he kept playing—and gawking at the room as much as he could without fouling up his melody.

But then...

Somethings strange began happening underneath his hands.

He whirled to face the instrument...

To see that it had begun playing itself.

It had caught up his theme, all of his harmony, and now keys on all three boards were rapidly depressing, the pedals at his feet didn't need him—the pipes swelled with glorious sound that then spilled out into the hall and drowned the whole castle.

He pulled his hands back, marveling.

"What is going on?" came the startled cry from the large doorway. "What...?"

Amber spun to see Silver standing there.

Her mouth hung open, her eye wide as she gaped at the transformed hall.

And at the sweeping, majestic changes that kept rolling across it from end to end.

Amber staggered off the bench, his knees weak.

As the instrument kept playing, an energetic ripple rolled through the tablecloths, and clattering tableware burst from the centers like feathers from a seam. Three hundred blinding gold plates, platters, lids and knives captured every bit of torchlight and flung it back from whence it came and a thousand directions besides, making the walls look as if they were streaming with waterfalls of firelight. A hundred candlesticks grew from the tables like daffodils, sprouting twisted candles that then laughed out white, twirling fairy flames.

With rapid *cracks*, two black iron poles shot out of the wall above the dais, and vividly-red and blue standards spilled from them, gleaming with silver embroidery, and the symbol of a dragon and a lion.

Amber eased toward Silver, hardly daring to blink lest he miss something. She slipped in to meet him, and grasped his left hand tightly in her right.

"Are you a wizard?" she whispered in his ear.

"Ha!" he laughed helplessly, his chest knotted with a mix of wonder, fear and awe. "*No.*"

She held on to him, and he returned the pressure, even as evergreen garlands trundled across the tabletops, weaving in and out of the candlesticks. Garlands also attached themselves to the eaves and draped across the pipes of the instrument, and the standards by the dais.

The dais itself bore two drab wooden thrones of equal height. But in an instant, dust disappeared from their backs and arms, revealing bright red cherry wood, and scarlet velvet cushions. Golden candle stands bounded up from the floor of the dais and rose high over the heads of the thrones—and then arms sprang from each stand like the stairs on a spiral staircase, each one putting forth a living candle.

And then a scent rolled through the room and almost overwhelmed them.

Rather, a *thousand* scents.

Baking bread, cinnamon, cloves, ginger, roasting hen, baking apples...

"What is that?" Silver asked, sniffing eagerly. Amber just laughed and swiped at his eyes.

Then, the music quieted, just a little...

So that they were able to hear clanking and clattering coming from the kitchen.

"What...What is *that?*" Silver wondered again. "Let's go see...!" She tugged on him, and together they hurried through the door and into the kitchen...

To halt in astonishment.

The kitchen had filled with bowls, bags of flour, spoons, knives, forks,
and all manner of baking tools. A fire blazed in the oven...

And the bowls, spoons and bags were moving about all on their *own*.

One bowl and spoon were furiously mixing up what looked like a Christmas pudding. A clockwork spit before the fire turned a turkey dripping with butter. Another set of invisible hands were speedily filling up little pastry tarts with mince-meats. Flour puffed through the air, towels beat themselves out, and bread dough pounded itself relentlessly upon the counter.

"Wh...Wh...Wh..." Amber tried, but he wasn't able to form anything more coherent than that. Silver just slapped a hand over her mouth.

Then, a raucous *thud-thud-thud-thud-thud*, like a trunk coasting down a flight of stairs, rumbled through the very stones. Amber spun around and hurried down the hall of stubborn doors, followed closely by Silver. They achieved the end, Amber pushed the door open, then darted across to the next, and pushed it open...

They toppled into the library.

A library whose shelves were packed from floor to ceiling, no room to spare...

With *books*.

More books than Amber knew anyone could ever read if he started the moment he learned how and went on to the day he went blind. A merry fire crackled in the wide, welcoming hearth in the center of the room, and surrounding it stood tall-backed chairs, and tables with lamps up on them. Tapestry-like rugs now covered the floor, and as they stood, a full tea blossomed on one of the tables, piping happily.

"What is this?" Silver wondered. "How is this happening?"

"I don't know," Amber confessed, out of breath. "I just started playing that instrument in there..."

"Ha," Silver said, echoing his earlier sentiment, then went on carefully. "Well...it...doesn't seem to be *bad*."

Amber grinned at the myriad books lining every single shelf.

"No, it doesn't."

After they had got over their astonishment, they promptly ate and drank the tea laid out on the table—which seemed by far the most delicious tea either had ever had—then set to exploring the library. They discovered all manner of books, from those about cooking, baking, gardening, weaving, painting and paper-making; to those filled with ancient runes, fairy legends, dead languages, extinct beasts, lines of forgotten kings, chronicles of battles, and how to properly shoe horses. Both Amber and Silver made use of the tall ladders that clung by rails and wheels to the shelves—Silver could climb one in an instant, with a rush and clatter, and chuckle at him from the top as he struggled to match her on another ladder.

After they got quite exhausted climbing up and down and juggling old volumes, they tossed a huge atlas out on the thick rug and sprawled in front of it, flipping the pages and marveling at the names of the strange, faraway lands. All the time Silver tapped her tail absently, like a cat. Once in a while, they supposed that it was still raining out, but neither of them cared.

By midafternoon, they had tired of the atlas, and put it back, and set out to see what had happened in the rest of the castle.

They poked their heads into the room with the talking Mirror...

To find her very contentedly surrounded by medieval portraits of children in huge gilt frames. Green curtains hung round the windows, a purple rug lay across the stones, a table stood against the wall, with two chairs and a candlestick burning. And Silver's mattress had transformed to a tall, long, single bed with four posts and elegant drapes. She gaped at the place for a full five minutes before Amber pulled her along to the next room.

Each chamber behind each formerly-stubborn door had magically furnished itself, fashioned into a recreation room or study. All bore colorful carpets. Some held hanging tapestries of horses, dragons or sprites; others had standing suits of antique armor, board

games on the tables, or small cases stuffed with books; all of them boasted at least one large portrait of a contented-looking nobleman or lady, and all held tables, chairs, couches, candles, and curtains. And every one harbored a different lovely smell, be it
mint, cloves, cinnamon, or rose.

The two hurried out to the great receiving hall to find that a giant iron chandelier had come to life, blazing down upon them, illuminating knotted designs in the stonework of the now-clean floor, and the massive wooden door. Amber childishly hopped his way across the floor, landing only on blue-colored stones while Silver laughed at him—and together they scrambled up the spiral staircase, joking and racing each other, to see what they would find in the upper floor.

They skidded out into the dim, dusty hallway Amber was used to passing through every day, to find that it had been dusted, the wood floors polished, and the glass lamps hanging on the walls had been lit. The two opened every door in that corridor they could find, exclaiming and calling to each other as they did, making certain neither of them missed a thing.

Each room proved to be a lavish bedchamber, complete with a massive curtained bed, tapestries, ornate fireplace, piles of trunks, animal trophies, bookshelves, portraits and even some statuary; and each room had been themed in a particular beautiful color: a scarlet room, an emerald room, a sapphire room, a violet room and a pearl room.

Finally, they bustled into a very large room with a king-sized bed and two large wardrobes. This one was done all in pink roses— roses embroidered in the curtains, on the rugs, and on the tapestries hanging on the walls. Roses had also been carved into the faces of all the furniture.

"Feels like a garden indoors," Amber remarked. Silver slid inside, running her hands across the shining woodwork. Amber's stomach growled.

"Is it dinnertime already?" he cried, slapping a hand to his belly. Silver looked at him.

"I have no idea!" she answered. "It's been so grim outside all day—I never saw the sun. But I think it *has* been quite a while since tea."

"Well, we should go down to the hall and eat the feast that's being made for us," Amber declared. Silver straightened.

"Feast?"

"Yes, didn't you see it?" Amber reminded her. "The turkey by the oven, the bread, the pudding?"

"In the kitchen? Yes," Silver nodded. "You suppose it's for us?"

"Who else could it be for?" Amber asked. "Unless you invited guests without *telling* me."

Silver beamed and ducked her head.

"No, I'm afraid everyone was too busy to come."

"Oh, well, more food for us," Amber declared, then spun and faced one of the wardrobes. "Though, while we're *dining* in a great hall—we might as well dress for the occasion!" And he flung the wardrobe open. He then raised his eyebrows. "Aha."

Silver came up beside him and canted her head far to the right.

"What...are *those?*"

"What, you don't recognize these as the...As the *finest* clothes in the land?" Amber said indignantly, pulling a pompous shirt coat out of the wardrobe. It had huge puffed sleeves, a lace-up front, and a blinding pattern of orange, green and purple stripes. He threw it on himself, shrugging into its bloated shoulders, and swiftly laced up the front while Silver gawked at him.

"There you are, don't I look handsome?" he said with utmost seriousness, posing with his nose in the air. Silver gave him a baffled smile.

"I—" she tried.

"Ah, but wait! There is more!" Amber declared, and Silver snorted. Amber snagged a voluminous, curly gray wig off its stand and stuffed it on his head.

"Haha, what is *that?*" Silver cried as he snobbishly arranged the curls on his shoulders.

"This, you uncultured creature, is the height of fashion!" Amber countered in a heavily-affected accent. He then tugged off his shoes to replace them with those in the wardrobe—one shoe was orange, the other green, and both were very long and came to a curled toe, each bearing a little jingle bell. He then spun to face her and haughtily planted his hands on his hips and puffed out his chest.

Silver burst out laughing.

She instantly clapped both hands over her mouth, but it was too late.

"Oh, wait—*cannot* forget *this,*" Amber cried, pulling out a drawer and finding a powder box and puff. He opened the box, dabbed the puff inside, and then rapidly patted it all over his face.

Silver kept chuckling even as she waved the cloud of white powder away. Amber tossed the puff back in, found a stick of lipstick and ducked his head in to find a hanging mirror, then drew a little heart on his whitened lips.

"Now!" he faced her again, forcing his features into a tight and wide-eyed expression.

Silver fell back against the post of the bed, fighting to stifle her laughter but completely helpless against it.

"What AH your LAHFING about, madAHM?" Amber asked snootily, sniffing and turning up his nose at her. He pranced across the room, making the bells on his toes jingle ridiculously. Silver fell sideways onto the bed, wrapping her arms around her middle. Amber stopped in the middle of the floor, foppishly tossed his wig, then made a stiff bow to someone invisible.

"Oh, my dear Lord Chumbermuffin," he said stuffily, holding out his hand as if he really didn't want to touch anyone. "Is this your famous brother?"

He hopped across and took the place of the invisible man, slapped a hand to his chest, and let out a dramatic gasp.

"Why *no!* It is my wife! How *dare* you?"

"Bahaha!" Silver chortled, collapsing onto her back.

"Psh, psh, psh!" Amber mocked the sound of slapping as he feebly batted the air where the offending face should have been.

Then he swept across the room, pretending to hold up massive skirts, and approached another unseen courtier.

"Why, dearest Lady Cheebleface," he raised his tone so he sounded like an old woman. "Your hair looks simply marvelous this evening."

He glided over to play Lady Cheebleface, and pursed his lips and batted his eyes.

"Why, thank you, Lady Ticklefeet," he purred.

Silver almost had a fit. Amber slid back over.

"Why yes, just marvelous," he said, tipping his head back and forth. "The very image of one of my prize sheep!"

"Stop, stop!" Silver tried. "You have to stop—I can't...I can't..."

"Oh, dear, seems to me this young lady is having trouble breathing," Amber noted flatly, then sniffed again. "How inconvenient. Someone do fetch some smelling salts or she may expire."

Silver slid off the bed and onto the floor, wracked with giggles. Amber grinned in triumph, grabbed the wig off his head and threw it back in the wardrobe, then jumped forward and skidded onto the floor, sliding onto his side next to her, facing her.

"It isn't funny," he warned her as she kept fighting her mirth. "This is very serious. That's exactly how court is conducted. You can't laugh at these people—it's not allowed."

She just snorted again, covered her mouth and shook her head. Amber propped his elbow on the floor and the side of his head in his hand, and smiled wolfishly at her. She dropped her hands and gave him a challenging look and a crooked smile back.

"Of course, *you* wouldn't waste time with those fops, would you?" he teased. "You'd spend all your time hanging around the *minstrel.* Hoping he'd write a song about the color of your eyes."

"You presume too much, sir," she answered frankly, still smiling. "I would have neither the time nor the inclination to hang about a minstrel simply for that reason. Not if there were such fools and characters in my court to be reined in. But I should consider it only if I enjoyed his company, and his music—and if he brought pleasure to an evening otherwise dominated by false niceties."

Amber stared at her. His smile vanished.

Silver's smile faded too, and she gazed openly up at him, her lips slightly parted.

Of a sudden, Amber found his attention flittering all over her features—her scars and scales, yes—but also the shape, the curves and edges. At the depth of her silvery-green eye. And the sudden softness, even in the face of a reptile.

He reached up his left hand, and gently touched her right cheekbone.

Silver swallowed hard, and drew in a sharp breath.

"I wonder why this eye isn't healing," Amber mused, his brow furrowing. "Your eyelid still won't open further, and your eye looks cloudy."

"I know," Silver murmured, sighing.

"Can you see very well?" Amber asked.

"No," she admitted. "Nothing. Not out of that eye."

Amber almost drew his hand back, but left it there for just a moment, tracing his thumb across one of the deep scars on her cheek. Silver just watched him, gazing unflinchingly into his eyes.

Finally, Amber sighed and withdrew his hand.

"You want to find something to eat?"

She grinned.

"Will you be going to dinner like that?" she asked, pointing to his powdered face and puffy shirt.

"What?" he asked huffily. "Is there something wrong with the way I look?"

She laughed again, he helped her up, he pulled off all the finery and put it back in the wardrobe, and together they headed down to the dining hall.

They found the great hall just as lively and luminous as before, though the instrument played much more softly. They ventured in, close to the dais, and stood on either side of one of the tables, facing each other, and gazed down at the gleaming domed lid atop each plate.

At the count of three, they each grabbed a lid and pulled it off—

To reveal a steaming serving of turkey, roasted carrots and cauliflower, potatoes, buttered bread and baked apples. The next instant, each of their goblets filled with rich red wine that bubbled in the candlelight.

They immediately seated themselves—and Silver let the length of her tail rest along the whole top of the bench. They ate greedily with their fingers, juices dripping from the turkey, the crispy skin crunching in their mouths. The apples burst with sweetness, and the wine tasted luscious—almost like raspberries. Amber and Silver laughed as they remarked on the convenience of having food simply *appear,* and swooned with each new flavor they put to their tongues.

After they had eaten everything and sponged all the juice and sauce from their plates with their buttered bread, slices of dark Christmas pudding suddenly materialized in the centers of their platters.

They looked at each other in despair, having no idea how they would even taste any, for they felt too full to eat another mouthful...

But Silver tried some, and said it seemed oddly very light. So Amber did the same, and before they knew it, they had each eaten all of it—in between remarks that the kitchen magic must not be aware of what season it was.

Then, since neither of them felt sleepy, Amber dashed all the way upstairs and retrieved his lute. And when he came back, he ordered Silver to ascend the dais and sit in one or the other of the chairs. She hesitated, but finally did so, curling her length across both of them, and setting her elbow on the rest. Amber hopped up and sat cross-legged on the edge of the table, facing her, and played and sang to her as many songs as he could remember. The instrument in the far corner quietly accompanied him, which made both he and Silver grin with pleasure.

He sang and played as well as he ever had—or perhaps it was the wine making him light-headed and silly. He also blamed the wine for the occasional times when, out of the corner of his eye, Silver did not seem to be a serpent coiled on a battered old chair, but a lady on a throne.

However, when he focused his eyes on her again, and clearly saw her ragged scales, deadly spined tail, long claws, lazily-moving fans and emerald eyes—one now ruined—he smiled to himself at his own nonsense, and kept playing.

CHAPTER SIXTEEN

"THEY WANDERED A GARDEN"

"Silver?" Amber shouted into the great hall, but nothing answered him except his echoes, and a friendly flicker from all the torches and candles. His heart pounded as he spun around and crashed into the kitchen. "Sil—" He stopped himself when all he saw were the bowls and spoons busily making up a porridge. He left, and swept down the hall again, looking for a second time past all the stubborn doors, but all of those rooms were still empty. So was the mirror room. He swung in there and pointed up at the pale-faced woman in the mirror.

"You know where she is, don't you?" he accused.

"Yes," she smiled.

"But you can't tell me?"

"No."

Amber huffed and ran back out, unable to control how his pulse hammered in his ears. He burst into the library and shouted again, but again, no one answered, and he didn't see a single sign of a long tail or dulled scales.

He had already searched the castle once from top to bottom — with the exception of the evil cellar. He knew she would never go back down there.

He shoved out into the courtyard—then skidded, flailed, and nearly fell down. He cursed under his breath, swearing at the still-wet paving stones, then glanced around. It had stopped raining, so the courtyard and the well stood silent. And empty, except for the sunlight that filtered through the wandering clouds.

He took a deep breath—then stopped himself. He didn't dare shout. Oralia's men might still be looking for him. Besides which, who knew what else crept and crawled through the wood...

Biting his tongue, he whirled around and dashed out the back gate, scanning everywhere as he ran, searching the hollow hen yard with a quick glance, then turning toward the gardens...

He slowed to a halt, panting.

Silver stood there with his back to him. He could see her through the opening in the garden wall. She gazed serenely up at the center statue, sunlight catching the edges of her uneven scales.

Amber heaved a sigh and put a hand to his chest as three painful pangs shot through it.

"Silver," he called, trotting toward her. She turned and looked at him.

"I've been looking everywhere for you," he panted, hurrying along the path and up to her.

"You said I should go to the garden when it stopped raining," she reminded him calmly. "I said I would."

"Yes, but I..." Amber fought to catch his breath. "I..."

He trailed off as he finally caught sight of his surroundings.

Something had changed. The grayish leaves of the roses had gained a deep green flush, and on the tips of their branches seemed to be...

Buds.

The garden was going to bloom!

"You didn't believe me?" Silver cocked her head and watched him closely. He called his attention back to her, and laughed.

"Well, I wanted you to come with *me!*"

"Oh!" she said, surprised—then smiled, and almost seemed to blush.

"All right, come on, then," Amber said briskly. "Let me show you what I've been doing."

The garden was indeed going to bloom, and soon. As he walked back and forth along the paths that he'd cleared, Silver right next to him, he ran his gaze across all the bushes to see that they all bore thousands of little buds that stretched toward the sun. Giddy with delight at that, he showed Silver the well, the shed and all its contents, the statue he'd cleaned off, and the lilies he had rescued, whose green sprouts now stood several inches tall. He told her how he had been turning the earth over underneath each rose bush, and tilling in the rotting leaves to act as fertilizer. He showed her what tools he had been using, and how he had been watering with both the bucket and the kitchen kettle. She listened and watched with eager interest and swift understanding, asking bright questions and laughing whenever he laughed.

Finally, Amber suggested that they have tea in an open space near the front gate, beneath one of the twisting old trees. She agreed, and he ran back inside the castle and found a tea tray waiting on the table in the kitchen—complete with buttery porridge. In afterthought, he darted up to his tower and grabbed his lute, and one of the thin hearth rugs, then carried all of it back out to the garden, whistling as he came.

They spread out the rug in the sunshine and set the tea down, and then both of them reclined and ate and drank, and reveled in the warmth of the clear sky. They talked about the flowers, and wondered what color they would be when they bloomed, and guessed they would be able to tell within at least two or three days.

After two cups of tea and three pieces of cake, bathed in the drowsy light, Amber laid back on the rug and pillowed his head in his hands, and drifted off to sleep. As he did, he sensed Silver ease down onto her side, and let out a long, relaxed breath.

In a while, Amber blinked his eyes open again, stretched, and turned his head to see that she wasn't lying next to him anymore. His brow knit, and he sat up on his elbows...

There she was. Near the well, just drifting in between the rose bushes, studying them. He smiled to himself, raked his hand through his hair, sat up the rest of the way and grabbed his lute. He fiddled on the strings for a few minutes before picking out a gentle waltz tune, and then starting to sing.

> *"Believe me if all those endearing young charms,*
> *Which I gaze on so fondly today*
> *Were to change by tomorrow, and fleet in my arms,*
> *Like fairy gifts fading away!*
>
> *Thou wouldst still be adored, as this moment thou art*
> *Let thy loveliness fade as it will;*
> *And around the dear ruin each wish of my heart*
> *Would entwine itself verdantly still."*

He stopped singing, his head coming up in startlement—but out of reflex, his fingers kept playing. Wide eyed, he searched the far reaches of the garden.

Because she was singing with him.

He could hear her. The clear, lovely voice of a young woman.

He scrambled to his feet, but managed to keep playing, even as he crept forward. He clamped his mouth shut, listening, even as her lilting tones filled the whole of the walled garden.

> *"It is not while beauty and youth are thine own*
> *And thy cheeks unprofaned by a tear,*
> *That the fervor and faith of a soul can be known,*
> *To which time will but make thee more dear!"*

Amber rounded the well, searching for her...

And found her. Right there, seated at the base of one of the largest rose bushes. She dug with a spade in one hand, and raked at the ground

156

with the other, tilling and clearing with the confidence and ease of a master gardener. And with the absent body-language of someone who habitually filled a courtyard with folk songs, she sang easily and conversationally as she worked.

> *"Oh! the heart that has truly loved never forgets*
> *But as truly loves on to the close;*
> *As the sunflower turns on her god as he sets*
> *The same look which she turned when he rose!"*

Amber finished out his chords, and stopped, but she kept humming as if she had no idea he was standing there.

Tears sprang to Amber's eyes, and a strange sort of panic shot through his chest.

"Silver?" he called quietly.

Her head came up. Her gaze flashed to his—

And for just a fleeting instant—

Her eye was brown.

Dark brown, of a chocolaty-chestnut hue, with a deep black iris. Warm and young and bright.

And human.

Amber gasped and jerked back.

She blinked.

Her eye became silvery emerald again.

She dropped the spade.

It hid the dirt with a dull clatter.

Amber froze.

Slowly, slowly, Silver rose up to her usual height, her breathing clamped, as she stared down at her dirty hands.

Amber couldn't tear his eyes from her. And as he stood, studying her features as if he'd never seen her before...

Something sudden...electric...painful...swept down through his blood.

"Silver," he whispered. She lifted her head, terror in her eyes.

"What?" she breathed.

Amber's thoughts swirled and swam, his heart accelerating like a rabbit's. He tried to shake himself—but he *knew* what he'd seen. And heard.

"Silver," he said again, taking half a step closer and leaning toward her, never breaking her gaze. "I think you are under a spell."

Flames guttered in the depths of the hearth. The rest of the chamber stood robed in blackness and silence.

Oralia sat in a tall-backed chair, gazing into the fire, her elbow set on the armrest, her fingers draped over her lips. She blinked slowly, her eyebrows drawn together. She wore a blue dress trimmed in green, her hair all undone around her shoulders. The residents of Tirincashel had settled in for the evening, but still she waited. Listening.

Footsteps sounded in the corridor outside the door. She did not move. She knew the purposeful measure of that gait.

"My lady," came the familiar voice, and the footsteps paused.

Oralia sat just as she was for several moments. Finally, she moved her fingers, just slightly, and spoke.

"Come in, Sir Roderick."

He instantly obeyed, and within seconds he had drawn around in front of her, standing off to her left, facing her. She ran a glance up and down his form.

"I see you bathed and changed into finer clothes before you came to me this time."

"I desire to please you in everything," he answered, his clear blue eyes fixed on her. Oralia's brow knitted. She took a low breath.

"You have been gone a long time," she said, very quietly.

Roderick's expression broke, and he stepped forward, then fell to his knees in front of her, reaching out and taking hold of her hands. She let him, and squeezed his fingers.

"I knew how brokenhearted you were about your sister's death," Roderick said earnestly, never tearing his gaze from her face. "I couldn't rest until I had found something that might ease your pain."

"What have you found?" Oralia breathed, leaning toward him.

"The beast," he said through his teeth, and tightened his grip on her hands. "I have seen it."

Oralia clamped down on his fingers.

"Where?"

"In a castle in the depth of Thornbind, across the river," Roderick answered rapidly. "It is a huge snake, with the upper body of a woman—but it has no hair, and instead has fins and spines like the blue asps. It is covered in crumbling gray scales, and it has fangs, claws, and only one eye, which looks like a clouded emerald. The other eye has been slashed so it is nearly gone—perhaps by a sword. The beast has spikes all down the length of its back and its tail. I am certain these are what killed Pather the Huntsman, and the highwaymen at the gate of the wood." Roderick leaned closer to Oralia and lowered his voice further. "She is horrid, and ragged—and by this I judge that it's probably an ancient monster, like the mother of that man-eater Grendel that plagued the kings of the north. Perhaps they are sisters."

"And what of the minstrel?" Oralia asked. Roderick paused, and his mouth tightened. Oralia's eyes flashed.

"You have seen him too," she realized.

"He is with the beast," Roderick told her. Oralia frowned.

"A prisoner?"

"No." He shifted closer to her. "They seem to be...friends. They walk together on the castle grounds, and talk—"

Oralia straightened.

"The beast can speak?"

Roderick shrugged.

"It seems to be able to. At least, it gestures, and seems to understand."

Oralia's hands went clammy. Her jaw tensed, and she stared past Roderick, unseeing.

"I saw them thus, just this morning," Roderick went on. "And after I had watched them, and learned enough, I came straight to you. I believe..." he breathed. "That the minstrel and the beast are of one accord. They both came to Tirin on the very same day to deceive and devour your sister. For what dark purpose, I cannot imagine." He reached up and touched Oralia's face, and she found his eyes again.

"But I also cannot believe they will stop here," he said, stroking his thumb along her cheek. "Perhaps they are waiting to attack again when you come to the age of authority. But no matter what I do, I cannot shake the terrible feeling that you are in danger so long as that beast remains so near."

Roderick took up her hands again, and kissed them fervently.

"My dearest love," he cried softly. "Please tell me what I must do to
make you safe!"

Fear writhed through Oralia's gut, icing her bones and her blood. She laced her fingers through Roderick's as she stared at the mantelpiece. Then, she turned a burning gaze upon him...

Snatched his collar and kissed him passionately, rapidly, over and over—overwhelming him, wrapping her arms around his neck even as he threw his arms around her waist. But just as he started to tangle his hands through her hair—

She pulled back and took his face in her hands.

"Take as many men as you need," she commanded, her words slicing the silence. "Bring the minstrel to me alive. And kill the beast."

CHAPTER SEVENTEEN

"AND FORGED A FARAWAY TRAIL"

The scent of burning peat and heather filled the room, along with the quiet spit and sputter of the fire. Amber sat with his back to the mantel, his legs crossed. A full tray of food sat off to his right, but he hadn't touched it. Neither had she.

She stood erect in front of him, her hands clasped, her head bowed slightly, a deep frown on her face. But her spine had straightened as it never had before, and there was something different about the bearing of her shoulders. Her tail lay completely still.

"Do you remember how long you've been in this castle?" Amber asked her carefully. Her frown darkened, and she took a low breath.

"No," she answered.

"What about before you came here?" Amber pressed. She shrugged.

"I can only recall vague impressions," she said. "Passing through gray woods...crossing a stream filled with cold water...catching fish with my hands...crawling up and down stone steps. I ate...I slept...I climbed trees...I killed things that made noise, or frightened me, or tried to take my food." Her tone hardened "But I...I never *thought* about any of it. I just *did* it." She lifted her head, and looked at him. Her brow knitted. "Until I saw you."

Amber's breath caught in his chest, and he couldn't speak.

"What did you mean," Silver said, very slowly. "That I am under a spell?"

Amber swallowed.

"I think..." he ventured, his pulse picking up. "I think...you're a woman."

"A woman," she repeated. "Like..."

"Like one of my kind," Amber clarified. "But someone has done something to change your form."

"What?" Silver gasped, her hand twitching toward her chest. *"What?* How?"

"I don't know." Amber quickly climbed to his feet and faced her. "But remember the prince of Dallydanehall? That was a true story—he *did* get turned into a bear by a dwarf. And I know that there are witches and wizards that live in woods like these, and they cast all *kinds* of spells."

"So you mean that I...A witch...made me look like this?" Silver pressed a hand to her heart, searching Amber's face desperately. "That I...I am a woman? With...With legs and skin and..."

"You could be," Amber nodded. "You remember nothing before these woods—*nothing* about a mother or father or brothers or sisters—but did you ever wonder how you learned to talk, or read?"

Silver stared at him, her breathing accelerating, her hand closing to a fist.

"I thought you taught me," she choked. He shook his head quickly, reached out and grabbed her hand in both of his.

"No, no—you *remembered.* Just like you remembered how to eat with a spoon, and drink out of a teacup. Just like you *remembered* that the shirt with the ridiculous sleeves was actually funny, and that people *do* talk like that at court, and that it was Christmas pudding we were eating."

Silver pressed her other hand over her mouth. Amber leaned close to her and pulled her hand against his chest.

"That's how you knew the words to *The Coin in the Well,* and *Charms.* And it's how you knew what to do with that spade in the garden, taking care of those roses."

"Why...Why would someone do that to me?" Silver breathed through her fingers. Amber shrugged, working his own fingers into her fist until she relaxed them and twined around his.

"I don't know," he said. "Something you did could have made a witch angry—something your *parents* did could have made her angry—"

"My *parents*." Her good eye widened. "I...have *parents?*"

"You might," Amber said quietly—and then a terrible ache traveled up and down his chest. "But...you might not. Anymore."

She swallowed hard. Amber pulled her closer, never breaking her gaze.

"Or you could have just been traveling through the wood and fallen into a trap," he guessed. "Been on the way to visit a grandmother or aunt, and taken a wrong turning. Just like we did when we jumped up into the tower with the books."

She nodded furtively, reaching out and gripping his hands with both of hers now.

"You...you *do* believe this," she whispered, searching his face. "You *really* think that...that this is not what I truly am? What I'm...supposed to be?"

Amber gazed at her torn skin and ragged scars, and lingered on her deep and brilliant gaze. And that same sudden, electric, painful thrill shot through his heart.

"I think I've always thought so."

For a long moment, both of them were silent—and Silver trembled deep in her frame.

"How can I know?" Silver finally asked. "How would I find out, for certain?"

"I'm not sure," Amber confessed. "From all the songs I've learned, different spells are broken in all different ways. Sometimes the person who cast it has to be killed, or has to undo it. Sometimes you need to put on a magic piece of jewelry, or drink from a special spring, or go into a cave carrying something..."

"Could it be in the library?" Silver ventured eagerly. "A book of spells?"

"Maybe," Amber allowed, tipping his head. "But that would probably get dangerous. I'd rather talk to someone who *knows*. Someone who has experience with..." He stopped.

A memory flashed through his head like lightning.

He stood ramrod straight.

"Oh!" he cried. Then, he let go of Silver's hands and darted out of the room. "Come on!" he yelled, and made straight for the kitchen.

The empty copper teakettle banging and clanging as he ran, Amber charged past the hen house, glancing back to find Silver hot on his heels. Night had fallen, but a full moon shone gloriously down upon all the yard and the garden, illuminating the whole like pearly daylight.

"Amber, where are you going?" Silver cried, her tail making a racket against the grass.

"I have an idea," he panted, dashing into the garden and down the paths toward the well. As soon as he got there, he set the kettle down and drew out the bucket, then hastily poured the water into the kettle and replaced the lid, splashing water all over his hands as he did. Then, Silver watching him in bafflement, he hurried noisily back to the front of the pointing stone statue. Silver instantly lighted by his side.

"What are you doing?" she demanded.

"I want to see if this works again," he said, pushing his hair out of his face. He then bent forward, and poured all the water out onto the lilies at the statue's feet. He straightened up, stared at the statue's face, and waited.

"What's supposed to—"

"Sh," Amber held up a hand. Silence fell all around them. Amber held his breath. Silver shifted, opened her mouth again—

The statue spoke.

"Follow the path by the river's edge
Then up to the bee-wolf's stony ledge
Between two men that stand alone
To Reola Curse-Breaker's hidden home."

"Haha!" Amber crowed, pointing at it. "Did you hear that?"

"Yes...!" Silver cried, sliding back three feet. Amber spun to face her.

"All right, what did she say? She said...She said follow the path by the river's edge..."

"Then up to the...the bee-wolf's..." Silver began.

"Stony ledge," Amber finished.

"Between two men that stand alone..." Silver went on.

"To Reola Curse-Breaker's hidden home!" Amber exulted. He whirled and faced the statue again. "A *Curse-Breaker. That* is what we need. And I'll bet everything I own that the statue is pointing our way into the mountains."

"What, to the Giant's Shoes?"

Amber spun around and almost fell over, then stared at her. Silver blinked.

Amber looked at her sideways.

"You know the name of the mountains."

Her mouth fell open.

"I..." she thought for a moment, and her eyebrows went up. "Yes. I do."

Amber grinned, rushed up to her and kissed her forehead. His lips met soft, cool scales—she gasped—and he pulled back and grabbed her arms.

"I knew it!" He shook her lightly. "Come on—we have to pack!"

Amber dug his forgotten satchel out from under his bed in his tower room, and when he turned around, to his amazed delight, he found food for the journey—bread, cheese, clotted cream, sausage, and two canteens of water—waiting on the table, neatly wrapped in wax paper and tied with strings. Two tightly-wrapped sleeping mats with carrying straps also sat there. He hurried over to the pile and began packing all of it in his satchel, along with the tinderbox he had found in the kitchen. While he was doing this, he noticed Silver ease just over the threshold, her hands clasped in front of her.

"Can you think of anything else we need to bring?" Amber asked as he carefully arranged the cheese and bread inside his sack.

"We're leaving...right now?" she asked quietly.

"Why not?" Amber wondered. "I'm not tired, you're not tired, and the moon is so bright it's very easy to see, especially since there are no leaves on the trees." He straightened up and faced her...

She had bound her arms around herself again, her brow knotted. Amber stopped.

"What?" he asked. "What's wrong?"

"We're going into the woods?" she said breathlessly. "I'm...I mean, how will we know the way? Do we even know that this curse-breaker is still there? And if she is, how do we know she'll help me? And what...What if you're wrong?" She swallowed hard, twice. "About me? What if...What if all I really am is this...*this?*" She gestured weakly at her face before wrapping her arms around her chest again. "Wouldn't...Wouldn't it be better if I just...If I just stayed here, in the castle? I have food, shelter...I don't ever need to go out into that wood again. I'll be fine. Here. I'll be fine."

Amber gazed at her, even as her brow twisted tighter, and her hands closed to fists.

166

He picked up his pack, and slipped the strap across his shoulders. He grabbed his lute, and laid it across his shoulders as well. Then, he stepped up to Silver, and rested his hands on her shoulders.

"But what if she *is* there?" Amber said ardently, capturing her gaze. "And what if she does help you?" He lifted his hand, and touched his fingertips to her chin. "And what if I'm *not* wrong?"

Silver took a deep, wavering breath.

"Amber," she murmured. "I am afraid."

He raised his eyebrows.

"You're afraid?" he laughed. "Have you looked at yourself lately?"

She blinked and twitched back.

"What—What do you mean—?"

"Do you know how fearsome you are?" he asked. "If I didn't know you, I'd run screaming like a banshee. I *did* run screaming like a banshee."

Alarm raced across her features, but Amber didn't let her go.

"Not because you are ugly," he assured her. "But because you look dangerous. Any wolves or witches we might meet along the way will think three times before even coming out onto the path."

She said nothing. He smiled at her.

"Come on." He reached around her and found her left hand. He pulled it toward him, and clasped it in his right. "Let's go."

He stepped past her, out into the small hallway. She turned, very slowly, her head low...

And she let him lead her down the stairs.

The moon shone brilliant and stark down upon the edges of the marble statue. Amber and Silver stood in front of it. She shuddered all the way down through her bones, but he didn't let go of her hand.

"Here, let's climb up here," Amber suggested. "I want to see exactly what she's pointing at."

He stepped up onto the planter, his feet scraping stone, then waited for her to slither up next to him. She had to reach out and steady herself on the statue—her whole length felt weak. Amber stood right behind the statue, resting his chin on its left shoulder, narrowing his eyes as he followed the direction of its extended arm.

"It looks like she's pointing..." he mused. "...right at the tongue of the front shoe. And that's past the woods. *So...*" he hopped down off the planter, then grasped both Silver's hands and helped her slide down. "That means that if we find the river and head that direction, it will lead us straight that way."

"How do you know?" Silver asked, trying to keep her jaw from clamping. She suddenly felt very cold.

"For one thing, the statue said so," Amber reminded her. "For another, there was a big map of this part of the country hanging in Tirincashel, and I walked by it a thousand times. I remember the river." Amber looked around, as if getting his bearings. "And luckily for us, it isn't far from here at all."

Again, he met her eyes. And somehow, even though the moon cast everything in a light of ice and frost, his gaze burned copper as a home fire, and when he smiled, the cold rushed out of her body. But she still trembled.

"Come on," he urged again. And he firmly, but gently, grasped her
left hand, and pulled her toward the garden gate.

And Silver knew, though she had made no conscious decision, and could not drive herself forward on her own power, that if he kept hold of her hand just like this...

She would follow him anywhere on earth.

Even straight into Thornbind Wood.

There was indeed a narrow path beside the river—a leaf-covered indentation mirroring its every curve. The black water flowed languidly, humming as if in sleep. The moonlight glimmered against its obsidian surface, winnowed as it fell by the spidery branches of the slumbering trees.

Together, Amber and Silver swished through the brown leaves, often spilling them into the water, where they drifted downriver like tiny Viking funeral ships.

No wind disturbed the upper branches, and nothing made any sound at all except Amber's confident footsteps and Silver's shushing tail. Amber held onto Silver's hand all the while, sometimes absently running his thumb against the back of hers, exploring the edges of her loosened scales.

After several hours of silence, with nothing but the moon appearing to bear them company, Amber looked up at the gnarled trees and chuckled.

It startled Silver, and she inadvertently squeezed his hand.

"What?" she demanded.

"Reminds me of a song," he said. "I haven't thought about it in a long time."

"What song?"

He glanced slyly over his shoulder at her.

"It doesn't have a name."

She frowned.

"It doesn't? Why?"

He glanced around.

"You want me to sing it?"

She looked around too, and a quiver passed through all the spines on her back and tail.

"In the wood?"

"There doesn't appear to be anyone here," Amber noted. "At all."

Silver swallowed, then pulled a little closer to him as they continued on.

"Well," she said, lifting her chin bravely. "Your voice could never bring anything evil. If you want to sing...please do."

He looked over his shoulder at her, and grinned.

"All right. Let's see if I can remember all the words." He thought for a moment, then took a breath and began.

> *"There is a crooked little man, with roving, wicked eye*
> *He has a house in Riven Woods, and magic fingers five*
> *He slips through cracks in walls when built strong as any dam*
> *He listens well to secrets, and keeps each one in the land.*
>
> *But at a price. A pretty price, will the favor then be sold*
> *A ha' penny. A penny's worth. Or half-again your soul.*
>
> *So beware of this wee, crooked man, whose name that no one knows*
> *Don't bargain with this peddler, no matter what your woes*
> *Be clever, then, and brave—take heart and keep your head*
> *If you sign your name and he names his price, one day you'll wish you dead.*
>
> *It's at a price, a pretty price, will the favor then be sold*
> *A ha' penny. A penny's worth. Or half-again your soul."*

Wild, disorganized images suddenly rolled through Silver's mind—

And words fell out of her mouth.

"Rumpelstiltskin."

"What?" Amber instantly faced her. They stopped right there in the path, Silver's head swimming so much she couldn't see.

"That's his name," she whispered. "Rumpelstiltskin. He...There was a peasant girl...she had to spin straw...into gold. He came, and told her he could do it...if she gave him her baby. And their contract would break if she guessed his name."

Silver blinked, and stared in shock up at Amber, who watched her like
an eagle.

"I've heard the story!" she realized, her chest constricting. "I was...I was somewhere...somewhere else. I was...I was in a great hall, but not the one in our castle. It was full of people. And...flowers. And...a dog? Two dogs...And..." She suddenly frowned. "And I can't remember any more."

She breathed hard, squeezed her eyes shut and swayed, her mind spinning.

"I told you," Amber murmured. She forced her good eye open and looked at him. He was beaming like the sun.

And somehow, she smiled back, wonder filling her chest.

"You did."

"Let's go, let's go!" he urged, tugging on her. And together, they hurried deeper into the wood.

They traveled all through the night, neither of them tiring. The river steadily curved and bent this way and that, but the path hugged it and never waned. They did not meet another living creature all the night long, and never heard anything besides the noise of their own passage.

Thus, the two of them sang the song about Rumpelstiltskin *together*, over and over, Silver delighting in it more and more each time—for each time her voice reflexively followed the right melody, it felt as if she had just found a jewel under a rug. After that, they sang *Charms*, and *The Coin in the Well*, and Amber taught her the song of the maiden asleep in a tower, and the maiden beneath the glass coffin, and the prince who had turned into a bear. Their voices rang through the empty forest, resounding against the deadened leaves and hardened wood. And Amber kept looking over at her as they sang, until soon he watched her constantly, an expression of pleased amazement on his face. When she became self-conscious asked him what he meant by it, he only said:

"You have a pretty voice."

As they kept on, following a steep bend in the river, dawn began to

break. And with it, Amber and Silver began to notice leaves on the trees.

The underbrush beneath their feet gained a deep green tone. The dead leaves became moist, and when Amber kicked through them, they glimpsed insects of all kinds. Amber and Silver bent to study the crawling creatures, and found a profusion of brilliantly-red ladybugs, which made both of them laugh.

"My mother always said that ladybugs were a good sign. They meant 'hope'," Amber told Silver, adjusting his grip on her hand as they stood up. "You sometimes find them in the most unlikely places—and sometimes even on a warm day in midwinter. They're a promise that everything will be better."

Silver smiled down at the busy drops of ruby red.

"I hope your mother is right."

"Ha! She always is." Amber winked at her. Silver's heart fluttered. And together they continued on as the daylight swelled overhead.

"This is starting to look like a real forest," Amber remarked. And it was true. More than true.

The trees had become tall, straight and stately, with beautiful white bark and full, light-green leaves that filtered golden light down across them, creating swimming, dappled patterns over the path. Breezes breathed through the upper boughs, making the ancient trees laugh quietly. Decaying mulch no longer covered the path—now it was dry dirt, and much broader, as if well-traveled. Almost a road. Squirrels scuttled through the branches, scolding the pair if they rounded a corner too quickly and intruded upon the ever-important business of burying a nut.

Wrens, sparrows and nuthatches danced through the leaves, sputtering and twittering to each other, flitting their little wings and turning their bright gazes down upon the strange duet that wandered among the beeches.

Little white and purple flowers bloomed upon lower bushes, filling
the air with a light, dainty perfume. Deep green vines wound around the trunks of the trees like emerald decorations around the hilt of a sword.

At midmorning, Silver and Amber moved off the path into a small, sunny glen, sat down and reclined there for a while, and ate their breakfast. They noted the different kinds of strange flowers, and they wondered why *their* portion of the wood had gone into such a deep sleep when *this* forest seemed so alive and awake.

"It must be under a spell, too," Silver ventured—and Amber thoughtfully agreed.

After they ate, they continued on, meeting no one as they traveled, listening to all the chirping and bustling of summertime all around them.

As day began to wane, the path became rocky, and headed upward at a sharp, weaving angle, leaving the river further and further down below them to their right. Amber suggested that they ascend this one hill, and make camp up there. They had time to do so before night fell.

So together they climbed—and slithered—and Silver had a much easier time of it than Amber did. Her lithe body undulated between the rocks and through the trees, winding around trunks and boulders to propel her along—and she could sink her claws into the bark to keep from sliding backward. Amber had to bend at the waist to keep his balance, and sometimes use his hands, and his pack and lute clattered against each other. Silver could have jetted all the way up the hill in three seconds—but instead, she remained just to his left and slightly behind, waiting to catch him instantly if he slipped.

Finally, they reached the top of this particular peak—though more peaks waited beyond—and they found a lovely spot upon piles of ivy, beneath a low-spreading oak to rest for the night. Amber spread out the sleeping mats, laid down his lute, and together they ate again, quickly, for both had worked up an appetite.

As the sky turned lavender, Amber gathered up some tinder and sticks, and lit a fire out on the path, clear of their mats and other underbrush. The bright, happy light filled the space beneath the boughs as a hearth fire would fill a cabin, and the warmth of it washed over Silver's scales, relaxing all her muscles and easing her mind. Amber lay back on his mat, pillowing his head in his hands. He gazed up at the old, tangled branches, and hummed a wandering tune into the night. Silver lay beside him, and slowly drifted off to sleep, the lilting notes and the song of the river weaving into her dreams.

CHAPTER EIGHTEEN

"TO AN OLD WOMAN WHO LIVED IN A SHOE"

The two woke up just before dawn, because the joyful racket of birds in the trees all around them made sleeping impossible. The fire had died to nothing, and so Amber scattered the ashes with his feet, and rolled up the bedding. Silver insisted on carrying his pack from now on, and so he relinquished it to her. She slung it over her shoulder, and they continued along the path.

They ate bread and cheese as they traveled, often glancing to their right, for that side of the path had transformed into a steep cliff, and the river down below had widened, and grown frothy, loud and snarling.

The trees thickened and became more gnarled, as if the two were drawing nearer the heart of the old forest. For a few hours, the only sounds that welcomed them belonged to the river, the birds, and the breeze.

Then, at about noon, something different reached Silver's hearing.

"Wait," she hissed, and touched Amber's arm. He instantly stopped.

"What?"

"Sh," she warned. She canted her head, listening. Then, she slid three inches backward. "Footsteps."

"Someone's coming?" Amber realized. "Toward us?"

Silver nodded.

"He'll be here soon."

"How can you tell it's a man?" he asked.

"The weight of it," Silver answered, her blood thrilling, all of her scales tingling. "Shouldn't we hide?"

"From a man?" Amber frowned at her. "Is he alone?"

Silver fought to control her rapid breathing, and made herself listen again.

"No. There's someone with him. Someone light...Like a child."

"A papa and his boy," Amber guessed. "Probably not life-threatening."

Silver shot him a dark look but he just smiled at her.

"The ones who have me worried are rattling knights on horses. If you hear anything like *that*, I'd be more than happy to dive into the shrubbery."

Silver swallowed, slipping in behind him—but Amber seemed so sure, so calm. Perhaps, if he thought it was safe, she should believe him. After all, these were his kind, his people. He should know...

In a few minutes, the footsteps grew louder, and voices reached them. A deep, jolly, conversational voice, answered often by a fluty, bouncing one. A man and a boy.

"Come on," Amber motioned to her. "No sense in our just standing here in the middle of the road."

So he started forward. Silver braced herself, then followed after him.

Then, around the bend ahead of them, the figures strode into view. A handsome, young man with a short blond beard and mustache, a low pointed cap with feather, and the green clothes of a ranger. He wore a quiver full of arrows, with a bow across his back. Beside him trotted a red-headed, freckled boy dressed almost the same, who had a knife at his belt. Together they talked and laughed as they strolled easily along, and the sight of them in the dappled golden light softened Silver's nerves, and almost made her smile.

The man looked up. He saw Amber. He raised his hand in greeting—

And then his gaze fell upon *her.*

He jerked to a halt and threw a hand across the boy's chest, stopping him.

The next instant, the man whipped his bow off his shoulders, set an arrow to the string, drew it back and let it fly.

Silver grabbed Amber and threw him to the ground on his face, falling down on top of him. The arrow *zinged* over their heads, shooting through the space where Silver's chest had just been.

"Get up, get up!" the ranger shouted, charging toward them. "Fight, man! Fight!"

"Wait—" Amber croaked—

The ranger drew another arrow. The sun flashed across his eyes and the silver tip. He aimed right at *her.*

Silver thrashed, rolled off the path and tore into the woods, leaving Amber behind her. Her heart thundered, her breaths ripped through her body as she sped through the slapping underbrush.

Another arrow zipped past her left ear and *thudded* into a tree trunk, its red feathers shivering. She ducked, then dove through a rose bush, slithering full on her belly at top speed.

There!

She spotted a huge oak tree with thick, impenetrable leaves. She skirted around it and mounted it in a moment, ripping at its bark as she clawed her way up.

At last, she wrapped her full length around a wide branch and pressed her chest against the trunk, ducking her head down and tucking her arms in.

She froze there, panting, the scent of rich wood and dust flooding her lungs. Her arms trembled, and her tail tightened in a death grip around the bough.

Silence fell.

No arrows sliced the leaves. Nobody tramped through the weeds toward her. No shouts echoed through the wood.

Gradually, the birds got over their fright and started twittering again. A curious squirrel scuttled around the trunk to have a look at her—

But when he saw her, he started so badly he almost fell off the tree, and scurried twenty feet straight up, scolding her harshly all the way.

Silver stared at the space where he had been.

Then, she buried her face in her arm, squeezed her eyes shut, and wished she was dead.

Haze covered the snake's mind. Her blood had cooled, her passion subsided. She had curled up on the branch and gone motionless, the layers of her raging thoughts whittled away until they became thin, hard—and then nonexistent. The day wore on, and the sun lifted in the sky. The wind rippled drowsily through the upper boughs.

She blinked slowly, breathed slowly. Listened to the heartbeats of the birds and squirrels, waiting for one to venture too close so she could snatch it from the air and break its neck.

And then, all of a sudden...

Something sat on the branch in front of her.

Something much larger than a bird or a squirrel.

The muscles in her forehead tensed. She lifted her chin from off her folded hands, just an inch.

The form was familiar—yet completely foreign.

It seemed to be of the same kind as that figure she used to know—the one who smelled good, and made songs.

And yet, this form was softer, more winsome; slender, curved and elegant. It had black, *black,* smooth skin that gleamed like burnished stone; long silver hair, with stiff strands that stuck out from the twisted plait so it looked like a shock of wheat. And it had brilliant, penetrating gray eyes—eyes that fixed on the snake's.

And then she made a noise.

"Silver."

The snake's bones vibrated. She frowned harder.

"Silver," she figure said again...

And all at once, the stranger clarified.

A woman. A woman wearing a simple, homespun, cream-colored dress with no sleeves. She sat on the branch, barefoot, one knee casually drawn up to her chest. Her slender arms wrapped around that bent leg, and her long neck tilted her head toward the snake. She had a broad nose, full lips, high cheekbones and pointed chin—and the luster of her whole presence shimmered quietly in the silence of the wood.

"Yes, you heard me," the woman insisted—almost as a retort—raising her eyebrows. "That's your name, at least for now, so you had better remember it."

Silver—yes *Silver*—sucked in a breath, and sat up even further, so her head was level with the stranger's. The woman lifted her chin.

"Yes, ma'am. There you are. Mhm."

Silver took another breath, parted her lips...

"Who are you?" Her voice felt like water bubbling through a rusted pipe. But the release of the words rushed through her chest, freeing something she hadn't known was lodged there.

The woman's full lips quirked into an almost-smile, and she cocked her head. She ran a critical glance all across Silver's form, then met her eyes again.

"That's a better question for *you,* don't you think?"

Silver's own eyebrows went up.

179

"What do you mean?"

The woman lifted her right hand, and held it out to Silver, palm up.

"I'm Reola Curse-Breaker," she said. "Welcome to the Giant's Shoes."

Silver stared at her hand. It was paler on the underside.

"This is when you take it now, child," Reola reminded her.

Silver hesitated, then unhooked her claws from the bark, reached out, and gently grasped Reola's hand.

And suddenly, she remembered Amber.

She remembered all of it—their castle in the dead forest, the magic dinners, the fireplaces, the talking mirror, the garden, the lute, and the songs.

She gasped, gripping Reola's hand harder.

Blinking, she searched Reola's face in a panic—to see the woman staring intensely at her.

"Mhm," she said again, deeper in her chest. "You need to come with me."

"What?" Silver rasped. "Why?"

"Isn't that the reason you came?" Reola wondered. "To find me? To find out if you're cursed?"

Silver sat up even straighter.

"I—*yes!*"

"Well, I can tell you right now that you are," Reola answered.

Silver put a hand to her heart.

"I am?"

"Course you are," Reola scoffed lightly. "Now we have to decide what to do about that."

And with that, she slipped forward and dropped off the branch.

Silver jerked, grabbed the branch and stared down after her—

To see her standing safely on the ground, looking back up.

"Come on," Reola called. Then, she turned and started walking away.

Clenching her teeth, Silver nervously sank her claws into the tree...

And then she slithered down the trunk of the oak, and followed in Reola's path.

Reola moved casually through the thickets and shrubs, and the birds did not fly away from her passage. Only when Silver slithered by did they screech and dart away. Reola walked barefoot, even through the wild roses, but they didn't seem to prick her, and never tangled around her ankles.

Gradually, the two of them worked their way up a hill, toward a large outcropping of rocks. Silver frowned as she studied their shape, and as they approached, she finally realized what it was.

A cave. A low, wide-mouthed cave, draped in vines, deep and solemn. And it smelled of...

Reeked of...

"A bear!" Silver hissed, immediately grabbing hold of a tree, ready to shoot upward.

Reola turned around.

"Oh, my poor bee-wolf. Yes," she said plainly. "You know, he's a prince! Everywhere he went, people tried to kill him. So, years ago, I told him he could stay here until his lady came to find him, just like she promised." Reola sighed and contemplated the rocky opening. "She must have fallen down a hole somewhere."

Silver didn't move.

"Are you..." she swallowed, shocked. "Are you sure? He was a prince?"

Reola glanced over her shoulder at Silver and winked.

"He *is* a prince."

And Reola turned and went on, treading a path near the cave, and passed between two ancient beeches.

Silver's whole frame shivered. She could smell that bear—taste his scent in her mouth—and could hear his heavy, rough breathing echoing against the hollowed stone. Pain flared across all her old wounds, and she dug
her claws deep into the bark of the tree.

He is *a prince...*

He IS.

Silver let go of the tree.

She darted up the hill, skidded onto the path, giving one fleeting look inside, but unable to glimpse the massive, dark form...

And whisked around the boulders, to find Reola striding up a broad, beaten path toward two towering stone statues.

Silver slowed, and gaped, the bear forgotten.

She had never seen a stone structure this tall that was not a castle. Indeed, these two motionless men stood higher than the towers of her own home.

Vines crept up their robed forms, and bloomed amongst their knees and their ornate belts. The two men seemed as if they had just parted company from each other, for each his own hand against his heart, and bore expressions of sorrow upon his face—and each turned away from his companion so he could no longer see him.

"*Then up to the bee-wolf's stony ledge,*" Silver suddenly whispered. "*Between two men that stand alone...*"

The bee-wolf. Reola's poor, forgotten prince who had been turned into a bear.

And two men who stood together, but alone. For once a goodbye is bid, even if the other man remains nearby forever, each is alone.

Reola passed between these men, still heading steadily uphill, humming as she went. Silver marveled at the sad relics, then hurried her pace, and kept following.

Around two more bends, the forest suddenly opened up, revealing a vast reach of afternoon sky, graced with gold-and-pink clouds that drifted across the bluebell reaches. A sunny, green valley plunged down before them, ringed around by a lush, flowering forest, and then granite peaks beyond the forest, stretching to the heavens—peaks of stones that gleamed with pinks and oranges at the edges of their shadows. Far below, within the embrace of the valley, a village of low, quaint houses nestled together like chicks, curls of smoke streaming up from their chimneys. A river, a glimmering band of alloyed silver and gold, wound its easy way through the center of the dale.

Reola turned to the left, and strolled up a narrow way along the edge of the plunge, Silver behind her—though Silver gazed into the valley below, captivated.

Then, one more curve in the path brought them to another sight that made Silver stop and marvel.

A two-story, crooked house of stone and wood clung to the side of a massive heap of ancient rock, as if it had grown from it. The lower story was walled with trellises, upon which grew brilliant yellow morning glories. The wood frames had been painted to match, and the sun shone straight through the house's many open windows. Two chimneys stood upon the roof, and one of them puffed serenely—and its smoke smelled of cedar, and baking bread. A rose bush crawled up one side of the stone house, covered with white blossoms.

All manner and colors of flowers, vegetables and herbs grew round the base of the house, and in the garden beside it, and the sunlight glowed through the leaves and petals. Reola climbed five uneven stone steps, reached out and grasped the brass handle of the front door—decorated with battered green paint—and tugged it open.

"Here she is!" she called inside.

The next instant, Amber came rushing out.

Silver's mouth opened—Amber's eyes went wide as he stumbled past Reola, down the first step—

Then he hurried down the rest of the stairs, lunged for Silver and grabbed her arms, then took her head in both his hands.

"Are you all right?" he wanted to know, his gaze racing over her face, and then the rest of her. Silver gripped his wrists, and nodded.

"Yes, yes, I'm fine," she assured him, her heart staggered at the alarm in his voice and the heat from his hands.

"I was sure Cedric had hit you," Amber panted, painful relief crossing his face.

"Cedric?" she asked.

"That ranger who shot at you," Reola chimed in. "He's my huntsman, and he thought your friend was in danger from you."

"In danger from me?" Silver cried, tightening her grip on Amber's wrists. "I would *never* hurt—"

"He was too quick, I will say that," Reola muttered, propping the door open. "But once Amber told him who you were looking for, he brought Amber right to me, and I came to look for you."

Amber settled his hands on Silver's shoulders, still watching her earnestly.

"You're sure you're all right?"

"She's fine," Reola said briskly. "Come inside."

Amber hesitated, but Silver smiled at him, and nodded firmly. So he slipped one hand down and took hers, and together they climbed the stairs and ventured into Reola's house.

Wooden floors, with afternoon sunlight filtering in from everywhere. Dried herbs and flowers hung in bunches from the low rafters, as did little jars full of living succulent plants. Straight before them stood a broad, rough-hewn table of blond wood, surrounded by cushioned benches and chairs. Carved faces peered out from between the vines on the walls, smiling secretively. To the immediate left, a staircase so narrow it was almost a ladder, stretched up through a square hole in the ceiling to the second story. Beyond that staircase, Reola's kitchen—counters and cupboards and a broad stove with a fireplace decorated with detailed white stone, and more mysterious faces. The scent of baking bread dominated the air, and Silver could hear a fire crackling behind the iron door of the stove.

Silver worked to get her awkward tail inside the door and curled up behind her, out of everyone's way. Reola moved straight to one of the counters, picked up a wood spoon and began vigorously stirring chopped vegetables and sauce together in a metal pan, then set it with a clack down on the top of the stove. Then, she titled her head back and shouted at the ceiling.

"Molly!" she called. "Poddle, come down those stairs!"

Silver jumped, and squeezed Amber's hand—but he smiled at her.

"Yes, ma'am!" came a bright cry from overhead, and the next moment, two little children came noisily dashing down the staircase. They wore homespun white clothes—one in a dress, the other in a shirt and trousers. Both had gleaming black skin like Reola, bare feet, large black eyes, and short, curly hair. The girl had short pig-tails that stuck straight up. They both looked perhaps seven years old. They hit the bottom of the stairs and skidded to a stop, staring up at Silver.

Silver wanted to shrink back, but Amber kept hold of her hand.

"Babies, this is Silver," Reola said, gesturing to her with her spoon, then stirring again. "Silver, these are my age grandbabies, Margaret and Peter. Around here, though, they're called Molly and Poddle, since everything at Age-Grandmum's house is more fun."

Poddle, the little boy, giggled and gave Reola a look—and Reola winked back at him. Molly gazed up thoughtfully at Silver.

"Ma'am?" she asked, her voice high as she tilted her head sideways.

"Yes, baby?" Reola said.

"Has she got a curse on her?"

"Yes, she *does*," Reola answered, stirring busily.

"Are you going to fix it?" Molly wondered.

"I'll do my best," Reola said.

"Can we watch?" Poddle asked, hopping up and down, then spinning to face her.

"First, us old ones are going to set for bit, and talk," Reola told him. "You and Molly want to go outside and play?"

"Nope," Poddle shook his head, once, then ran over and hopped on one of the giant chairs, then gave Silver a broad, toothy grin. Molly, frowning, wandered over to stand by her brother, then clambered up onto one of the benches across from him, watching Silver and Amber warily.

"Sit down," Reola invited, nodding to the table. "Silver, you can stretch out on one of the benches. Babies, watch out for that tail."

Together, Silver and Amber obeyed, and Silver tried to make herself comfortable on one of the far benches, leaning up against the corner of the room. Amber sat in the chair next to her. The children twisted to face them, as if afraid their visitors might suddenly disappear.

"So, where have you two come from?" Reola asked, reaching up and pulling a large piece of cheese wrapped in cloth out of one of the cabinets. She took up her spoon again and stirred.

"A castle in the middle of Thornbind," Amber explained. "No one was living in it, except Silver. The whole castle was empty at first, but when I went in I eventually found a tower room that had a bed, and a fire, and a pot that always had soup in it, and tea on the table."

Reola turned and frowned at him.

"How did you find that castle?" she demanded.

"I'm not sure," he admitted. "I was running away from highwaymen, and lost my way, and I found a creek to drink from—"

Reola set her spoon down with a *clack* and faced him completely, putting a hand on her hip.

"You *drank* from that stream?"

Amber's mouth fell open—he glanced uncertainly over at Silver. "I...Yes?"

The children's mouths got small and their eyes big as they stared at Amber.

Reola studied Amber with narrow eyes, then folded her arms.

"Then what?" she asked, jerking her chin.

"I...Well, as I said, I went inside, and ate the food and slept in the bed, and then I found Silver. She almost killed me."

Silver ducked her head—but then Poddle giggled again.

"Hush, you," Reola admonished him. "Then what?"

"Then she got hurt by a bear, and I found this bottle of stuff called Snakesalve on my mantel, and so I put it on her cuts," Amber went on. "And after I got her out of the cellar, we were friends." He gave Silver a warm look, which she tried to return.

"What else?" Reola pressed.

"Well," Amber said, thinking. "I started working the garden, and watering it with the water from the well, and it started to bloom—and I played the instrument in the great hall, and then..." He looked over at Silver again.

"The castle filled up with furniture," Silver said quietly. "And paintings. And food."

Reola's brilliant gaze pierced through Amber, then moved to Silver, then back to Amber.

"And how did you find me?"

"The statue in the garden," Amber told her. "When I watered the plants around it, it...well, it talked."

"And it told you where to go," Reola finished. Both Silver and Amber nodded. Reola watched them for another long moment. Then, she turned and stirred her concoction on the stove again.

"Well, let me tell you, Amber sweetie," she muttered. "You're lucky you're not dead."

"What?" He sat up. "Why?"

"Because the river in that part of the wood is under a spell," Reola told him. "Anyone who even touches it falls sleep like *that*," she snapped her fingers. "And goes headfirst into the water."

Amber went pale. Reola looked at him and raised her eyebrow.

"You didn't even think of that, did you?"

"No," Amber swallowed.

"Same with that well," Reola told him. "It's been cursed for half a century."

Silver's brow furrowed.

"It isn't anymore?"

Reola didn't answer—just bent and opened her stove, peering at her bread.

187

"I want butter with mine!" Poddle yelped, jumping up to stand on his chair.

"You sit down," Reola barked, pointing at him. "I don't want you tipping forward and smacking your head."

Poddle grinned again, looked over at Silver as if he knew he was being cute, and squatted and fiddled with his toes.

"So you didn't think about drinking from the river," Reola went on, putting on oven mitts to pull out the bread. "You didn't think about going into the castle, or eating the food or sleeping in the bed." She set the bread down on the counter, and gave Amber another look. "What is it you do to put food on your table?"

"I'm a minstrel," Amber told her, pointing to his lute that stood in the corner. Reola's eyebrows went up as she pulled off her mitts.

"So you go around collecting stories about all the awful things that happen to people when they fiddle with magic," she waved her fingers through the air. "But you're not afraid of any of that happening to you? You could have been poisoned, knocked asleep, trapped, or turned into a toad."

Amber blushed. Reola clicked her tongue and shook her head.

"Babies," she said as she picked up a knife to cut the bread. "Tell Silver and Amber what I told you about that castle."

"Me, me, me!" Poddle raised his hand. "I want to!"

"I want to, too!" Molly cried, giving her brother a fierce look and sitting up on her knees.

"You both can," Reola said, slicing the bread.

"Age Grandmum used to live there," Poddle said, leaning his elbows on the table. "A really long time ago. But then—"

"All the weeds started growing," Molly interrupted. "And the magic started breaking."

Silver and Amber exchanged a glance, but Poddle cut in.

"The doors wouldn't open one hall," he said. "They'd slam your fingers if you tried!"

"And the lady in the mirror shut her eyes and wouldn't talk," Molly added. "The spoons and bowls in the kitchen wouldn't move, the fires wouldn't light, and—"

"The wine all rotted," Poddle made a face. "And the basement stank."

"And it was because of a witch!" Molly cried. "A bad witch, and the

Breakers were trying to kill her—" she swung her arm through the air. "But they turned the wrong way and so she *escaped!*"

"And she put a spell on the river, so all the trees went to sleep," Poddle finished. "And the magic water is how the castle worked. Only a part of it that wasn't by the water still had magic."

"The tower—that was Grandmum's room," Molly added.

Just then, Reola came to the table bearing a wide board covered with slices of bread that had been covered with melted white cheese and lightly cooked, chopped tomatoes and sweet onions. She set it down in the middle of the table, then fetched a pitcher of milk and five glasses, and poured each of them a portion.

"Go on and eat," she told them, waving to it, and sat herself down beside Amber. The children quickly grabbed a piece each and took big bites.

"You be careful and chew that," Reola warned them. "Don't choke on the cheese."

"What is a Breaker?" Silver asked, carefully taking a piece for herself.

"Mhmfmhmf," Poddle tried around a mouthful.

"Shush, you," Reola waved him off, and Poddle snorted and smiled through his cheese. Reola set her elbows on the table, and looked at Silver.

"It's a Curse-Breaker. And that's what I am." She motioned to Amber. "Your friend makes his living by singing songs. I make mine by snapping evil spells. Getting to the root of them, and untying them, or knocking them loose." She shifted in her chair. "It's the oldest profession on earth, and it takes a long time to master. There used to

189

be a school in the Emerald Hills called Wyverncwellan, taught by a wizard with three names. I learned there, and so did the man I married."

"Age Grandpapa Aleric," Molly piped up. Reola smiled—with beautiful warmth that startled Silver—and nodded at Molly.

"Yes, baby. Grandpapa Aleric. We were called the Caldic Curse-Breakers. Me, Aleric, Anthon, Reyella, and Gwiddon Baba Yaga."

A strange, quiet chill traveled down through Silver's whole spine.

"Curse Breaking is its own kind of good," Reola went on, addressing Amber and Silver. "Because when you break a curse, it gives you life, and health, and youth. Even if you only break one solid curse a year, you can stay looking and feeling exactly as you are forever. And everything you touch will be blessed, and nothing that grows upon this earth can ever hurt you."

Amber began to eat, but Silver's stomach had tightened, and she watched Reola carefully.

"Is that why you're so *old?*" Molly asked—overtly teasing.

"Oldest lady in the *world,* right here," Reola said grandly, holding up
a hand.

"Yeah," Poddle laughed. "You're really our great-great-great-great-great-great—"

"All right, little man—!" Reola tickled his neck and he shrieked and ducked away.

"Honestly, I can't remember," Reola confessed, sighing. "My family and their children and their children have lived in this valley for hundreds of years."

"What about the witch?" Amber asked. "The one who put a spell on the water?"

"Well, there's always the other side of the coin," Reola sighed. "Folks who enjoy *making* curses instead. Now, *making* curses will give you a long life just the same—but your face and skin will rot, and so will your brain. You'll be ugly, and crooked, and even if you cast a spell that was designed to be good—a spell to make someone beautiful, or

190

loveable, or a good dancer—it will poison the person you gave it to, until that person becomes just as wicked and vile as you are." She stopped, and pointed to the food Silver held. "You had better eat that before it gets cold."

As the afternoon sun bloomed through the valley and stood on the peaks like jewels at the points of a crown, the family, Silver and Amber left the house to meander through the paths of the garden.

The garden didn't have a wall, and as it stood on a height, the hill swooped down and away beyond the border, and a spectacular, craggy mountain dominated the view. A large, low, old tree stood to the right hand as the group faced the garden, and another tree mirrored it across the way, hunching in the corner beside the house and sheltering dozens of stone planters filled to overflowing with shamrocks. From its strongest bough hung a wide, wooden swing.

Amber fell back, admiring the low blooming shrubs that made a short
little winding maze in the middle, and the beds that bordered it, brilliant with all kinds of mountain flowers.

Reola, a cup of tea in her hands, headed straight for the swing and sat down. Silver meandered out beside the hip-high maze, running her keen glance all across the flowers. The children left Amber's side and traipsed curiously up next to Silver. Amber suppressed a smile and drifted to the opposite end, toward the cliffside tree.

Finally, Molly took a deep breath and trotted around in front of Silver. Silver stopped.

"Do you want to play?"

Silver stood up straight. Poddle raced around and stood beside his sister, so that both of them waited with big eyes.

"Play?" Silver repeated. "I'm not sure I know any games."

"What about stories?" Poddle asked. "Do you know any stories?"

Amber suddenly filled with sadness, and his smile disappeared. Silver lifted her chin.

"Yes. Yes, I do."

Amber blinked.

"Tell us, tell us!" Molly jumped up and down. "We haven't heard any new stories for a really long time."

"All right," Silver mused, then slid forward on the path, thinking. The children fell in on either side of her—

And reflexively reached up and grabbed her hands.

Amber saw her startlement—his own heart jumped—but Silver didn't let go. The children waited, walking beside her.

"All right," Silver nodded. "Once upon a time, there were a brother and sister who looked just like you. One was named Mary, and the other's name was Patrick. They lived far in the north, where all of the magical creatures fill the forests. One day, their very wise grandmother told them about a treasure cave filled with the most delicious sweets anyone had ever tasted."

"Oooh!" Poddle cried, wriggling with excitement.

"Oohoohoo!" Molly tugged on Silver's arm. "Where was it?"

"Well, their grandmother told them that it was deep in the woods, by
a waterfall," Silver answered. "But she told them, 'You must not go into the forest to find this treasure, because it is guarded by a terrible fairy beast with a thousand teeth and one eye, and if you don't answer its questions three, it will eat you up for supper!"

"Ack!" Poddle cried. "That isn't good!"

"No, it isn't," Silver said seriously.

Amber, utterly fascinated, folded his arms and leaned against the tree, watching her every move. Silver and the children had reached one corner of the garden now, and paused by a flower bed.

"So what do you suppose Mary and Patrick did?" Silver asked them.

"They stayed home and didn't go," Molly concluded.

"What? What kind of story would that be?" Silver huffed.

"They went into the forest *anyway?*" Poddle cried. "They're going to be in trouble!"

"*My* babies know what's right!" Reola piped up, lifting her teacup. "Amber, you should pay attention."

Silver laughed. Amber chuckled to himself.

"Yes, maybe they will be in trouble," Silver acknowledged. "But they went anyway. And after searching all day long, they found the cave..." Silver bent down to the children, lowering her voice ominously. "And there it was: the big, hairy, terrible fairy beast with a thousand teeth and one eye!"

Both of them gasped and covered their mouths.

"What happened?" Molly wondered through her fingers.

"Well, the beast came out of the cave, licked its sharp teeth, and said..." Silver took a deep breath, and her eyes flashed. "*What do you want, you delicious-looking little children?*" Her voice suddenly became savage, rumbling and deep, both children squealed. They bounced up and down, and swung Silver's hands back and forth.

"Don't *do* that!" Poddle squeaked.

"*Hahaha, why not? Are you scared?*" Silver asked in that same horrible tenor, showing all her razor-sharp teeth.

"Yeeeeep!" Molly screeched, then broke out into wild giggles.

Amber grinned stupidly, his whole frame filling with warmth.

"I'd run away!" Poddle decided, putting a hand over his eyes and peering between the gaps in his fingers.

"Yes, but if you did," Silver said, her tone instantly normal. "You would never find the treasure!"

"So what happened?" Molly demanded.

"Mary spoke up," Silver said. "And said to the fairy beast, 'We want the treasure in your cave.' And the beast said, '*If you want it, you will have to answer my questions three, or I will eat you up for supper!*'" Her dragon voice rang out again, sending both children into fits of laughter. Silver let go of them, slid back a little, and raised her arms like crooked branches, curling her claws menacingly.

She cocked her head, and talked again through her teeth.

193

"'Tell me, little children: what is something that is gold—but more valuable than gold?'"

Out of the corner of his eye, Amber saw Reola's expression change to one of interest. But Amber could do no more than notice her peripherally, for his attention remained totally enchanted by his friend.

"It *is* gold but it's more valuable than gold?" Molly said. "There's no such thing!"

"Of *course* there is," Silver dropped her arms and rolled her eyes. "You think I'd start this story just to end it with, 'and it didn't exist, so it ate them?'"

Poddle snorted and poked his sister's ribs.

"Yeah, dummy."

"Peter," Reola warned loudly. Molly folded her arms.

"What is it, then?"

"Well, Mary was a great gardener," Silver went on. "The best in all the kingdom. And so she said to the fairy beast, 'A daffodil. It is the loveliest gold color in the world, but it's more valuable than gold because it doesn't last. Even if you cut it and bring it inside, it's only there for a few days before it withers and it's gone. And no matter how much money you have, you can't get it back.'"

"Was she right?" Poddle demanded.

"She was!" Silver pointed at him.

"What was the next question?" Molly asked, plopping down cross-legged on the grassy path. Poddle did the same. Probably without thinking about it, Silver settled in front of them, curling her tail around behind her, assuming the dreadful persona of that fairy beast again.

"'Tell me, little children: what is something giant, that is also small?'"

"Oh, no," Poddle said, and he and Molly exchanged a frightened look.

"That doesn't make sense, either!" Molly said. "What would that be?"

194

They both turned back to Silver.

"No guesses?" she asked, narrowing her eyes.

"Nope," Poddle shook his head.

"Well, luckily you were not there, or you would have been eaten!" Silver wriggled her fingers at him, and he leaned back.

"But Patrick was very good at climbing trees," Silver went on. "It was his favorite thing to do. And so he answered the fairy beast: 'An acorn. It is very small, but a giant oak lives inside!'"

"Aha!" the children said, nodding.

"He's smart," Poddle decided.

"He was," Silver agreed. "But there was one more question."

"What?" Molly asked. Silver bared her teeth again—and when she spoke, the low growl thudded in her chest and snapped through her throat.

"'Tell me, little children: what is something that is so strong that no matter how many times it is crushed, it can never die?'"

"What, what, what?" Molly bounced.

"Don't you even want to guess?" Silver cried.

"No, no, no!" Poddle answered. "I want to know what it is!"

"Well, the two children were always outside, playing and building houses for their dolls," Silver said. "And so they told the fairy beast: 'Stone! It can be hit with a hammer, or split by an earthquake, but its pieces cannot be killed!'"

"And what happened then?" Poddle asked. "Did the fairy beast die?"

"Of course not!" Silver shot back.

Amber smiled to himself.

"No? Why not?" Molly wanted to know.

"Because it said to them, *'I have taught you well, little children. For you have learned that the most valuable things can fade and so must be cherished, that greatness can be disguised as littleness, and true strength can never be destroyed.'* And then the fairy beast transformed into their very wise grandmother."

"Ah!" the children shouted.

"And so," Silver concluded. "Their grandmother took them home, and set out a table for them full of sweeties and pies. And they ate them all, and fell asleep by the fire, and had lovely dreams all the night through. The end."

Reola laughed out loud and applauded. At that cue, the children did the same thing.

Silver grinned, and glanced up at Amber.

He beamed at her, and clapped too, lingering on the sight of her.

After this, Molly and Poddle got to their feet, and insisted upon showing Silver every corner of the garden, and all the spots that belonged to them, and all the flowers they each had planted. As midafternoon reached the sky, Reola called them inside, and headed that way herself. The children scurried after her, Silver in tow. As she passed, Amber ducked close and caught her attention.

"Did you...*remember* that story?" he asked. "From before?"

"Oh!" Silver stopped, then frowned. "I...no. I read it in the library." She smiled crookedly, some of the light fading.

"It's a very good one," he told her quickly. "I really enjoyed the way you told it."

"You did?" Silver perked up. He nodded.

"I've always liked riddles."

"Did you guess the right answers?" she asked slyly.

"No," he confessed. "But I knew the fairy beast was their grandmother."

Silver's mouth fell open. He winked at her, then ducked into Reola's house, treasuring the look of astonishment on her face.

CHAPTER NINETEEN

"THE CURSE WAS REVEALED"

"Stay on the path, and bring him back before dark!" Reola called out the door as Poddle and Molly grabbed Amber's hands and tugged on him. Amber twisted and looked over his shoulder at Silver, but again she smiled for him, so he answered it, waved and tried to keep up with the two little ones as they pulled him along.

"Ballyboon looks far away, but it won't take them long," Reola said as she waved too, then turned to Silver. "I hope they can find the right kind of flour—I'm clean out."

Silver backed up into the house to make room, and Reola stepped in, and shut the door. Then, her vivid gaze met Silver's, and she took a deep breath.

"Now," she said quietly. "Let's see about you."

She moved past her, through the kitchen, and down a short hallway. Silver waited, squeezing her fingers together as her heartbeat picked up. She heard the creak of hinges, and the slam of a trunk lid. Then, Reola came back, carrying a folded garment. She shook it out— it was a long tunic-dress the color of ivory, with simple red embroidery around the neck, and it hung down to Reola's knees as she held it up.

"Here, child," she said, gathering it up and pushing the opening of the garment toward Silver's head. Startled, Silver leaned toward it, and Reola put it over her head, then helped her put her arms through the loose sleeves. The fabric tumbled down over Silver's torso. Then, Reola moved around behind her and tied the sash around her waist. Finally, as Silver tried to absorb the strange sensation of being wrapped in cloth, Reola came around and faced her, solemn as a grave. It chilled Silver's blood.

197

"What is this?" Silver whispered, pressing her hands to her chest, the soft fabric wrinkling beneath her fingers.

"You're a young woman," Reola replied. "And a lady, I think. You shouldn't be naked."

"Naked!" Shame filled Silver's face, but Reola smiled quietly at her.

"It's all right. You didn't know." She nodded to the door. "And neither did he."

Silver's heart bashed against her ribs, and she closed her fingers. Reola's smile faded, and she reached out and touched Silver's face.

Silver froze.

Reola gently tipped Silver's head one way, then the other, piercing her with a look as intent as lightning. She ran her thumb along the edges of her scales, and pressed her fingertips against the deep scar on her cheek. And as the minutes passed, her frown deepened.

At last, she took a low breath, and let it out slowly.

"Gwiddon."

The sound of that name again sent a quiver all through Silver's body.

"Who?" she asked.

"Gwiddon Curse-Maker," Reola answered. "In another part of this world, she's called the Baba Yaga. I told you a little about her. I knew her when we were young. She could break curses better than any of us—but we found out it was because she understood them better. Then she started building them, gathering them, and selling them. She's the one who poisoned the water in Everhart Wood—and *she* called it Thornbind."

"And...why did you say her name?" Silver asked, clenching her hands together again.

"Because your curse passed through her," Reola said, moving over and

sinking down into a chair at the table. "But she didn't make it. It's old. Maybe something she found digging up a druid's bones in the north.

She also didn't cast it." Reola pointed down at the tabletop. "This is a very deep, very exact curse." She gazed up at Silver. "If I had to make a guess, it was cast either by your mother or your sister."

"What?" Silver cried. Reola nodded.

"Your curse was sent out with jealousy and hate," she said. "And the person had to know you *very* well, so that you'd lose all your memories."

"My memories..." Silver choked.

"They're all gone," Reola said. "All of who you were before the curse was cast is gone. Unless you can break it."

Silver stared at her.

"You mean... *You* can't?"

Reola watched her for a long moment, then finally shook her head.

"I can't."

Silver's heart stopped, and she squeezed her dress so hard she might rip it. Reola raised her eyebrows.

"But I know how it *could* be broken."

Silver gulped, and started toward her.

"How?"

Reola paused, as if weighing the effect of the words she was about to speak.

"Someone who loves you has to recognize you. And that person has to tell you your name."

Silver stopped.

"My name?" she breathed. "My *real* name?"

"Mhm," Reola said. "The name your parents gave you when you were born—the one they used at your christening. The one you had before this made you forget."

"So...someone who knew me *before* would have to recognize me *now*," Silver realized. "And not just *recognize* me, but..." She halted, her throat closing. Reola kept silent.

"Love me," Silver mouthed, a stinging sensation dancing through her chest. She suddenly shook her head. "I...I can't remember any of my family. I don't know where they are, or how to find them! How could I ever find someone who loves me enough to know me *now?*"

"What about Amber?" Reola asked.

Silver twitched, heat flashing through her body.

"Amber?"

"Mhm," Reola nodded again. "You love him?"

Silence fell, and the whole world ceased turning. Silver's pulse slowed to nothing, and her breath suspended.

The meaning of Reola's words turned over and over, rising and falling through the room, penetrating Silver to the bone. And then—

"Yes," she said—before she could think, before she calculated at all. Her face twisted, and she nodded hard. "Yes. Yes, *yes.* More than...more than anything in my whole life."

"Does he love *you?*"Reola wondered. "Would he stay with you, even if you never changed?"

Ice cold gall slid down Silver's throat, then radiated out through her entire frame like liquid fire. She held her hands out to Reola, flooded with indignant pain.

"Why would you ask me something like that?" she cried brokenly. "*Look at me!*"

Reola said nothing.

And Silver covered her face with her hands.

"I see the house!" Poddle cried, dashing ahead. Amber adjusted the bag of flour on his shoulder, and waggled Molly's hand, which he'd been holding for a while.

"See? Almost there!" he said brightly.

"Ugghh, my feet hurt!" Molly groaned, sagging and stomping along beside. "Can you carry me?"

"Sure," Amber laughed. "If Poddle wants to carry the flour."

"Noooo," Poddle said, still running.

"Ugh!" Molly protested, and Amber just chuckled. Soon, though, they had attained the path in front of Reola's house, and Molly let go of his hand. The day had faded from the sky, leaving behind a rich violet in the west, and the light from within the house glowed warmly.

The children bashed through the front door, shouting for their grandmother. Amber smiled to himself, climbed the steps, opened the door and stepped inside.

The corners of the house now hid in shadow, and Reola had lit candles on the table, and opened the door of the stove so that the firelight spilled out over the wooden floor and into the dining room. Silver sat in front of it, curled tightly, her upper body low, her head bowed, and her good eye distant and listless. Amber slowed, his smile fading.

"Thank you so much, Amber," Reola said, striding out of the kitchen and holding out her arms.

"Oh—you're welcome," he said, pulling the flour off his back and handing it to her. She easily took it and carried it back to the bin.

"Do the three of you want some water?"

"Me, me, me!" Molly insisted. "I almost died three times coming back!"

"Oh, you did, hm?" Reola said, grabbing a pitcher and pouring water into a few glasses. She handed them to the children and they drank greedily.

"Hello, Silver," Amber said carefully. Finally, she lifted her head and looked at him.

And gave him the most forced smile he'd ever seen.

"Hello."

Amber took a step toward her.

"Everything all right?"

"We had a talk," Reola told him, handing him a glass of water of his own. "She'll tell you when she has a moment to herself."

Silver's glance flickered, and she turned back to the fire. Amber's fingers closed around his glass.

"Amber said he'd sing us a song," Poddle bubbled, water dribbling down his chin.

"Wipe your mouth," Reola ordered. "Sakes alive, child."

Poddle hurriedly swiped his mouth with his sleeve, then told Reola again.

"He said he'd sing for us. Can he sing for us now?"

"Why don't you ask him?" Reola nodded to Amber.

"Sing for us!" Molly cried. "I'll get your guitar!"

"It's a *lute*," Poddle corrected, rolling his eyes. "He told you that *five times.*"

"It looks like a *guitar*," Molly retorted, picking it up and carrying it over to Amber. Amber took a sip of water, set the glass down on the table, and took his instrument from the little girl.

"Thank you, my lady," he said quietly, patting her head.

"I want to sit by you," she said, pressing her forehead against his side, then wrapping her arms around his leg.

"I'd love that," Amber laughed—and he could feel Silver watching him again. He stepped over to one of the benches that leaned against the wall but faced the fire, and settled down onto it. Molly climbed up on his right, and Poddle scrambled up to sit by his left. Instantly, the little girl cuddled snugly up to his side, and the boy scrunched down so he could lay his head on Amber's left leg.

And Silver looked at him.

Looked at him in a way she never had.

Gently, with a soft furrow to her brow, her eye alight. As if she had never seen him before—and yet could see all the way through him, to his inmost heart. And that same gaze drifted across the children, his lute, and then back up to his face—and deepened with something that looked like sorrow.

Amber swallowed, a strange, quiet pain pressing against his breastbone. Molly wiggled, and lifted her head.

"Sing!" she commanded. Amber dipped his head, trying to gather his thoughts, then shifted his lute on his lap and tuned it. After a moment, words wandered into his head—words to a song he had learned a very long time ago, but now felt more right than anything. And so he took a breath, and sang them.

> *"Deep in a forbidden depth of wood*
> *There stands a single tower*
> *It has no door, but one window, and a vine-draped, hidden bower.*
> *The peak of this high, lonely room*
> *Can be seen above the trees.*
> *And sometimes, a long and golden plait from the window is released."*

Amber's fingers moved easily across the strings, and his voice filled the little house. The wooden beams, like the chest of a violin, took up his tones and resonated with him. He lifted his head, and gazed at Silver—and couldn't
look away.

> *If you sit and watch, mayhaps a witch*
> *Will trail on through the wood*
> *And she will climb the hair of gold.*
> *For a maid does live within those heights, and does what she is told."*

Silver's attention slowly distanced as he played—and she turned away, toward the fire.

When she did that, Amber took a deeper breath, purifying his tone, and sang with everything in him. He had never sung so well—not ever, in his whole life.

> *"True, the old woman is a witch*
> *As payment for a theft*
> *This girl was taken, then, and named for that bereft*

But who shall steal her from the witch
And what price will he pay to have her?"

Amber finished out the tune, embellishing the melody as he played. Briefly, he glanced past Silver to see Reola watching him, her arms folded. Finally, he lifted his fingers, and the echo died away.

"You, child," Reola smiled, her expression alight. "Have a gift."

The corner of Amber's mouth twitched. Usually, such words sent a warm glow blooming in his heart...

But now, right this moment, he felt nothing. Because Silver wasn't looking at him. It was like he wasn't even there.

Poddle rolled onto his back, and looked up at Amber between the lute neck and Amber's arm.

"What happens?" he asked.

"When?" Amber wondered absently, making himself glance down.

"To the lady in the tower?" Molly mumbled into Amber's sleeve. "Does she stay there forever?"

Amber lifted his head, and again looked at Silver.

"I don't know," Amber confessed faintly, unable to pull away. "I've never heard the end of the song."

Silver said nothing. Amber's hands felt weak.

"Sing another one," Poddle urged.

"It's time for baths and beds," Reola countered, stepping around Silver's curled tail. "Come on."

"Awww," they complained, but both of them got up, slipped off the bench and followed their grandmother to the back of the house.

Amber lay his lute across his lap, his brow knitting as he studied his companion. But she just stared into the flames, motionless as a statue, as if she were completely alone.

Amber lay on his back, staring at the ceiling. Reola had brought him blankets and pillows, and he now stretched out on the bench. But he couldn't sleep.

All the candles had been extinguished, and now only the light in the stove remained—and it was dying. Silver lay before it, curled and wrapped, her arms folded as she rested on her belly, her chin propped on her layered hands. Amber turned his head and studied her profile, his chest tightening. At last, he screwed up his courage, and took a breath.

"What did she say?"

Silver blinked slowly, and did not answer for a long time.

Finally, her lips parted.

"She cannot break the curse."

Amber's head came up.

"What?" he wondered sharply. "Why not?"

"Because," Silver breathed. "Only someone who loves me can do that."

Amber's heart skipped a beat.

"What—" he choked, then swallowed, and tried again. "What does that person have to do?"

"Recognize who I truly am," Silver said, the firelight dancing across her scales. "And tell me my name."

Amber fell silent.

Silver smiled crookedly at the flames.

"Remember what you said about the prince of Dallydanehall?" she murmured. "'He isn't really a bear. He's a man. But being a bear makes it hard for him to get someone to break the spell. *Most* people aren't fond of bears. Which was probably the dwarf's idea all along.'"

Amber's fingers clenched around his blanket. But he couldn't think of a single thing to say.

He wanted to get up. He wanted to get off the bench, and go sit beside her, and...

She turned her head away, and lay the side of it down on the floor. Amber gulped, heat filling his face. And he stayed where he was.

The night deepened. The embers faded to nothing, and the darkness overtook them. Amber lay back and stared at the ceiling, seeing nothing, as something broke deep inside him.

From his perch high in a sleeping oak, Sir Roderick watched the brilliant moon sail across the sky. The striking white light split by the naked branches gave the whole earth below a deathly aspect—the fallen sticks were bones, the leaves withered snakeskin.

Sir Dane, Sir Ethen, Sir Cam and Sir George sat below in a tiny clearing, eating their supper by moonlight, since Roderick had forbidden a fire.

Soft footsteps.

Roderick glanced down, and peered through the dark along the path. He recognized the tread.

Nearly silent, he slipped down out of the tree and landed. The other knights got to their feet, and faced the newcomer.

As soon as the moonlight struck his familiar black-bearded face, all of the knights' hands relaxed on their weapons.

"Good evening, Shal," Roderick greeted the seventh member of their company. "What did you find?"

"I followed the two of them at a great distance, up the river," he answered. "I didn't want her to catch my scent."

"Very good," Roderick commended him. "And what did you discover?"

"I stopped following them when their path on the other side of the river became very jagged and steep," Shal went on. "And it pulled away, into the woods and up the foothills. I also began to see signs of a bear thereabouts, and I wasn't inclined to make his acquaintance."

Roderick folded his arms.

"Have they started back this way?"

"Not yet," Shal replied. "But I came across a huntsman and his boy wandering the forest roads, and made inquiries. The huntsman said that the minstrel and the dragon were headed up the mountain to see a woman—one of the old ones, he said. A woman who knows all about curses."

Roderick stared at him, his words sinking in. Then he turned...

And gazed through the woods at the empty castle on the hill.

"They've gone to retrieve a curse," he murmured.

"So what do we do?" Dane asked. "Hunt them down on the road?"

"No," Roderick answered quietly. "They will come back here. They will come back here to rest and eat, before they strike the heart of Tirin."

"You do think they're after the princess after all?" Cam said. Roderick faced him.

"It's clear they are trying to wipe out the royal line," he said. "I will not let that happen. Shal, go relay my orders to the four on the other side of the castle. We will all stay here, and keep watch. And when the minstrel and the dragon return, we will draw them out or go in after them—but either way, we will capture the minstrel and kill that monster."

CHAPTER TWENTY

"AND THEY RETURNED FROM WHENCE THEY CAME"

They stayed with Reola one more day. She employed Amber in entertaining the twins while she baked and cooked and made preserves. Poddle and Molly were hilarious and energetic, and under any other circumstances Amber would have been delighted to spend all of his time with them.

But Silver simply lay by the stove, saying nothing, as absent as if no one else was in the house. She did not eat when Reola asked her, and Reola did not press—and she gave Amber a stern look if he opened his mouth to do it himself.

Another night passed, and silence weighed heavy between them. And in the morning, Silver simply rose up when the others were eating breakfast, and addressed Reola.

"I thank you for your hospitality, Curse-Breaker," she said evenly. "But it is time for me to go."

Reola offered no protest, though the children wailed. Reola packed food and drink neatly into Amber's bag and handed it to him, and amidst the tears of the two little ones, Silver and Amber passed through the door. As they left, though, Reola caught Silver's hand.

"Don't give up yet," she whispered earnestly to her. "What you seek might still be found."

Amber watched Silver's reaction keenly—but her expression stayed blank. She didn't even nod. She waited for Reola to release her, then faced the path and started down it.

Amber bent and placed quick kisses on the weeping children's foreheads, and then turned to Reola—

Who gathered him into a tight hug, wrapping her arms around his neck.

"Open your heart, child," she murmured, squeezing him. "Open your eyes and your heart."

Mystified, his throat thick, Amber backed away, tried to return her brilliant, fiery gaze, and then turned to follow Silver's swishing tail.

Silver did not speak to him all journey back. She seemed faraway—realms apart from him. They passed between the vast, mourning statues, moved by the gaping bear cave where an old, snoring beast slept; and trailed down the path beneath the dappled leaves and broad arms of the ancient beeches. But this time, the birds hushed their songs, and the squirrels did not scold, but watched them from high branches. Amber tried to make casual remarks at first, about how pretty the sky looked, or how old the trees might be, or what the name of this river was. But as each sentence was met with silence, his heartiness failed, and he went quiet. He even paced slightly behind her, and she led the way down the mountain, down the foothills, and back into the graying wood where nothing moved and nothing grew.

At night they slept beside the black waters of the river as it murmured lost nonsense to the stars. Amber rested fitfully, all the ground feeling hard and uneven and cold. Silver did not move—she gazed up at the heavens, fractured
by the bare branches, absently curling her fingers around the fabric of her white dress.

At last, evening the next day, a light met them through the barrenness, and Amber recognized the angles of their castle atop the hill.

They swept through the trees and out onto the front lawn as the clouds gathered low, and the wind hissed through the grass. Silver pulled out ahead of him, and rounded the corner of the tower, leaving him behind. Amber's steps faltered, and he stopped. He looked up.

That light glowed from the window of his tower. And the smoke rose from its chimney, just as it had the first day he saw it. His legs felt weak, and he closed his eyes.

Finally, he rounded the tower himself, and entered the back door of the kitchen. All the utensils sat still and silent, though he could smell that a meal had been cooked. It probably waited for them in the feasting hall. Amber ignored it, and walked through into the entryway. He traipsed up the spiral staircase, his pack and lute a burden on his back. He shuffled down the hallway, up more stairs, and attained his tower at last.

He pushed inside, to find everything neat and tidy, as always. The bed was made, the fire burned, and tea waited for him on the table. He pulled off his pack, tossed it wearily down on the bed...

A flash of color caught his eye.

He turned to his window...

To see a single red rose in full bloom.

Still grasping his lute, he crossed the room, fixing intently on that beautiful, flawless new flower. The firelight captured every tint of vibrant scarlet and crimson in its velvet petals. With his right hand, he reached out, and gently touched it with his fingertips, half afraid it would vanish like a mirage.

It didn't. Soft as feathers, and more perfect than any he'd ever seen.

Absently, he set his lute down on the floor, gazing at the rose in wonder, feeling that it meant something—something fathomless and important...

He turned and took a dinner knife off the table, then carefully cut the long, green stem, catching the blossom as it broke loose. He pressed it to his face, closing his eyes and drawing in a deep breath of it—and swooned as the fragrance shot a million sensations through his body. He blinked his eyes open, set the knife down, and strode toward the door.

He made his way all the way down the stairs, back into the entryway, then into the dark hall of difficult doors. When he reached the last one, he slowed, hesitated as he saw it was open...

And he heard her speaking.

"Is there anyone in this world who loves me?" she whispered.

Amber halted, his eyes going wide.

"*Yes,*" said a voice like the winter wind—the Mirror.

"Are they nearby?"

"*Yes.*"

"Did someone in my family...do this to me?"

"*Yes.*"

"Would anyone in my family...Would they know my name if they saw me?"

"*No.*"

Silver made a strangled sound.

"Are the people...who know my name...looking for me?" Silver tried.

"*No,*" the Mirror said sadly.

Amber ground his teeth, his eyes squeezing shut.

A long moment later, Silver asked one more question.

"Will anyone who knows me ever find me?"

And the Mirror did not answer.

Amber forced his eyes open, and pulled in a rattling breath. Then, he made himself round the doorframe and enter the room.

The fire in the hearth burnt low, and the Mirror gazed down at Silver, who lay before it, arms outstretched as if in prayer.

He saw her notice his entrance—she ducked her head, and slowly lowered her arms.

"I found this for you," Amber ventured awkwardly, stepping closer and holding out the rose. "It was blooming in my window." He bent, and held the rose close to her.

She had to turn her head more fully toward him in order to see, for her right eye remained useless. She regarded the rose, then looked up at him...

Slowly straightened, and took the rose from him. She held it delicately in both hands, her head bowed. Amber waited, his heart thudding with an odd, unnamed dread...

"You have to leave," she murmured.

Amber stiffened, his eyes flashing.

"What?"

She lifted her chin, and stared coldly at the mantel.

"You have to leave this castle, and never come back."

"What?" Amber repeated, stepping toward her. "Why?"

"Because you are no longer welcome," she stated. "This is my house. You were my guest. And now I want you to leave."

Amber stared at her, feeling that meaning sink down through him like a knife.

"I...I don't understand," he stammered, his pulse raging in his ears. "What did I do?"

"It's what you *haven't* done," she shot back, her voice breaking.

"What do you *mean?*" he cried.

"You haven't sung in court more than once, you haven't been made the high composer of a king!" she shouted, whirling to face him, pinning him with a blazing look. "You haven't heard all the stories yet, you haven't finished the songs—you haven't seen all the beautiful lakes and woods in the east, you haven't traveled to the north to see the ruins of the Druid kingdoms—you haven't fallen in love and gotten married and had *children!*" Her words tore through him. She threw the rose down on her bed.

"Your voice—*you*—are trapped here," she gestured to him violently with both hands. "Locked up in the dark and hidden away from *everyone*. You *must* go, you *must* sing for them, out *there!*" She pointed toward the wall, toward the entry, toward the edge of Thornbind. "You *cannot* stay here with me, and you can never, ever come back! I will never be *anything* but a dragon," she roared—and her wild expression shattered. "And you cannot sing for me anymore."

"Silver—" Amber tried, his eyes stinging.

"That isn't my *name!*" she howled, covering her ears with both hands. "It was *never* my name! Get out, get out! I don't want you here. *Get out!*"

And with that, she lashed her mighty tail, smashing the corner of her bed—sending it crashing to the floor, splinters flying. The fire flared in the hearth, roaring, sending Amber reeling backward. He withdrew, ducking clumsily back through the door as her voice broke into a wail.

He staggered into the hall, his vision blurring, pushed through the kitchen and out into the bracing night wind.

He drew to a stop, his head jerking up, desperately searching for the stars. But a veil of clouds hid them all. He kept looking, struck through with confusion and alarm. His throat clamped shut, he pressed a hand to his raging heart...

And tears spilled down his cheeks.

He gasped. It ripped through him. He took a shaking fistful of his shirt as more tears tumbled—burning his cheeks as his ribs filled with fiery ache.

He bent his head, weight crushing his shoulders as he let out a helpless sob, more tears tumbling. He covered his eyes with his hand, choking...

And sat down hard on the grass, his whole body shaking. The wind rushed through his clothes and hair, distant and cold, moaning as it left him, and gusted through the dead branches of the cursed wood.

As darkness besieged the castle, and surrounded Amber like a fog, his tears finally ran dry. He had wept so hard his muscles felt strained and sore, his face stiff and weary. He lifted his forehead off his knees, breathing shallowly, and stared at the nothing that was the edge of the forest.

The wind had abandoned him, and the stars and moon hid themselves. All lay as motionless as death.

Except.

His tired brow furrowed. He blinked, and forced himself to focus.

A light.

A light, close by. It looked like a single torch, flickering between the trunks of the trees.

For just a moment, he sat where he was. Then, he got his feet beneath him, and stood up. He listened.

He didn't hear anything. No horse hooves, no voices. Swallowing, he started forward.

His feet swished through the grass, but he knew that the ripple of the river would cover that sound. He leaned forward, striving to peer through the gloom...

He slid down the bank of the river, then stopped in the middle of the water. The light had gone out. He held his breath.

For a long while, he stayed just as he was, the icy water licking his legs.

Then, he splashed out onto the opposite bank, onto the path that had led him to Silver in the first place.

Then, the clouds parted. Ivory moonlight spilled down into the skeletal wood. Amber turned around—

To see a man. A familiar man.

A handsome young man in knight's clothes, with dark hair, and eyes the color of steel.

Sir Roderick.

Something *cracked* against Amber's skull.

Everything went black.

CHAPTER TWENTY-ONE

"THE TRUTH WAS SPOKEN BEFORE THE THRONE"

Silver sat in front of the fire, leaning her side against the broken bed. The mirror had winked out, and gone dark. The fire hunched low in the hearth, and spat restlessly. Deep shadows played across the walls.

She fingered the petals of the flawless rose, running her thumb along the feathery edges. The scent wafted through her, and she closed her eyes, breathing it in, and out, and in, and out...

Footsteps in the corridor.

Her eyebrows drew together. She listened.

The tread was unfamiliar.

A strange man. No—more than one man.

Six men.

She opened her eye, her body leaden.

She waited.

She heard their tight breathing, the brushing of their clothes. The quiet jingle of their weapons and buckles.

One by one, they slipped through the door behind her. She didn't move—just stared at the mantelpiece.

They halted. She could feel their eyes on her back. She ran her thumb back and forth, back and forth, across the bloom of the rose.

"Well, what do you think, lads?" a voice belonging to the foremost man spoke into the silence. "Her hide isn't so fine after all, but that's rather an interesting head she's got. Can we try to spare it so we can hang it in the great hall?"

A few murmurs of agreement answered him.

Silver looked down and watched the progress of her fingers.

"All right, what do you say, dragon?" that man asked, stepping closer. "Would you like to give us a fight worthy of your being hung on a wall? Or should we just skin you and eat you?"

A sharp point dug into her back.

Silver accidentally ripped all the petals off and clenched them in her fist as she whipped around—

To see a dark-haired, grey-eyed young man wearing some armor and leather, jabbing her with the end of a spear.

She reared up—

He plunged the spear down through her tail.

She screamed, slamming her back against the wall.

The other men cheered, and brandished their weapons. They charged at her—she slashed at their faces and coats, tearing their clothes—

The first man lashed out with chain mail gloves, grabbed her around the throat and flung her to the floor. Her wounded tail flailed amongst their ranks—

A shaft of pain flared down her spine as another spear stabbed through it.

She wailed.

"Haha! Watch out for that tail!" one man warned, laughing.

"By Jove, it's a strong thing! Watch out, watch out! Hold it down, now!"

Two of the men, laughing and shouting at the sport, got down and threw their whole weight against her, crushing her against the rug. Metal sang against metal.

Then, some sort of pliers grasped a large spine right between her shoulder blades.

"No—" she gasped.

He wrenched it loose.

Silver couldn't even scream—pain blinded her and blasted the breath from her body. Blood gushed down around her neck and pooled on the floor.

"Roderick, we're staining the rug," one man grunted as he drilled his elbow down onto Silver's back. "I think it's a treasure—it looks very old. Your lady would like it."

"Right. Right," Roderick said, straightening. "Let's tie her up and drag her outside. That way we can slaughter her and field dress her without ruining any of the furnishings in here. After that we'll...We'll take what we want from the castle and head back to Tirin. Cam, do you have the rope?"

The knight leading Amber's horse pulled back on his own reins and skittered to a halt, the horse's shoes skidding on the cobblestones of the courtyard. Amber bared his teeth, fighting for the hundredth time to loosen the ropes that tied him to the saddle. The knight hopped off his horse and grabbed the bridle of Amber's, then reached up and untied Amber, snatched his arm, and dragged him off the horse.

Amber staggered, tripping down onto one knee, blood from the wound on his head running into his right eye. His whole skull throbbed, and he still felt dizzy—though not as dizzy as he had been when he'd regained consciousness atop a horse, galloping at full tilt through the night across the moor, surrounded by four mounted knights. Through his concussed senses, he had managed to discover that Sir Roderick wasn't with them. Which meant he could be anywhere—

Including inside Silver's castle.

Amber gulped back a flash of terror, battling to regain his footing as the red-bearded knight dragged him up, re-tied his hands behind his back, then pushed him toward the entrance to a castle...

A castle Amber suddenly recognized, even with its pale face only lit by torchlight:

Tirincashel.

Where Princess Oralia lived.

He went cold, and almost stumbled up the stairs before the great double doors. The escorting knights fell in behind him, another knight took hold of his jerkin. They shoved him through the entry corridor, turned him, and then ushered him to the double doors before the throne room.

They pushed through the massive entrance, and thrust him in...

218

Princess Oralia sat on the throne at the far end, her shapely arms draped across the rests. She wore raging scarlet trimmed in gold—and upon her head rested a glittering, pearl-studded crown far more regal than any princess would wear. It took Amber just an instant to realize that she had donned the queen's crown. Her hair tumbled down around her shoulders and arms—a waterfall of purest gold. Her eyes of wintry blue pinned him where he stood, and knifed through his heart. And before her, a fire blazed in the pit, casting a wild and sinister aspect across her stunning beauty.

The knights dragged Amber to the foot of the dais, and threw him down on his knees. He yelped as his kneecaps hit stone. One of the knights snatched him by the hair, and yanked his head up to face her. Amber gritted his teeth.

Oralia lifted her chin, and gazed coldly down upon him.

"Amberian of the Lute," she said smoothly. "You've gotten blood on your tunic."

Amber's lip curled, and he said nothing.

"I offered you the most precious gift I have: my own heart," Oralia went on, slowly rising from her seat. "And as if that wasn't enough, I also granted you the entire kingdom. I *handed* them to you." She slipped down the stairs, serpentine and soundless, her gown rippling over the steps. She stood tall over him—the knight jerked Amber back, forcing him to look up.

"Yet you threw them back at me," she muttered. "As if they were worth nothing. And you chose something else entirely."

She bent down, peering deeply into his eyes, and reached out with a delicate hand to touch his cheek.

Amber bit down and tried to recoil—but the knight held him fast.

"Where did you go, minstrel?" she asked, her fingernail tracing his cheekbone as she leaned ever closer. "Where did you go, but to the home of a *beast*. A beast so foul and dangerous that no one else on earth dared venture into that wood where she lived. And you...*stayed* with her." Oralia breathed, her face an inch away from his. "You ate with her. You talked with her. You laughed with her. You...*loved* her."

Heat surged through Amber's face. His heart thudded in his ears—and Oralia's eyes flashed.

"So it's true!" she hissed, sliding her hand down Amber's neck, pressing her fingertips to his pounding pulse. "A *beast*. You would rather have a *beast*...than *me.*"

Her eyes caught fire—Amber's muscles quivered as his fingers squeezed around his ropes.

Suddenly, Oralia stood up straight.

"Finnick!" she erupted, pointing to a knight at the back of the hall. "Ride out swiftly and meet Sir Roderick and his men. Tell them that I still want her carcass cut to pieces and thrown in in the river, but he must bring her head to me!"

Gwiddon Baba Yaga stirred.

She had been sitting motionless in her chair for seven days, tucked in amongst a hundred rancid furs, hardly breathing. Her house of bones creaked and sighed around her, but nothing else had dared disturb her stillness.

Now, she slowly opened her eyes. Blackness shrouded the whole room.

She muttered a spell, and waved her hand. Winced at the rusty movement.

The oozing candles upon the mantel blinked to life, illuminating her dusty eaves, dried heads, dangling jars and piles of feathers.

Gnashing her teeth, she eased forward, the furs dropping from her shoulders. Her joints cracked—she spat hollow blasphemies and forced herself to her feet.

She shuffled across the floor, her threadbare shoes chattering through finger bones, to the far corner. She grabbed a rag off a table as she walked, and stopped in front of a dust-covered mirror on the wall. She swiped the rag across the smooth surface...

Then leaned in to squint at what she saw.

Thornbind—a large stretch of woods near Reola's old castle. It looked just as grey and lifeless about it. Except...

Her old eyes went wide.

Green around the edges. Deep within the roots of the grass, and the trees, and the roses.

"No," she seethed. She stretched out a bony hand, pressed it against the cold glass...

And began to hiss and sputter the most powerful spells she knew.

Come clouds, come rain, come blazing lightning...
Fill the air with poison, and electrocute the wind.
Destroy them all, lest the wood re-awaken.
Bring down a squall from the mountains.

And even as she spoke, in a hundred dead druid tongues, the air outside her hovel sparked and crackled, the wind snarled around the trees, and the clouds descended upon the castle in the wood.

"*NO!*" Amber leaped to his feet—
Oralia slapped his face. Hard.

He tasted blood in his mouth, and reeled to the side.

The knights behind him knocked his feet out from under him, and he crashed to the floor again.

"Silence, dog," Oralia snarled. "Now you'll see what happens to those who break my heart."

"No, no, no!" Amber thrashed frantically against his bonds and the grips of the knights, blood running down his lip. "No, *leave her alone!*"

"Shut up!" one of the knights punched the other side of his head—Amber saw double, and collapsed onto his side—

The red-bearded knight drew out his sword in a flash. The blade sang. Amber fought to regain his balance, fought to get up—

"What is going on here?"

The voice boomed like a lion's roar through the entire hall.

Oralia spun—the knight staggered back. Amber squeezed his eyes shut, shook his head, forced them open again...

To see the king—the *king!*—still clad in grand mourning, a circlet on his head, his gaze bright with anger, stride into the chamber, beside his wife the queen, and twelve burnished knights, their swords in their hands.

"Mother!" Oralia cried, putting on a startled smile. "Father! I didn't expect you back until tomorrow—"

"Answer your father's question," the queen ordered. "What are you doing to Amber, and why are you wearing *my crown?*"

"I...I, erm..." Oralia quickly reached up and took it off her head, and set it on the throne. "I was dealing with a few disciplinary measures—"

"By beating my minstrel to death?" the king cried. The queen, her jaw set and her expression like steel, waved one hand at the knights, and they instantly backed away from Amber. The queen strode right up to Amber, then, and knelt before him. Gently, she reached out and helped him sit up, and untied him. Tears tumbled down Amber's cheeks, and as soon as his hands were free, he took tight hold of her sleeves.

"Please, you have to stop them," he begged. "Please—they're going to kill her!"

"Kill who?" the king demanded.

"A beast in Thornbind wood," Oralia cut in. "An old, poisonous dragon.
Amber got lost in Thornbind one day and she captured him, and put him under her spell. I've sent Sir Roderick to kill her, so Amber will finally be free of her. Poor boy."

"You are a *liar!*" Amber thundered, his vision turning red. "If anyone has put anyone under a spell, it is *you!*" He climbed to his feet, aided by the queen. "People love you, but you don't deserve it—you are selfish, vain and hateful, and you're sending men to kill the one I love because I refused to marry you!"

Her parents looked at her. Oralia turned white—then laughed airily and waved to him.

"See what I mean? He thinks he's in love with a snake."

"Why were you beating him, then?" the queen wanted to know.

"He was resisting my help," Oralia shrugged. "He isn't in his right mind."

"I will *kill* you if anyone hurts her—!" Amber lunged at her. Oralia leaped backward, and the king caught her in his arms. The queen tugged Amber toward her, studying him.

"Amber, dear—think for a moment. Do you suppose this may have happened? That you were put under a spell?"

"*No,* Your Majesty," he cried. "I wasn't. But *she* was! Silver! The one you keep calling a beast—she was a young woman, who someone turned into a snake! We visited Reola Curse-Breaker in the Giant's Shoes, and she told us so!"

The king and queen exchanged a sudden glance. Oralia lost more of her color.

"Please," Amber begged, more tears falling down his cheeks. "Please, you must stop your knights—they're going to kill her."

The king and queen regarded each other again—and Amber saw Oralia tuck herself into her father's chest.

223

Amber went cold down to his bones.

"Oralia..." the queen said gently...

"Your Majesties?"

Everyone turned to see the castle steward ease into the room. His usually starched and perfect purple robes now disheveled, his hat crooked—and his eyes haunted.

"Do forgive me," he said, stepping in, a roll of fabric held in his trembling hands. "But I felt this must be brought to your attention immediately."

"What is it?" the king frowned. The steward ventured closer, and he trembled much more.

"Per Princess Oralia's request, we were just now in the midst of gutting Princess Eleanora's chambers and sealing the windows...and one of the servants discovered this relic beneath the wardrobe. And as soon as she put her hand upon it, she fell into a stupor on the floor, and we have yet to wake her. We are certain it did not belong to Princess Eleanora—and we are fearful of what it might be, and *whose* it might be."

"Show it to us," the queen commanded, leaving Amber's side and striding up next to her husband.

"If you do not mind, I will lay it here on the floor." The steward knelt, and unwrapped the fabric...

To reveal a small, weathered scroll.

The scent of poison, of rot, of lightning, darted through the room.

The torches guttered, and darkness swooped near.

A terrible chill passed over all of them, and the faint sound of chains slithering on stone sneered through the edges of the hall.

"What. Is. That?" the queen breathed.

The king bent down, pulled two knives from his belt, and placed their tips carefully on the paper. Gingerly, he unrolled it...

And for a full minute, he said nothing as he read the words written in blood upon the parchment.

"What is it?" the queen asked again, hushed, searching her husband's face with a look of fear. "Dearest, what is it?"

"It is a curse," he rumbled. "A terrible curse."

He rose to his feet, and turned around...

And when he looked upon his daughter—it was as if he was seeing a stranger.

"I have heard of such a curse," he growled. "I learned of it when I was a boy, being schooled in the north, in the land where the druids once lived. It is a curse that will change the form of another person— change his form to that of a beast, or a stone. It will also banish that person's memory, until nothing of him remains. And it must be cast by someone near the victim's heart. By one who hates that person more than anything else in the world."

For half a moment, the world stood still.

Oralia smiled a little, and opened her mouth—

"It's Ele."

Everyone spun to stare at Amber—the one who had cut into the silence.

Wide-eyed, his face white, he took a step toward the queen.

"It's Eleanora," he repeated, the truth screaming through his veins with sudden, impossible clarity. "Reola told us that someone she knew—her mother or her sister—*had* to have cast the spell or it wouldn't work!" he cried, leaning toward the queen. "The snake beast didn't *kill* Ele that night—she *was* the beast! Don't you see? Oralia cursed her, and Ele lost her mind—and now your knights are going to kill your daughter!"

"*Herrard!*" the queen screamed her husband's name, her hands flying to her head. "Herrard, you have to *stop them!*"

"No! Mother, no!" Oralia screeched, lunging toward her. "He's lying! Mother—"

"Get away from me!" The queen recoiled, horrified. "You have murdered your sister!"

"Not yet she hasn't!" the king snarled. "Sir Ethyn, tie this wicked girl to a horse and bring her with us. Sir Gerard, release Amberian! Son, can you ride?" He stepped toward Amber.

"Well enough," Amber nodded as Sir Gerard loosed the ropes.

"Then you must show me and my men the way!" the king commanded.

"Yes, Your Majesty," Amber said, darting after him as he hurried out of the room, all the knights in tow.

CHAPTER TWENTY-TWO

"AND THE SCALES FELL"

Amber did his best to hang onto his reins and the horse's mane as it galloped through the night toward Thornbind. Storm clouds surrounded them, and the wind whipped across the moors, gusting through the capes of the king and his men—and Oralia's dress, as she rode bound to a horse. Lightning cackled, shooting stark brilliance and shadows over the road.

Then, all at once, they plunged into the shattered darkness of the forest, ducking low so the trees would not claw them from their seats. Amber strove with all his might to remember exactly where to turn, and in a moment's time, he tugged on his horse's head, pulling him to the right and charging down the steep incline to the river. His horse glimpsed the water below and kicked off the bank. The two soared through the air, then lunged up the opposite hill and burst out into the open.

Amber absorbed the next sight in an instant.

Sir Roderick and five other men, swords drawn, encircled Silver. Her hands were bound before her, and two of the knights had drawn her arms forward so far as to pull her face to the grass. They had stabbed three spears down through her tail, pinning it to the ground. And Roderick had taken a horse-shoeing tool and ripped a long, thick spine from her shoulders—he held it in the iron teeth of that tool. Blood ran in rivers down her neck and back, soaking her dress, and the fins by her face had gone slack.

The knights, lit by the fiendish illumination of constant, coursing lightning and their lit torches held aloft, laughed and called to each other—and Roderick's grin flashed through the night.

Roderick threw down his tool and drew his broadsword. He set its blade against the back of Silver's neck, to gauge his swing.

Amber's heart stopped.

Silver's fingers loosened, and scarlet rose petals fluttered silently to the earth.

Roderick reared back—

"*Stop!*"

Amber shouted with all the breath in his body. Roderick flinched. The other knights reeled around to see—

Amber threw himself off his horse and pelted toward them as hard as he could.

Silver's head came up.

She saw him.

"Amber!"

"Sir Roderick, *drop your sword!*" the king's voice resounded through the glade. Roderick hesitated.

Amber saw nothing but Silver as he ran toward her—nothing but her outstretched hands, and the spears that had gone through her, and the blood on her face—

"Roderick!" Oralia shrieked, tearing through the storm. *"If you ever loved me, you will kill them both!"*

Roderick's head lifted. Amber saw him look down the hill, and catch sight of Oralia.

The knight's gaze turned to steel.

His sword flashed—

Amber staggered sideways—

An inhuman, terrifying, feline screech lanced through the space between them—and the knights fell back and screamed.

Silver's fearsome tail tore loose of the spears, thrashing like a sea monster through the rattling meadow. In an instant, she had ripped the ropes asunder, spun and leaped upon the knights, slashing their faces. They slammed to the ground, howling and scrambling to flee.

Like a band of lightning herself, she darted through their feeble ranks,
lashing them with her wicked tail, shooting spines through their throats. They fell dead, all of them—except Roderick.

He ducked back—and when Silver had seized the last knight and flung him to the ground—

Roderick swept forward and lunged his blade at her back.

"Look out!" Amber cried, pointing.

She spun.

Roderick stabbed—

Silver flashed to the side, snatched the blade by the hilt, reversed it—

And plunged the sword straight through Roderick's heart.

Roderick's mouth fell open, but he couldn't scream. Silver lowered her chin, watched his head loll back...

And tossed him onto the ground. He crumpled like a rag doll, and did not move again.

Thunder rumbled. Silver raised up, clenching her fists, the bodies of the vanquished knights strewn all around her.

Amber let out a sigh of desperate relief, allowing half a smile...

All at once, his vision faded in and out.

And he fell to his knees.

Silver blinked. She stared out across the glen at the company of men that sat astride horses—along with a golden-haired young woman. Men who merely gaped at her, not daring to come any closer. Her eyes narrowed as she tried to puzzle out who they were, even as terrible pain traveled up and down her spine in darts and spasms.

A dull *thud* reached her, and she frowned, and turned to her left.

Amber—it was Amber. He'd collapsed to his knees.

And his hands came up, and pressed against the left side of his chest...

Dark red blood spilled between his fingers.

"*Amber!*"

She threw herself toward him, fell down—clawed through the grass and dirt, scrambled to get up, to see him clearly...

"What...What happened?" She snatched hold of the front of his shirt. He lifted his head, and looked at her.

Smiled crookedly.

"I didn't see it. His sword," he whispered, tears brimming up in his eyes and running slowly down his face. "I think I ran right into it."

"*No!*" Silver insisted, taking his face in her hands, pressing her forehead to his. "No, no—it will be fine. You will be fine! It isn't...It isn't so deep..." She pressed her right hand against both of his—and felt hot blood seep through and soak her palm.

Amber choked on a laugh, swaying forward. Silver wrapped her left arm tight around his waist, pressing her chest against his, holding him up. He looked down at her, blinking slowly.

"I have to tell you something," he gasped, blood trailing down his lip.

"Tell me later," Silver frantically shook her head, her whole body pulsing with agony. "You'll have time to tell me—"

"Eleanora," he breathed. And then he beamed at her, his tears shining in his eyes. "Your name...is Princess Eleanora. And I love you."

She stared up at him, his words hanging in the air.

"Eleanora?" she mouthed. He nodded. Tears dripped from his jaw.

Her brow tightened, and her eyes went wide.

"You love me?"

His whole face twisted, he nodded again—so earnestly, and his throat strangled. His frame sagged against her, and he sat down hard.

"No, no, no!" she howled, taking her bloody hand from his wound and wrapping it behind his neck. He fell back onto her lap, resting his head against her.

"Oh, please! Amber—please don't leave me here!" she begged, her eyes stinging—and burning water suddenly streamed from them, slicing down across her scales. "Don't...Don't leave me here in the dark!"

Amber lifted his hand up to gently touch her cheek.

"You'll never be in the dark again, Ele," he smiled. "You're the brightest lady I've ever known."

And he died.

His hand fell limp to his side. His coppery eyes fixed, and went out like a candle.

And Ele remembered.

She remembered, in a warm and joyous flood—dappled meadows filled with flowers and sunshine, running and giggling alongside her mother as a little girl.

Her bedroom, and the curtains, and the cinnamon-and-cloves scent she liked.

Her dogs, her horses—her favorite foods at Christmastime.

Her father's laugh. Her mother's voice.

The bustle of Tirin on market day.

The way she had cried night after night into her pillow after Roderick had broken her heart.

The sound of Amber's singing filling the courtyard the very day she had met him.

"If a gold coin lies down in the shaft of a well
And deep water hides it, its worth can you tell...?"

The two of them had danced by the fire. He had held her in his arms.

Oralia had been angry with her about that, and had told their parents...

In an instant, Ele came back to herself, and she looked to the edge of the glen...

And found the familiar face of her father, the king.

Her father!

Bewildered, the king swung off his horse, hit the ground, took three toward her—then hesitated, studying her, searching her...

"Papa," she said, but made no sound. She stretched out toward him, imploring him...

He stayed still. All of the knights froze, holding their breath. Not daring to come any nearer.

They still did not know her.

Ele squeezed her eyes shut. Her tears trailed down her cheeks and her neck, and as they traveled, her scales felt as if they were splitting.

She released her breath, and a sharp, terrible cry tore from her throat.

She bent over Amber, nuzzling her forehead against his, pressing her hand to his lifeless chest. Praying to feel his heart beat against her touch...

But she didn't.

Ripples passed through her whole bleeding body. Faster and faster they came, like the irritated skin of a horse—like contractions upon giving birth.

Ele could feel her foundations breaking apart, certain she was going to die.

Hoping that she would.

A raging shriek suddenly cut through the gusts of the coming storm. Ele blinked through her tears and realized that the sound had come from the edge of the glade.

The golden-haired woman wriggled free of her bindings.

Oralia. It was Oralia—her sister.

Her *sister.*

She leaped off her horse, threw down the ropes and charged up the hill.

"Oralia!" the king tried to grab her arm as she passed, but he missed. "Oralia, I command you to stop!"

Oralia snatched up a sword from a fallen knight, turned and pointed the blade at her father.

"You stay where you are," she thundered—and suddenly the king froze in place.

Oralia spun, her eyes full of fire, and marched up toward Ele, and Amber's body.

She reached them, and loomed over Ele's head, shifting her tight grip on her gleaming weapon. The wind swept her pale hair, and lightning flashed against it, swirling it around her face and shoulders like the tresses of a Fury.

"Stay on your belly, snake," Oralia gritted, leveling the blade at Ele's neck. "You stole my minstrel from me, and now you've murdered knights of the realm." Thunder rumbled, and the branches of the trees clicked together like gnashing teeth. Oralia pressed the sharp tip against Ele's throat.

"It's time we were rid of you," Oralia hissed. "And I'm glad to do it, if it will keep you from poisoning the rest of my kingdom."

Ele's hand darted out.

She knocked the blade away—her hard scales clanged against steel. She lunged up and grabbed the hilt, shoved the weapon aside, and clamped down on Oralia's wrist with both hands.

Oralia yelped—

With a jerk, Ele yanked Oralia toward her, and bared her fangs in her face. Oralia's blue eyes went wide.

"Do not fool yourself, little sister," Ele bit out, her nose inches from hers. "You know very well who I am." She squeezed so Oralia's bones came together. "And *so do I.*"

Oralia blinked. She lost all her color—

Started to shake her head, tried to twitch loose...

Her skin got hot. Hot as metal in a forge.

Ele let go and recoiled, baffled—

Oralia staggered backward, dropping the sword, staring...

As her arms began to glow.

Then—

Light blasted through the glade.

And Oralia burst into towering, all-consuming green flame.

The knights reeled away from her—their horses screeched. Oralia screamed hysterically, plummeted to her knees—

Ele dove to cover Amber's body with hers.

And with a boom that shuddered the roots of the trees, Oralia burst like a star.

The *crack* of the explosion rolled across the wood.

Ele lifted her head, blinking the dazzle from her eyes...

And watched a cloud of sparkling dust meander back down to the earth and dissipate.

Ele stared at the empty space, her mind spinning...

A crisp *jolt* traveled through her tail.

And it...shortened.

She spasmed.

Her tail split in two—all of a sudden broke into halves. She writhed and turned...

To see *legs* appear where her tail had been. Human legs. And bare feet!

She sat up.

The scales on her arms loosened, turned white, and flaked off. Her claws shortened, changed color, and a maddening tingling broke out all over her. She shuddered and began feverishly scratching at her arms, scraping the scales off...

To reveal shining, pale, *human* skin beneath.

She shook her head once, twice—and the fins by her ears cracked, and clattered onto the grass. Her spines snapped off at their roots.

Long, waving, ebony hair cascaded down from her head, framed her face, brushed against her shoulders and covered her back.

Her whole body softened, lost its iron strength—yet gained a penetrating familiarity that sent fire pulsing through her every limb.

"Ele," she tried hoarsely as her face flushed—and her mouth felt familiar again—her fangs had dulled, and now she had her own teeth, tongue lips, throat... "Eleanora."

She held out her hands, and gazed at them. Human hands. *Her* hands.

She put those hands to her face—bumped into a scaly dead mask—and tore it loose. It fell away like paper.

She pressed her fingers to her cheeks.

Her nose, *her* eyelids. She found her eyelashes, her eyebrows, her smooth skin...

"Aha!" she laughed brokenly, delight glowing through her...

Her hands shivered, and she studied them again, sitting there alone in the tatters of her dress.

It began to rain. Light, cool drops hit her skin, her hair, the colorless grass all around her...

A breath.

Ele froze.

Another one—deep and low. And it moved through Amber's body, swelling against Ele's legs...

Her attention flashed down—

He breathed. His chest lifted...

And fell. Ele's hands came up, her pulse suspending—

He opened his eyes.

Ele gasped, slapping a hand over her mouth.

Amber blinked, frowned, and focused.

He cleared his throat, and his hand moved groggily across his chest.

"What happened?" he mumbled.

Ele cried out—

Amber's eyes flew open. He jerked into a half-sitting position and fumbled with the hole in his shirt—

Tore his jerkin open further, put his hand to his wound...

"It's gone!" he yelped. "I—"

Ele pushed her hand past his, through the hole in the fabric, and pressed it up against his bare side...

To feel nothing there but warm, soft skin...

And a powerful, thundering heart.

He grabbed her wrist.

Her head jerked up—she met his eyes.

His wide, searching gaze captured her.

And he quickly struggled up onto his knees, gripping her fingers.

"Silver!" he cried softly. "It's you!"

She kissed him.

She threw her arms around his neck, caught his mouth with hers and pressed deep. Amber sucked in a surprised breath, then wrapped her up tight—her blood thrilled as her heart crushed against his, the barrier of her armored scales now gone. She could *feel* his hands, his arms, his chest, as she never had before...

His hand wound through the tresses at the back of her head, and she tasted salty tears on her tongue.

After an eternal, breathless moment, Ele broke the kiss, took his head in her hands—memorizing his handsome face, his stunning, tear-flooded eyes.

"You...You did it!" she managed, still stunned and trembling. "You did it—you broke it. You found me." Warm, delicious tears danced across her cheeks. "I love you so!"

Amber laughed. It rang through the empty wood like a church bell. He tugged her back in—his lips crashed into hers, and she curled her fingers through his hair, leaning into him with all her strength.

And the dawn shattered the storm. Sunlight sheared through the clouds, capturing the tumbling raindrops and transforming them to refracting crystals. The light spilled through the glen and the wood, deluging all of it in living color. The grasses swelled with emeralds and yellows, the trees blushed deep chestnut, the castle face gained the tint of cream and the clouds turned white as waves upon the shore.

Amber laid one last, swift kiss upon her lips, then hopped up, his happy features ruddy as the playful wind tossed his curls. He held tight to her hands, and tugged on her.

Ele shifted, got her legs underneath her...

And slowly rose to her feet. Scales showered from her lap and her shoulders, cascading down around her feet, jingling like a waterfall of diamonds.

And the next moment, her father the king stepped around Amber and swept her into his arms.

She burst into sobs as he lifted her off the ground, and he cried her name over and over, and kissed her over and over, his beard delightfully scratchy against her neck. Once he had released her, set her down and given her a good, long look to make sure she was, in fact, healthy and sound, she leaped again into Amber's arms, breathing a thousand thank-yous into his ear—and then tasting his mouth again and again, intoxicated by the beat of his great heart.

And if only the two could have seen it, had they not been so entwined together—but in that moment, all of the roses in the dead castle garden burst into bloom...

Every single one of them a dazzling, and unmatchable, red.

EPILOGUE

The victorious party returned to Tirincashel amidst trumpets and fanfare, as the fragrant dawn banished the clouds and the shadow and sent brilliance reigning over the hills. Eleanora rode upon Amber's horse, in front of him, his arms wrapped around her. Those in the city who swarmed out to meet them would later say that the Princess Eleanora, though she wore rags, shone like a star upon that steed, in the arms of her true love—and that Amber of the Lute beamed brighter than the sun, with shimmering tears fresh upon his face.

The king himself, proud as a lion, loudly announced their return upon their entrance through the castle gate, and the queen flew out the doors into the courtyard and embraced Eleanora with wild affection and hundreds of kisses—all of which Eleanora affectionately returned. All of the servants turned out, leaning through the windows or spilling through the doors, cheering and waving their handkerchiefs, and those who could clamber to fetch them threw flowers down like a carpet in front of their beloved princess.

When the jubilant fervor had dimmed just slightly, all of those who had been absent made inquiries about Princess Oralia, Sir Roderick, and the other knights, for their horses had returned riderless. When the king bowed his head and revealed that all had been killed—some by sword, some by battle and one by apparent magic—a terrible wave of grief swept through the court...

Which was inexplicably replaced by a queer and bitter-tasting gall as they all sharply remembered countless despicable and spiteful things that Princess Oralia, Sir Roderick and the other missing knights had done to each of them—actions that, somehow, had been erased from their minds until this instant.

It did not take them long to realize that some sort of spell had just been broken. The royal family and Amber recollected that Reola had told them that the spell that had transformed Ele had passed through Gwiddon Curse-Maker's hands, and that Oralia herself had cast it. The king pointed out that, in order to acquire a curse from a witch, a person already had to be acquainted with the witch's name, for she could not be summoned in any other manner.

And, like a second wave upon the sand, more memories came flooding back to the king. He told them all of a day when Princess Oralia was thirteen years old—the king and his knights were suiting themselves to ride out upon a witch hunt, for they were certain that she had just filled Tirincashel's cellars with blue asps, thereby killing a housemaid, and then she had fled to nearby Everhart Wood. The men had openly discussed her name, her magic and her powers, and how they ought to counter her should she attack them. Upon the king's leaving the hall, he had found his younger daughter outside the door. He had asked if she had heard what the knights had been discussing, and she said she had. She also asked where he was going, and he told her. He said their scout had left red ribbons tied to mark the path they ought to take, and so they should be able to dispatch of Gwiddon Baba Yaga quickly. The knights and the king had set out the very next morning to kill this witch. But, though they followed the ribbons, they came upon nothing that looked even remotely dangerous, and though they searched all the day long, they found nothing. As they had been returning to the castle, frustrated and disappointed, they came across Oralia wandering the moors. The king's first instinct had been to scold her for straying so far from the castle—but he had suddenly felt disinclined to do anything but shower affection upon her.

And now, even as the king spoke, both he and the queen remembered that Oralia, at that age, had been plain, sallow-faced and sour-tempered—but *after* that day, she had bloomed with extraordinary beauty, and her charms had delighted them, while those things she did that were selfish or mean-spirited seemed instantly to fade. Thenceforth, no one could resist her requests, nor easily contradict her—for when Oralia confronted them, something within them lost the inclination, no matter what she had done.

Amber then reminded them that Reola had made this elaboration: that those who practice curse-making cannot even cast a "good" spell without it eventually turning evil—a spell of beauty or good luck would fester within the receiver.

Soon, the royalty deduced that, the day the king had ridden out to kill the witch, Oralia had headed out before them, moved the ribbons, and then called upon Gwiddon. She had doubtlessly told the witch that she had saved her from the king's men, and that she was owed a favor—and since she held counsel with this witch, even if the king had called the witch by name, the witch would not have been at liberty to come to him. In gratitude for sparing her life, the witch had then gifted Oralia with beauty and charm, and the love of all who knew her.

However, this selfish desire, married with a spell that had an evil root, soon served to make Oralia as depraved and malicious as anyone in the kingdom—and worse, her sins went unnoticed because of this spell. Those within her command, such as the knights and the servants, were forcibly compelled to desire her favor by obeying her every whim; and those in her family lost their will to challenge her. Only someone with an incredibly strong will could stand up to her, in her presence, and openly defy her. And only someone who was not from this kingdom at all could disobey her orders. And Sir Roderick had opened his heart to her, allowed his mind to be fully poisoned by her, and thus could offer no opposition at all, even to save his own life.

This revelation naturally distressed the king, the queen, and Ele—but as their memories came rushing back, one after another, each as fresh as if it had happened mere hours ago, they found that they were less and less inclined to mourn, and far more inclined to forget they ever knew Oralia, Sir Roderick, or the other brutal knights.

It was into this contemplative silence that the shaken steward dared to approach, and remind the royalty that Princess Oralia had, a month ago, put into motion plans for a massive wedding and feast—and it was to have taken place that very day. Food had been prepared, a wedding dress tailored, musicians ordered, halls decorated, guests invited! Whatever were they to do?

Amber, distressed at the poor steward's wringing hands, offered to make remedy—and so he knelt before the king.

The next moment, the king pulled Amber to his feet and embraced him with a hearty laugh, and granted his request—if only Ele would consent.

And so Amber got to his knees before the princess...

And she leaned down to kiss his lips before he could even finish his question.

Thus, Amberian and Eleanora were married that very afternoon, in the great sunlit hall. Ele wore the dress Oralia had been making—the dress of spun fire. And it looked, for all the world, like a downturned rose with a thousand petals that shimmered with every move she made.

Together, they feasted, and laughed with all of their friends—for Ele had brought all of the household servants to the high table to sit with her and her parents and her husband, since she had felt their absence so keenly since her memories had returned. The king made plans to set out afresh on a new witch hunt, now that her sleeping spell had released Thornbind, and the winding paths had become much more hospitable. Amber and Ele also determined to live again in their woodland castle, to tend to the roses, and keep the invisible servants company. The queen did not protest this, as it was, after all, quite close by.

After long hours of feasting and singing, as the fires swayed and twinkled, and the laughter jingled through Tirincashel...

Amber and Ele danced together again. They danced the very steps that he had taught her, that singular night long ago. And their smiles lit the night; their radiant gazes, when turned upon each other, unrivaled before and since.

And as the merry music ended, and they stood in the center of the floor, wrapped in a tender embrace, a little page stepped up, begged their pardon, and handed a letter to the new husband and wife.

Together, they opened the envelope, and looked with surprise down upon the writing.

Did I not tell you, Amber Curse-Breaker?
Open your eyes and your heart.
And did I not tell you, Princess Eleanora?
Do not give up yet—what you seek may yet be found.

~Reola

THE END

AUTHOR'S NOTE

Beauty and the Beast has always been my favorite fairytale, but I have grown to love it so much more since I had the pleasure of playing Belle in a stage production of Disney's version. I was fascinated by both of the main characters, the depth of the dynamic between them, and the concept of one person being able to see *into* another person—past the physical, past prejudices, past society's perceptions—into a terribly guarded and wounded heart.

And the young man who played the Beast actually planted the seed of this very tale. One afternoon, after the production was finished, he jokingly (but wishfully) said to me "All right, let's do the show again—but this time, you play the Beast." My imagination caught on that idea. What would it be like if the "Beauty" was actually a young man, and the "Beast" was a princess, trapped by a wicked curse? From his inspiration, this story took root, budded and bloomed. He also allowed me the use of a certain, special name. And for those reasons, this novel is dedicated to him.

OTHER BOOKS BY
ALYDIA RACKHAM

The Beowulf Seeker

The Riddle Walker

The Last Constantin

The Campbell River

The Paradox Initiative

Lady Rackham

Christmas Parcel: Sequel to Charles Dickens' A Christmas Carol

The Mute of Pendywick Place and the Torn Page

The Mute of Pendywick Place and the Scarlet Gown

The Mute of Pendywick Place and the River Thames

The Mute of Pendywick Place and the Irish Gamble

The Mute of Pendywick Place and the Ghost of Robin Hood's Bay

Christmas at Pendywick Place

Dear David: The Private Diary of Basil Atticus Collingwood

Scales: A Fresh Telling of Beauty and the Beast

Glass: Retelling the Snow Queen

TIDE: Retelling the Little Mermaid

Curse-Maker: The Tale of Gwiddon Crow

Bauldr's Tears: A Retelling of Loki's Fate

Alydia Rackham's Fairytales

Amatus

Galatea: A Novella of Eliza Doolittle and Henry Higgins

Linnet and the Prince

The Web of Tenebrae

The Rooks of Misselthwaite Book I

The Oxford Street Detectives

The Last Scene

ALL AVAILABLE ON AMAZON, IN PAPERBACK AND KINDLE!

ABOUT THE AUTHOR

Alydia Rackham graduated from McPherson College with a bachelor's degree in English. She has published 75 fanfiction stories and 27 original novels.

In addition, she is a singer (winning superior ratings at state competitions in both high school and college), an artist, an avid traveler, and has performed in 21 theatrical productions, 6 short films and one feature-length film to date (winning a Jester Award in high school for the role of Mrs. Higgins in *My Fair Lady*, and a gala award for Best Female Performer in a Musical for her role as Mary Poppins in Salina Community Theatre's Production of *Mary Poppins*.)

She wrote the screenplay for the feature-film *Inkfinger*, which was featured in four film festivals, including the Hollywood Dreamz International Film Festival and Writers Celebration in Las Vegas, Nevada, where it was nominated for Best Cinematography. It also won the Award of Merit at the IndieFest Film Awards in La Jolla, California.

Made in the USA
Coppell, TX
10 December 2019